TOM O'DONNELL

SPACE ROCKS! 2

WITHDRAWN

For the love of **GELO!**

razor bill

An Imprint of Penguin Group (USA)

razOr
bill

A division of Penguin Young Readers Group
Published by the Penguin Group
Penguin Group (USA) LLC
345 Hudson Street
New York, New York 10014

USA / Canada / UK / Ireland / Australia / New Zealand / India / South Africa / China
Penguin.com
A Penguin Random House Company

ISBN: 978-1-59514-714-1

Printed in the United States of America

1 3 5 7 9 10 8 6 4 2

CHAPTER ONE

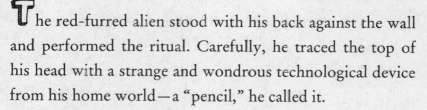

The red-furred alien stood with his back against the wall and performed the ritual. Carefully, he traced the top of his head with a strange and wondrous technological device from his home world—a "pencil," he called it.

Then he turned and regarded the measurement with satisfaction. To my eyes, it was indistinguishable from the previous mark, made just a few days earlier.

"I've grown a full four centimeters in the last three months," he said. "I really think I could be called Medium Gus now."

"It could just be the gravity on Gelo, Little Gus. It's a tad lower than Earth's," said another human, this one a female named Nicole García. "You're still only in the fifth percentile for boys your age, though." She was comparing his height to a sloping human growth chart that shimmered in the air above her holodrive.

"Top five percent," said Little Gus. "Not bad at all."

"Dude," said Rebecca García, the perfect duplicate, er, "twin" of Nicole, "you're about as good at math as you are at piloting."

"Thanks, Becky!" said Little Gus, failing to detect the insult.

"Do all humans *want* to be tall?" I asked them in their own language. I'd become quite fluent in human. These days, when I spoke to them, it no longer felt quite like I had a gul'orp full of rocks—at most, just one or two small pebbles.

"Nah," said Becky, "but it's still nice when you're taller than your sister."

"You are only two millimeters taller than me!" cried Nicki.

"Still counts," said Becky.

These aliens had been living with my family since the great battle three months ago. They had helped to defeat the dark forces of the Vorem Dominion and save my civilization from certain destruction. By Xotonian standards, it was a pretty crazy weekend. The months since had been quiet, though, and a sense of normalcy had returned to the underground city of Core-of-Rock.

Just then, the fourth human arrived. Daniel Hollins, the oldest and largest of them, burst into my dwelling. He was accompanied by Hudka, my grand-originator, a wrinkled little old Xotonian barely taller than me (yet much crankier).

"Xotonian burritos!" cried Hollins, plopping a big sack of food down on the table. "Fresh from Sertor's stall in the market!" Burritos were one of the few Xotonian foods that the humans actually seemed to enjoy (though I had still neglected to tell them that they were actually fried cave slugs).

"So Hudka didn't help you order?" asked Nicki, taking her burrito out of the bag.

"Nope," said Hollins. "I did it all by myself."

"I heard my name," whispered Hudka in Xotonian. "What did Becky say?" My grand-originator's human language proficiency was nowhere near mine. It had only managed to learn the two most important phrases: "Save game" and "Play again?"

"Not Becky," I corrected. "That one's called Nicki. Remember the rule? Check the lenses." I pointed to Becky: no glasses. I pointed to Nicki: glasses.

"Whatever," said Hudka. "I get it right nearly half the time."

Nicki frowned as she bit into the burrito. "Um, I don't mean to complain but . . . mine seems to be full of rocks."

"Mine too," said Becky, shoving hers away. "I think I chipped a tooth."

"Hang on," said Hollins, "isn't 'oitra'a'giv' the Xotonian word for 'extra cheese'?"

"Nope," sighed Nicki. "That's the word for 'full of rocks.' You should consider doing the vocabulary homework sometime."

"Huh. No wonder Sertor was acting so weird when I ordered!" said Hollins. "I thought it was giving me the stinkeye because I didn't have the correct amount of x'yzoth crystal change—"

Suddenly the lights of my dwelling dimmed. An instant later, an earsplitting boom ripped through the air. The walls shook and wobbled, causing little cascades of dust to pour from the ceiling. A particularly ancient—and fortunately very ugly—vase fell from the mantle and shattered.

The humans and I stared at one another, startled. I poked a frib into one of my ringing ear cavities. I felt like my internal organs had been rearranged.

"If I wasn't deaf already, I am now," said Hudka as the dust settled.

"What *was* that?" asked Becky.

"A Vorem attack?" said Nicki. "Or another asteroid

colliding with Gelo? Maybe this system's sun just went supernova!"

Her comrades frowned at her.

"Sorry," she said, "just thinking out loud here."

"Maybe these terrible rock burritos have angered the food gods," shuddered Little Gus as he threw his into the garbage.

"Whatever it is, it sounded like an explosion," said Nicki. "We should—"

"Follow me!" cried Hollins.

In an instant we were outside, racing through the streets of Core-of-Rock. Whole sections of the city were totally dark.

Another explosion flashed in the distance! Away to the east, a plume of sparks rose thirty meters above the city. For a moment, the blast lit Core-of-Rock in angry red. This time, we covered our ears before the thunderous boom reached us.

"This way!" I cried.

We passed the Hall of Wonok, formerly the seat of Xotonian government and now the most heavily guarded building in the city. Dozens of city guards stood outside, their usk-lizards snorting and stamping in agitation. The guards wanted to help too, but they couldn't. They couldn't leave the hall unattended, even for a moment.

The Hall of Wonok was now a prison. The thirty-two Vorem legionaries who had been captured during the epic battle were all locked inside. The city guards watched them day and night.

In the past few months, we had learned much about our Vorem prisoners. To our surprise, we found that beneath their scaly black battle armor, the Vorem were very human in shape. Nicki suggested this may have been an example of "convergent evolution" in which two unrelated species gradually evolve similar traits.

In any case, the Vorem did have two arms, two legs, and two eyes. They even had humanlike fur on the top of their heads (incredibly disturbing to the average Xotonian). But unlike humans, their skin was a pale shade of purple, and their eyes were red. Their hands were clawed, and their mouths were full of sharp white teeth.

I recognized a guard captain standing outside the hall. "Eromu," I called out, "do you know what's happening? Have any of the Vorem escaped?" It was hard for me to imagine that our ancient enemies didn't have something to do with the explosions rocking the city.

"Absolutely not," it said. "All thirty-two prisoners are accounted for!"

"Thanks, captain," I said.

"Whatever's happening," said Becky, "at least it's not the Vorem."

We hurried through Core-of-Rock toward the site of the explosions. At the edge of the city, near an exit to the Unclaimed Tunnels, we came to a dense jumble of dwellings. This neighborhood was called the Farrago, and it was on fire.

Soot-stained Xotonians led their offspring from smoky buildings. Others watched in a daze as their homes burned. A few guards, those not on Wonok duty, stood by helplessly. I heard sobs and coughs and the roaring of flames.

"Does Core-of-Rock have, like, a fire department or something?" asked Little Gus.

I shook my head. I'd never heard of an uncontrolled fire in our city. It is a damp place, and most of our buildings are made of stone. Mold problems? Sure. We knew how to deal with those. But not a fire.

"Well, is there at least any running water nearby?" asked Nicki.

"Yes, there's a fountain two blocks from here!" I pointed the way.

Nicki stepped forward to address the crowd, but Hollins cleared his throat and spoke first. In the Xotonian language, he said, "Hello. Water people . . . runs . . . does running. House people! Does eat . . . sandal. Water." The crowd stared back in confusion.

Gently, Nicki placed a hand on his arm. Then she spoke to them in slow yet comprehensible Xotonian. "Quickly, we must carry water from the fountain to put out the flames."

Several members of the crowd nodded and ran off toward the fountain. Becky and Little Gus followed close behind them.

Before I could join, someone grabbed my thol'graz. It was Linod, my best friend (in the nonhuman category). Its thin face was covered in soot.

"Chork-a-zoid," it rasped. Its silly nickname for me sounded doubly silly in the midst of a crisis. "Please. My originator . . ." Linod descended into a coughing fit and pointed toward its home.

"Okay, don't worry, Linod-tron," I said. "We can help."

Around the corner, flames bloomed from the windows of its dwelling. If Linod's originator, Lhoy, was still inside, its life was in grave danger.

"It looks like it's burning too hot," said Nicki. "I'm not sure we can—"

"Nicki, you go get some water," ordered Hollins. She stared at him for a moment and left.

"Chorkle, stay behind me," he said. "My clothes probably won't burn."

Like the other humans, Hollins wore a formfitting utility suit. Becky said the silvery unisex outfits made them look like they were all part of a French Canadian circus troupe. But apparently, they were useful.

"Uh, what do you mean *probably* won't burn?" I asked.

"I mean if Mission Control didn't cheap out on the fire-resistant coating," said Hollins, and he burst through the front door. Inside, the place was an inferno. Everything that wasn't made of stone was on fire. Furniture, clothing, support beams, even several masks and old costumes—Lhoy was an actor by trade—burned around us. The choking smoke made it impossible to see more than a meter ahead.

Apparently Mission Control didn't "cheap out." Hollins was able to pass through the fire unharmed, and by sticking close behind him I was able to follow without getting burned. We found Lhoy, unconscious but breathing, in its sleeping-veth upstairs. Together, we carried it past the licking flames and out onto the street.

Lhoy coughed for a minute and slowly blinked its eyes. "Hello. Good day," it croaked in human when it realized

9

that one of the aliens had helped to save it. This was its way of saying thank you.

"Hat meal," said Hollins back in Xotonian. Lhoy looked baffled.

The other residents of the neighborhood—under the orderly direction of Nicki and Becky—were now carrying water back and forth from the fountain and throwing it onto the flames. Each bucketful made a loud hiss as it helped to put out the fire. While we were rescuing Lhoy, it looked like they had gotten things under control.

"Where's Little Gus?" I asked. The twins gave each other a panicked look.

As the fire finally died, we went door to door, house to house, searching for Gus. A haze of smoke and steam had settled over the Farrago. It swirled behind us as we passed.

We found Little Gus standing just inside the shimmering Stealth Shield. He was silently staring out into the Unclaimed Tunnels.

"Dude, we thought you were barbecue," said Becky.

"Where did you go?" I asked. "Were you looking for privacy to eliminate your human waste?"

"No," said Little Gus, turning toward us. His face was terrified. "I saw someone."

"Who did you see?" asked Nicki.

"A Vorem," he said, "running through the fire. I saw a Vorem. His eyes were glowing red."

Nicki spoke gently. "Gus, all the Vorem on Gelo are captured or dead. You don't have to worry about them anymore."

Gus shook his head. "No, there's one of them still out there. I saw him. He left the city."

Hollins frowned and gave Nicki and Becky a look. I stared out into the Unclaimed Tunnels, past the glowing purple shield and into the darkness. I saw nothing.

"Gus, the city guards spent weeks scouring the tunnels for any survivors of the battle," said Hollins. "After the first two days, they didn't find a single one."

"I know, but they found that legate guy a month later," said Gus. "The one who led the invasion."

"Yeah, but he was dead," said Becky. "He'd been dead since the battle. We all saw his body when they buried him. Remember, he had the cloak and the fancy armor on? That was the last of the Vorem. The ones who are alive are all locked up."

"I know what I saw," said Little Gus.

He sounded so sure of himself that I wanted to believe him, but it wasn't very likely. The chances of a legionary still hiding out there—somehow surviving undetected for months—were virtually nil. The guards still patrolled the tunnels outside the city every day.

"Come on, buddy," said Hollins to Little Gus, placing a hand on his shoulder. "We should take a rest. I think maybe you breathed in a little too much smoke when we were fighting the—"

"Chorkle!" cried Kalac. I turned to see my originator running toward us. "I was in a council meeting. I came as soon as I heard what happened. Thank Jalasu Jhuk you're safe. All of you." Kalac hugged me tight.

"A council meeting, huh? That sounds way worse than a fire," I said. Kalac laughed, something that had not always come so easily to my originator.

"I heard from the residents of the Farrago that you all helped to get things under control. That you even saved Lhoy's life," said Kalac. In human, he added, "Thank you all so much."

Nicki bowed. "All Fortune Is Owed to Great Jalasu Jhuk," she said, using an extremely formal Xotonian phrase.

"Show-off," muttered Becky.

"Guys, look!" said Little Gus.

Hollins sighed. "Seriously, dude, there isn't a Vorem, okay?" he said. "You have to just let it—"

"No!" said Gus. "Look at that."

The Stealth Shield—the ancient technology that conceals our city's existence from outsiders—flickered once. Then it died.

We were hidden no longer.

• • • •

An hour later, we stood inside Trillid's power plant, which held the ancient Xotonian reactor that had powered our city for eons. The place was a twisting maze of catwalks and cables and massive crystal tubes pulsing with energy.

Usually the plant was empty. Not today. Ydar, the High Observer, poked at a thick snarl of charred wires with its frib and made a little disappointed noise. Other Observers milled about, taking notes and making serious faces. They were among the few Xotonians who had more than the barest understanding of the amazing technology of our ancestors. Unfortunately, they were quite pretentious about it.

"So what happened to the Stealth Shield?" asked Kalac.

"Well, Chief, you must understand that this is far outside my area of expertise," said Ydar. "I *observe* the heavens. If this were a quasar or even a brown dwarf I could expound quite confidently—"

"I understand it's not a quasar," said Kalac, gently cutting the High Observer off. "Please continue."

"I hesitate to offer my opinion, but I'm afraid it's the nyrine quantum inducer," said Ydar, as though that might mean something to anyone. "It's gone."

"Obviously I know what a nyrine quantum inducer is," I lied, "but please explain it to everyone else."

"It's a crucial component here in the plant," said Ydar. "Our reactor is highly efficient, praise to our ancestors. It gives us energy and makes society run. It can power all of Core-of-Rock for years on just the smallest amount of iridium."

"But . . . " said Kalac.

"But the nyrine quantum inducer is one of the pieces that slows and regulates that process. Without it, the reactor must have burned up all its iridium in a single instant. Several years' worth of power were fed right into our grid all at once!"

"And that's what caused the fire. Those two explosions were, like, transformers overloading," said Nicki in Xotonian.

"Exactly," said Ydar, a little taken aback by her linguistic and technical aptitude.

"She's the genius, but I got the looks," offered Becky.

Ydar nodded uncertainly.

"So what do you mean the nyrine quantum inducer is gone?" I asked.

"Well, here is where the nyrine quantum inducer should be," said Ydar, pointing to a tortuous nexus of cables. "And yet, you can plainly see that there is no nyrine quantum inducer there."

In fact, I couldn't plainly see that, but I was willing to take the High Observer's word for it.

"What happened to it?" asked Nicki.

"I suspect it blew out somehow," said Ydar, shrugging. "Perhaps it got so overpowered that it imploded. I don't know. It's just . . . gone."

"Nobody saw anything strange?" I asked.

Ydar shook its head. "The facility is unmanned."

"Can you fix the reactor, Ydar?" asked Kalac.

"No. Without the inducer, we can maybe get it running at twenty percent capacity. But I don't know what damage that might do to the system. The reactor may fail again, and there's no telling when."

"Will it still produce enough power to maintain the Stealth Shield?" I asked.

Ydar shook its head gravely.

"But without the shield, anyone with a long-range scanner will be able to locate Core-of-Rock," I said. "We'll be sitting shuggs."

Ydar sighed and nodded. Then it turned toward Kalac. "There is one more thing, Chief. I hesitate to mention it, what with all this on your mind. . . ."

"Go on," said Kalac.

"Four hours ago," said Ydar, "a Vorem trireme was observed departing the battle cruiser."

"What?" I cried. The ruined Vorem battle cruiser—or half of it, anyway—now traveled the same orbital path as our asteroid. Though its hyperdrive and communications system had been disabled in the battle, there were still a few Vorem alive aboard the vessel. Only one of the ten triremes—the small, agile starfighters accompanying the massive battle cruiser—had survived the battle. And now, it seemed, it was unaccounted for.

"Don't tell me General Ridian means to use his last ship to try to land troops on Gelo again," said Kalac.

"No," said Ydar, "We believe the trireme has landed on the new planet."

CHAPTER TWO

"Please sync your workdrives to location 219 and follow along as I read from the text. This information will be on the test. . . ." From a human holographic computer—a so-called holodrive—a 3-D projection of one Ms. Neubauer, a human female with thick glasses and an elliptical pile of frizzy brown hair, was currently teaching us something known as "geology."

After the invasion, we Xotonians decided we could no longer take for granted the ancient technological devices passed down by our ancestors. To survive, we needed to learn.

And so we began the fifth grade. It was Becky's idea—though perhaps she only wanted us to suffer as much as she had. In advance of the asteroid mining mission, each of the human children had had a year's worth of schooling prerecorded for them on their holodrives to cover the class time they would miss. The humans figured that these lessons could give the average Xotonian a basic foundation in (at least) math and science.

But at the moment—in the time-honored tradition of students on all worlds throughout the history of the universe—I wasn't paying attention in class. I stared past Ms. Neubauer's shimmering holographic form at a screen on the far side of the Observatory.

On the distant screen hung a fuzzy green ball: the new planet. It was orbited by a lopsided planetary ring, warped by the gravity of a single icy moon. Three months on, and we hadn't come up with a better name than "the new planet"—although "Gusworld VII" was advanced from at least one quarter.

The new planet seemed to be habitable: It had a nonlethal temperature range, its atmosphere appeared to be breathable, and we knew its gravity wouldn't crush us to jelly, at least. Indeed, its surface was green with life. But at the same time, it didn't look like the top vacation spot in the sector, either.

Huge, churning dust storms, charged with electricity, raged across continents. Wide, barren swathes of land—like colossal scars on the planet itself—seemed to support no living thing at all. The rest of the surface seemed to be covered in thick forest or fetid swamp.

We had seen some possible signs of intelligent life there. But cloud cover and dense vegetation made it hard to gather conclusive proof. Our official policy was not to attempt contacting the world until we knew more. So we continued to study it from afar.

The Observers pored through their ancient cyclopaedias, searching for any information about the new planet. As always, they pretended they had the situation well under control. In truth, they knew nothing. So far they had only been able to narrow down our present location in the universe to a handful of possible galaxies.

You see, at the end of the great battle, our asteroid had been pulled through a wormhole—a wormhole accidentally created when we fired the Q-sik at the Vorem battle cruiser—and flung across the universe. If you don't understand how that works, don't worry. I don't either.

I consider myself pretty smart. I'm a decent speller (a lot of Xotonians forget that the word ⊽⧿⧿⊣⦣⧿ has two ⊣s in it; not me). I have a working knowledge of human slang terms meaning "good" ("cool," "rad," "dope," "totally Little Gus," etc.). And I am a qualified expert in Xenostryfe III (high score: 1,672,890. Try to beat it. You can't). But rips in the very fabric of space-time are some-what beyond my understanding. Suffice it to say we hadn't covered wormholes in fifth grade yet.

Ms. Neubauer droned on. "Metamorphic rocks are formed when intense heat and/or pressure produce physi-cal or chemical changes in an existing rock, which we call a protolith. . . ."

Thank Jalasu Jhuk not all our lessons were prerecorded like hers. Sometimes the young humans themselves taught subjects in which they were particularly knowledgeable.

Hollins and Becky had brought in one of the human rocket-bikes (disassembled and recovered from the surface of Gelo). With several eager students, they had already re-assembled it. With the two of them teaching, it also func-tioned as a master class in the human vocabulary needed for pointless bickering.

Nicki too had been teaching the fundamentals of programming using the holodrives and some spare Observatory computers. Though baffling to most, many of the less athletic Xotonians had made great strides forward in this oddly universal science. Indeed, thanks to her lessons, many of the screens in the Observa-tory now displayed "Hello, world" in glowing human letters.

Little Gus had even tried his hand at teaching a course he titled "Fancy Gourmet Cooking for Master Chefs Who Are Cool," but he quickly gave up when he discovered that he couldn't get the ingredients he needed for his first lesson. Whatever "nacho cheese" is, it is unknown on our world. If it is as wondrous as the humans say, we are all the poorer for it, though.

Collectively, we Xotonians called all these lessons "human school." Listening to hours of the video instructors and the young humans talking every day also had the incidental effect of quickly teaching other Xotonians the human speech. (In addition to being highly attractive, we Xotonians are naturally good at learning languages.) After a few weeks of class, many were nearly as fluent in human-ese as me.

"Igneous rock," continued Ms. Neubauer, "may form above or below the surface of the Earth's crust. . . ."

Just then, her hologram flickered, and the lights in the Observatory dimmed. Several of the screens around the chamber went dark.

"What?" cried Linod, snapping awake again. Ever since the explosions and the fire, blackouts and brownouts had been occurring frequently in Core-of-Rock.

A few minutes later the holodrive, too, abruptly died, cutting off poor prerecorded Ms. Neubauer midsentence.

Someone had forgotten to connect the device to the Observatory's power grid to charge. Now its batteries were completely drained.

Ydar, who had been proctoring the class, stood up from its own console and approached the dead holodrive. The High Observer plugged the device in, but it didn't reactivate. After scowling at it three times and hitting it once, Ydar sighed in defeat.

"Well, I suppose that's where class ends today," said the High Observer.

"What? Speak up!" cried old Gatas from the back.

The rest of my cohort began to file out of the Observatory, each taking a dismal geology worksheet as it left. It was strange to resent something voluntary, but perhaps that was simply the nature of school. I noticed Linod choking back sobs as it collected its things.

"Linod-tron, what's the matter?" I asked.

Linod shook its head. "I was thinking about the fire again," it said. "I just miss them so much. . . ."

"Who?" I asked. Thankfully, Linod hadn't lost any friends or family in the blaze—Lhoy was completely fine.

"My fascinating fungi!" Linod cried out "All of them burned!"

"Don't worry, you'll find more," I said, patting its

thol'graz. "There are plenty of spores in the cave, as the old saying goes. I'm sure your new collection will be even more fascinating than before."

"You know what would make me feel better?" it said between sobs, eyes glistening pitifully. "If I could just have one of your humans. Just a single one. I could take one of the Garcías, since you've got a spare."

"We've been over this, "I said. "They're not pets, Linod. I can't just *give* them to you."

Linod squinted at me. "Okay, how much do you want?" it said, reaching for its x'yzoth wallet. I shoved it out the door and returned to my desk to wait for the humans.

"Cer'em, Chorkle. Oed Little Gus, ha'ois la'stisiaekt soiris. Di omih," said Little Gus as he burst through the door a few minutes later. Roughly translated from Xotonian, this means: "Greetings, Chorkle! I am Little Gus, your sovereign ruler. Obey me."

"Gus f'a'raely. Chorkle ael phsii etv lisstil ta' delnis!" said Nicki, meaning: "Foolish Gus. Chorkle is free and serves no master!"

"Ya'oi esi nerds," sighed Becky, shaking her head. ("You guys are nerds.")

The humans had been learning too. Since no one knew how long they would be living on Gelo, they decided they should be able to talk to their new neighbors. So they spent a portion of every day studying what they called XSL: Xotonian as a second language. Biologically, the human brain wasn't as quick to pick up new languages as ours. But after a few months under the tutorship of Loghoz, a member of the Xotonian Council and self-declared grammar enthusiast, they'd made a lot of progress.

Nicki—especially diligent about studying everything—was nearly fluent. Becky and Little Gus did virtually no work outside of class, and yet they were still pretty good. Only poor old Hollins seemed to be having trouble.

"Hisi aen ra'dil. Da'il lehaetk. Cer'em lehaetk. Asi ha'oi doilysa'a'd?" he said to me. Which, roughly translated, means "Here it comes. Does saying. Hello saying dentist. Are you pudding?"

I nodded, confused but trying to seriously consider his question. Was I pudding? In some sense, weren't we all just pudding?

Switching back to human, Hollins asked, "Are we ready to give home a call?" The human children sidled up to the Observatory's communications station. Every three days, they tried once more to contact their parents. It never worked.

"I'm afraid it won't be possible today, children," sighed Ydar, speaking passable human. "We're running on very limited power." A few screens scattered around the Observatory still showed feeds of stars. Most were dark.

"What? We walked up five thousand stairs to get here," said Becky.

"Yeah, how do you do it every day?" said Gus to Ydar. "Your quads must be ripped. Wait, do Xotonians even have quads?"

Ydar quickly spot-checked itself for "quads," then shook its head no.

"Are you sure we can't try? Just for a minute?" asked Hollins.

"We did kinda save your civilization," said Becky. "So . . ."

The High Observer sighed and looked around shuggishly. "Oh, all right." At Ydar's command, the rest of the Observers deactivated their own consoles. Ydar then powered up the communications center and adjusted a few dials and sliders. It nodded to the humans.

And so Hollins repeated the following into the microphone: "Hello. This is Daniel Hollins, Nicole García, Rebecca García, and Augustus Zaleski of the Nolan-Amaral mining vessel *Phryxus*. We are safe, though our location is unknown. We seek immediate rescue. Is anyone out there? Over." And his words were beamed out into the cosmos.

"Do you think anybody heard that?" asked Little Gus.

"Well, the universe is a pretty big place," said Nicki. "And we could be anywhere in it. Even if the new planet—"

"Gusworld VII," interjected Little Gus.

Nicki sighed. "Even if Gusworld VII is just a single light-year from Earth—and assuming we knew Earth's location relative to our own, which we don't—it would still take a radio transmission a full year to reach our parents."

"Isn't there a faster way?" asked Becky. "I'm missing a ton of TV shows back on Earth."

"Well, I've talked to the Observers," said Nicki. "Some of their old manuals do mention faster methods of communication: hyperlight, tachyonic ansible, and a couple of others. But the Observatory doesn't have any of this stuff."

"That's probably intentional," I said. "Jalasu Jhuk wanted Gelo—and the Q-sik—to remain hidden from anyone who might be looking for it. Outgoing calls would not help with that."

"I guess for now, then, we're stuck with good old-fashioned radio waves," said Hollins. And he repeated his message a handful more times before the communications console flickered and went dead.

"Or not," said Becky. The Observatory was now powerless, totally dark. After a moment, Little Gus flicked on a human flashlight (humans suffer from a sad and crippling inability to see in total darkness; in my experience, they don't even want to discuss the possibility that they might need more eyes).

"Well, I suppose that's it for today, everybody," said Ydar to the other Observers. "Take the rest of the day off. Spend some time with your offspring. Try to get some exercise."

The Observers, used to spending their time hunched over glowing screens, stood and stretched uncertainly.

"Sorry, children" said Ydar to the kids. "Feel free to borrow some cyclopaedias when you go." It pointed to the shelf of the dense astronomic tomes.

"Yay," said Becky.

Previously, these ancient cyclopaedias had been sacred holy books of the order, completely off-limits to the uninitiated. Now Ydar was encouraging anyone who had the time or the interest to study them for clues as to just where in the wide universe we might be. I hadn't borrowed any before—they were notoriously dry reading, and I worried that with extra homework my Xenostryfe III skills could suffer—but I figured I might as well give it a shot. I grabbed a thol'graz-ful at random.

"Ah, *Spiral Arm 314229 of the Turech Galaxy*," said Ydar, smiling with approval at one of the books I held. "An underrated classic."

As we descended the spiral steps of Dynusk's Column, the children were quiet. Their mood was glum. They missed their parents and their planet.

I too was quiet. I felt responsible for their predicament. My actions had accidentally stranded them on Gelo. Through my curiosity, and a boundless love of Feeney's Original Astronaut Ice Cream, I'd involved them in Gelo's ancient war with the Vorem Dominion and somehow gotten them trapped on the far side of the universe.

I wanted to help them contact their parents. I wanted to help them find a way home. But at that moment, I simply wanted to cheer them up. So badly that I was even contemplating drastic measures. I still had a few Feeney's Original Astronaut Ice Cream bars—the universe's most delectable treat—hidden in various secure locations around the city. I was on the verge of offering one of these to them when Nicki spoke.

"I wonder what Mom and Dad are doing right now," she said.

"Probably polishing your awards," said Becky. Nicki nodded in satisfaction.

"I hope everybody on Earth isn't, like, an ape now," said Little Gus.

"Don't worry," said Hollins, "we're going to make it home. We'll think of something. 'All the resources we need are in the mind.' Teddy Roosevelt said that."

"But *what* will we think of?" asked Gus.

"If we knew that, we would have already thought of it," said Hollins.

We walked through Ryzz Plaza, past the iridium statue of Great Jalasu Jhuk. Whole neighborhoods of the city were totally dark. With the power outages, certain foods had become scarce or even disappeared completely. As we passed through the market, we saw some stalls deserted, while others had incredibly long lines. Xotonians grumbled at one another and jostled to get to the front.

"Hey! How come mine doesn't have any fried mold on it?" cried Dyves, prodding the cave slug it had just purchased from Sertor's stall.

"The mold fryer needs power to run," said Sertor, brandishing its spatula like a weapon. "And there isn't any power!"

"But I'm on the Xotonian Council—"

"I don't care if you're Jalasu Jhuk itself! There's no fried mold left. And if you don't like it, I'm happy to serve you up a nice thol'graz sandwich!"

Dyves gritted its ish'kuts and blinked back tears.

Tension was building in Core-of-Rock. Regardless of losing the Stealth Shield, our broken reactor was making everyday life much more difficult. Air and water circulation had slowed. All the occupations and hobbies that required power were curbed. Public sanitation, medical care, and agriculture suffered the most. Rumors of the departing Vorem trireme didn't help matters.

"Hold on, I'll catch up with you guys," said Little Gus, and he peeled off and headed toward the butcher's stall. Then he stopped. "Wait. Can somebody lend me ten x'yzoth crystals?"

The humans looked at one another, then at me.

I sighed. "Ten x'yzoth," I said. "That's an awful lot. How about . . . none?"

"Gotta be at least ten, Chorkle," said Little Gus. "Prices have really gone up!"

When he met us later at the usk-lizard stables near the city guardhouse, he was carrying a wrapped parcel.

A young guard named Ixoby nodded and opened the gate. Inside, dozens of the huge, dull-eyed usk-lizards placidly chewed dried lichen in their stalls. The humans and I set about bridling two of the great beasts that we knew well: Goar and Gec.

"Well, they may not be the swiftest usk-lizards . . ." said Hollins, holding his nose and patting Gec's haunches.

"Or the smartest," said Becky as she watched Goar chew on an old piece of rope for a minute before determining it wasn't food and spitting it out.

"But Goar and Gec definitely stink the least," I said.

Gec snorted as Hollins and Nicki climbed onto its back. Becky, Gus, and I climbed onto Goar's.

"Ha!" cried Hollins.

"What's funny?" I asked.

But before anyone answered, we were galloping through the streets of Core-of-Rock and out into the Unclaimed Tunnels. It was unnerving not to see the Stealth Shield, the traditional Xotonian boundary between civilization and wilderness.

We traveled onward into the cavern system. Behind me, Gus squinted and shined his flashlight around in the darkness. I suspected he was hoping for a glimpse of his phantom Vorem.

The usk-lizards carried us through a thick scrub of spiny dralts, past fields of pulsing purple geodes. At one sharp bend in the tunnel, we disturbed a huge flock of rockbats. For a minute, the air was thick with them as they flew past by the thousands.

"Whoa, careful, Nicki," said Hollins as he made a protective gesture to cover her from the flapping mass of gray wings.

"They're just rockbats," said Nicki, frowning. "They're totally harmless."

After an hour of riding, we came to the place called Flowing-Stone. It was nine turns from Core-of-Rock, and even the humans knew the way by now. Flowing-Stone was a gnarled old philiddra forest growing on the site of what had once been a thriving city. Long ago, Flowing-Stone had been completely destroyed in a Xotonian civil war. An occasional stone ruin poked through the mist like a broken bone, the only remnants of its existence. The whole place had an eerie, haunted quality. With the death of our reactor, I wondered if Core-of-Rock would end up like Flowing-Stone.

Goar sniffed the air and slowed to a walk. Then it stopped altogether. Becky yanked on the reins as the usk-lizard began to shake its head from side to side and tried to back up, bumping into Gec, who bellowed.

Now both the usk-lizards were snorting and stamping and making low whining noises in the backs of their throats. They smelled something out there in the forest. Something that scared them.

"Oh, here we go," said Becky, shaking her head.

I checked my own skin. It had turned the same dappled gray and black as the forest around us. This was a Xotonian camouflage reflex, the unconscious reaction to a nearby predator. I sighed.

Suddenly a blue six-legged beast—a thyss-cat, the apex predator of Gelo's ecosystem and just about the most ter-rifying sight a Xotonian could hope to see—came tearing out of the darkness toward us. Becky and Hollins fought the reins as their usk-lizards howled in distress and tried to flee. The thyss-cat hunched and sprang high into the air. It landed right on top of Little Gus, knocking him out of the saddle.

Gus and the cat rolled over and over on the ground, a ball of blue fur and human limbs. I heard a high-pitched mixture of yowling and giggles.

"Pizza, heel! Heel, dude! C'mon, Pizza!" said Little Gus, wrestling with the young thyss-cat, which was now much bigger and far stronger than him. "When are you go-ing to learn how to heel?"

"Maybe when you stop carrying raw meat in your pockets," said Becky.

"Good call," said Gus, pulling out the parcel and unwrapping it: two fresh usk-lizard flank steaks from the butcher's stall. Pizza bolted them down in a gruesome and bloody display. Goar and Gec stamped nervously.

"And that's why Pizza's got to live way out here," said Hollins, shaking his head and suppressing a gag.

When he was a mere thyss-cub, Pizza was grudgingly tolerated by the Xotonian populace of Core-of-Rock. After all, the humans were heroes, so perhaps they should be allowed to have exotic (terrifying, dangerous) pets? But as Pizza grew, this tolerance gave way to fear. Every day Pizza looked less like a harmless blue furball and more like a nightmarish killing machine. Eventually, the Xotonian Council held a vote. It was decided unanimously that Pizza had to go. After some of our neighbors complained that Pizza had trampled their puffball garden and eaten three welcome mats, even Kalac was for it.

So Little Gus had released the beast—then about the size of an Earth housecat—back into the wild. We had chosen a spot near the waterfall where we'd first found him. It was a tearful scene. At the time, Hollins had said the whole thing was very *Born Free*, referring to some ancient human film.

But that wasn't the end. Each time we passed through Flowing-Stone, Pizza would bound out of the philiddra forest and give Little Gus a forcible tongue bath. Sometimes he even brought us a bloody shugg carcass as a "present." And Little Gus brought presents of his own: leftovers, fresh meat, brand-new welcome mats purchased just for Pizza to shred. I was loaning Gus a lot of x'yzoth crystals.

"You guys go on," said Gus. "I can ride on Pizza, my faithful mount and battle companion." Then he tried to climb on top of the thyss-cat's back. Pizza immediately shook him off into the dirt.

"You heard him," said Becky, and she spurred Goar forward. Gus stayed behind, wrestling with his self-declared best friend.

The other humans and I left the usk-lizards to graze on moss above and descended the long stone staircase to the only intact part of the ancient city, a place we simply called "the hangar."

The hangar was a huge iridium chamber, empty save for a couple of spaceships and one messy corner. This small area was cluttered with human things. After the battle, we had brought all that could be saved from their crashed pod: a televisual screen, a dilapidated yet comfortable couch, a stained area rug, and a ping-pong table with one wobbly leg. This ping-pong table was the bloody field of competition for Hollins and Becky. Their high-speed grudge matches made oog-ball look civil by comparison.

It was a little slice of Earth, right here on Gelo. And I suspect that this—even more than solitude or the chance to work on actual spaceships—was why the humans enjoyed spending time in the hangar. In fact, we made the trip to Flowing-Stone nearly every day.

"So, who's up for some ping-pong?" asked Hollins. "What do you say, Becky? You haven't been humiliated in a while."

"I feel humiliated every time I'm seen with you in public," said Becky, heading for the storage locker where we kept the snacks.

"No ping-pong for me. I've got ships to fix," said Nicki.

Two of the starfighters had been badly damaged in the great battle, shredded by Vorem laser fire. Nicki, Hollins, myself, and Becky (when she was in the mood) gathered here to patch the holes in their hulls and repair their malfunctioning systems, using replacement components from the crashed human pod or the mining equipment the humans had left behind.

Eventually the three Xotonian starfighters had been given names to tell them apart. Little Gus's suggestions—

Guswing Zero, the U.S.S. *Gus-terprise*, and *Little Gus: The Spaceship*—had all been vetoed. Hollins suggested we call one the *Roosevelt* after an ancient human leader (or maybe two ancient human leaders? I was never sure). Becky christened another *Phryxus II* after the human mining vessel. I felt that at least one of the starfighters should have a Xotonian name, so I called the third *T'utzuxe* after the red planet we had left behind.

There was a fourth starship in the hangar that had no name. Not content with trying to master just one type of advanced alien technology, Nicki also spent time working on her "special project": repairing a disabled Vorem trireme. This ship had been shot down on the surface of Gelo but remained largely intact. She hoped that it could be salvaged. So far, progress on this ship had been minimal. Its sleek black contours were still twisted and charred from the battle.

On some days, the hangar was abuzz with activity—Hollins and Becky had been actively training Xotonians to pilot their own ancient ships. Today, though, we had the hangar all to ourselves. Every sound we made echoed endlessly through the cavernous space.

"A negatively charged induction coil," said Hollins as he started to work on the *Roosevelt*. "I never would've thought

37

of that. Good thing one of us is smart."

"I'm not just the smart one," said Nicki. "I can do other stuff."

"Sure, but being smart is, like, your main thing," said Hollins.

"I guess," said Nicki quietly, and she went back to fiddling with the *Phryxus II*.

"Okay, so who ate my phui-chips?" asked Becky. She was referring to a popular Xotonian snack food/salt-delivery mechanism. "My phui-chips are missing."

No one said anything.

"It's okay. Whoever did it can tell me. I won't be mad," said Becky. "I promise I'll be totally calm and emotionless when I end your life."

"It wasn't me," said Hollins. "Those things are full of carbs, possibly."

"Nicole Ximena García?" said Becky.

"Do what now?" asked Nicki. "Microchips? Don't have any. Wish I did." She was already completely engrossed in a thick tangle of colored wires.

"You're being awfully quiet, Chorkle," said Becky. "If you confess, this will go easier on you."

I gulped. A few days ago, I *had* stolen two of Becky's sweetened yth-cakes—a poor substitute for the Feeney's

Original I craved—but I hadn't taken her phui-chips. "I didn't eat them," I said. "Why don't you try some of that mushroom jerky instead?" I pointed to a pouch of gummy gray flakes that had been sitting open on the ping-pong table for weeks.

"That fungus has got mold on it," said Becky, and she plopped down on the couch in front of the TV.

"Hey, Chorkle, a little help over here?" Hollins called out.

"'Sup, cool dude playa?" I said, trying for maximum human slang as I joined him on the far side of one of the ships. I was expecting to assist him in patching a blaster hole or holding two wires together to be soldered.

Instead, he looked around and then spoke quietly. "Hey, look, Nicki's birthday is coming up, and I want to get her something special. Any ideas?"

Apparently, each year humans expect special accolades and material rewards merely for having been born. "A bag of phui-chips?" I suggested, wondering if I should claim that today was my own "birthday" and demand that all of the humans give me their shoes.

"A bag of phui-chips?" said Hollins, crinkling his brow. "No. Come on. It's gotta be bigger than that."

"What about . . . ten thousand tons of phui-chips?"

"Forget the chips, Chorkle. What about some cool alien thing? Like a space gem or a jewel? Something that's, like, classy. Hey, maybe a crown that does telepathy! Do you know where I can buy a telepathy crown?"

I shrugged.

"All right. Well, if you think of anything, let me know."

"Won't it be Becky's birthday as well?" I asked. "They hatched on the same day, didn't they?"

"Hatched? What? Oh yeah. I guess so," said Hollins. He shrugged. The humans were always evasive on the details of their reproductive cycle.

"So don't you need to get Becky something too?" I asked.

He looked confused for a moment. Then his eyes lit up. "Yeah. You're right. I could stuff a bunch of stink-pods into a sock and wrap it up real nice. Put a card on it that says 'From Your Secret Admirer.' Then, when she opens it, she'll probably barf. That would be hilarious. Good idea, Chorkle."

I was puzzled by the discrepancy in the quality of these two birthday presents, and I was about to inquire further when Becky called out.

"Sis!"

I turned to see her lying on the couch, pointing the

remote at the televisual console and clicking. The TV remained resolutely off.

"Hold on," came her twin's muffled voice. Nicki was torso deep in the guts of the *Phryxus II.* "I'm recalibrating the flight controls."

"Sis."

"Just give me one second."

"Siiiiiiiis," whined Becky, stretching the word out to four syllables, at least. "Sis. Sis. Sis. Sis. Sis. Sis. Sis. Si—"

"All right, all right!" cried Nicki, emerging from an access panel. She pulled out her holodrive, and with a few quick swipes, the *T'utzuxe* hummed to life. So did the TV. Nicki had figured out a way to redirect a small percentage of the ship's power. It wasn't much, just enough to run the human televisual screen.

"Thanks, sis," said Becky. "This is why I'm still twins with you." And she started to watch her favorite prerecorded episodic program. The humans had brought several with them from Earth. This one was a teen melodrama called *Vampire Band Camp.*

"Do you think Clyve is *finally* going to ask Lucy to be second trombone?" I asked, sitting down beside her. *Vampire Band Camp* certainly trumped the wrinkled geology worksheet I clutched in my thol'graz.

"Nah, Clyve's dead," said Becky. "Oboe right through the heart."

"Wow," I said. I'd only missed one episode, but apparently a lot had happened.

"Hey, everybody check this out," said Little Gus. He'd finally arrived, with Pizza leaping and gamboling behind. "I taught Pizza how to say 'hamburger.'"

"What?" said Hollins. "Dude, why didn't you teach him how to say 'Pizza'?"

"Huh," said Gus, scratching his head, "Oh yeah. Well, hindsight is twenty-twenty. Too late now." Then to Pizza, "C'mon, boy, say 'hamburger.'"

Pizza stared at him silently.

"'Hamburger.' C'mon. Remember what we discussed. It's very important that you say 'hamburger.' C'mon. Say 'hamburger,' boy. You're embarrassing me in front of my colleagues."

Pizza rolled over onto his back, sticking all four feet in the air. He wanted a belly rub.

"Impressive," said Becky, turning back to the TV.

"This is, uh . . . also something I taught him to do," said Little Gus, pointing to the thyss-cat. "He couldn't do that this morning." But everyone had already returned to what they were doing.

Gus approached the couch. "Aw, c'mon. Not this dumb show. I hate these cool-hair vampires. All they do is make serious faces and french. It's gross," he said. "How about we watch *Kaper Kidz* instead." He referred to another human program, a kinetic, brightly colored cartoon show. Unless I'd eaten an astronaut ice cream directly beforehand, *Kaper Kidz* always gave me a splitting headache.

"*Kaper Kidz* is for little babies," said Becky distractedly. "This is grown-up stuff." On-screen, two chiseled teen vampires tried to learn the new color guard routine.

"I'm not a baby!" said Gus. "In two years we'll be exactly the same age."

"No. Because I'll still be two years older then," said Becky.

"Has anybody seen the ion welder?" asked Hollins as he rummaged through the toolbox.

"Is this it?" asked Little Gus. He picked a screwdriver up from the floor near the couch.

"No, dude," said Hollins, "that's a screwdriver. Come on."

"Oh, well excuse me, Sir Einstein Newton," said Gus. "Some of us aren't complete nerds like Nicki."

"I'm not a nerd!" cried Nicki from somewhere inside the bowels of the *Phryxus II*.

"Total nerd thing to say," whispered Little Gus. "You're cool though, Becky."

"You're not," she said. Gus frowned.

"Man, I could have sworn I left the ion welder in this box," said Hollins.

On-screen, vampires kissed and broke up and struggled to learn a very challenging tuba part. I briefly considered doing my geology homework. Then I began to flip through one of the Observatory cyclopaedias that I had borrowed. I'd heard that *Spiral Arm 314229 of the Turech Galaxy* was an underrated classic.

CHAPTER THREE

"**K**yral," I said. I awoke in the night with this sudden revelation. I leaped out of my sleeping-veth and reread the cyclopaedia entry.

Then I tried to rouse the humans from their slumber. As usual, it was hopeless.

"I may have finally figured out our location!" I cried. "We can finally calculate our position relative to Earth!"

"Neat," said Nicki without waking up.

"Can we talk about it in the morning?" slurred Hollins before rolling over.

"Little Gus," murmured Little Gus.

So instead I woke Kalac and made my originator take me directly to the High Observer's dwelling. Hudka came along too. My grand-originator could never bear to be where the action wasn't.

Core-of-Rock was dark. Power outages had become the norm in the weeks prior. Only the most essential services were allowed to use electricity. Normal life in the city ground to a halt. The fifth grade was put on hold indefinitely.

In my free time, I studied the Observers' cyclopaedias. I'd become obsessed. I had the feeling that somehow our salvation lay with the new planet. Every day I would borrow new cyclopaedia volumes and spend hours reading through them. Their content was occasionally interesting, filled with brief descriptions of distant worlds and strange alien races—apparently there were many intelligent species in the universe. Usually, though, the cyclopaedias were deadly dull. A typical entry might read:

"Cymis-19 is a type 6 binary pulsar (Pulsar-901368A and Pulsar-901368B) in the Ghez sector of the Ylori star cluster of Spiral Arm 991234 of the Edopo Galaxy. Pulsar-901368A has a mass of 2.6×10^{30} kg and a spin period of 0.023 seconds, while Pulsar-901368B has a mass of 2.8×10^{30} kg and a spin period of 2.8 seconds. Cymis-19 may reach a rate of up to 227 EMR pulses per second. ACRG: 5018, 8183, 0081."

If you feel like gnawing your own eyes off after reading that, imagine trying to get through a whole book of entries just like it. Then imagine reading ten such books.

But in the end, my suffering had paid off. Buried in all

the facts and figures, I had found something important. And I had to share it.

So I knocked on the door of the High Observer's dwelling, while the rest of the city slept. I clutched the cyclopaedia in my thol'graz.

"See," muttered Hudka, pointing to the fancy platinum doorknob of Ydar's dwelling, "I've always said the High Observer position is overpaid."

"Oh, Ydar's not so bad," said Kalac. "It's come a long way in recent months."

I pounded on the door again. At last, it eased open.

"Yes, what is it?" said Ydar, its five eyes blinking slowly. It was odd to see the High Observer out of ceremonial robes and wearing pajamas. Recently Ydar had been pulling double duty, working in the Observatory and trying to keep the reactor in Trillid's plant running.

"Sorry to bother you at this hour, High Observer," said Kalac, "but Chorkle—"

"It's Kyral!" I said. "The new planet is Kyral!"

The High Observer frowned and shook its head. "No, Chorkle, we already considered Kyral. It's not the new planet. Believe me, we focused on all the entries for habitable worlds in the cyclopaedias first. I can't believe you awakened me in the middle of a sleep cycle for this. It's enough to make me reconsider my policy of allowing lay-Xotonians to access the order's sacred cyclopaedias." Ydar started to close the door.

"Listen up, mold-brain," said Hudka. "If my grand-offspring here says the new planet is Kyral, then it's Kyral. The evidence is irrefutable!"

"And just what is the evidence?" asked Ydar, squinting at Hudka.

"How should I know?" shrugged Hudka. "Chorkle?"

"Right," I said. "So it's got a single moon. It's the same diameter. The same mass. It's habitable—"

"Slow down and read the entry," said Ydar.

I opened the tome and read. "Kyral is a planet located in the Nyspol sector of the Ueldo star cluster of Spiral Arm 5456901 of the Pharrash Galaxy. Kyral has a mass of 6.00809×10^{24} kg and a diameter of 13,458 km, with a single orbital moon (*see*: Ithro). Kyral is a densely populated and highly urbanized world, a regional cultural mecca for several adjacent sectors, home to an intelligent species known as the Aeaki, whose capital city of Hykaro Roost—"

"And that is where I will stop you," said Ydar, cutting me off. "The new planet we orbit is not 'densely populated.' We've seen a few scattered signs that could mean intelligent life, yes, but hardly 'urbanized.' And no cities to speak of at all. Just lots of forests and swamps and blighted deserts down there. We haven't seen anyone coming or going. The planet isn't a 'cultural mecca' by any standard."

"Yes," I said, "but this cyclopaedia comes from the time of Jalasu Jhuk, doesn't it? That was ages ago. Maybe something happened since then."

Ydar pondered this.

"See," said Hudka, "I told you the evidence was irrefutable."

Ydar's expression had changed. "Chorkle, what did you say that diameter was?"

"Thirteen thousand four hundred fifty-eight kilometers," I said. "But here's the most important part." I returned to the entry, skipping over long boring swathes that focused on Kyral's water cycle and tectonic plate dynamics.

"The Aeaki," I read aloud, "are a highly technologically advanced race, capable of faster-than-light space travel. Xotonians enjoy the highest level of cultural amity and cooperation with this friendly species."

Kalac, Hudka, and Ydar looked at one another.

"The reactor," said Kalac.

"If they're so technologically advanced, then maybe the Aeaki can help us fix it!" I said. "And with faster-than-light travel, maybe they can even help the humans get back to their own planet."

"It's a long shot," said Ydar. "But I suppose it's worth a try."

"I always said you were a wise one," said Hudka. "The Council should give you a raise."

. . . .

"By Great Jalasu Jhuk of the Stars," cried Loghoz, "let this, the eight hundred nineteenth Grand Conclave of the Xotonian people, commence!"

Ryzz Plaza was packed once more. The entire population of Core-of-Rock had gathered for the great meeting. Four young humans stood among the populace, now counted as full citizens of Gelo. This time they were able to follow the proceedings on their own. Well, three of them were, anyway.

Hollins was lost. "Did Loghoz just ask us all to name our favorite type of mouse?" he asked. "Because I don't know if I have one."

Nicki shook her head. "I can't wait to exercise my civic duty!" she whispered as she rotated her shoulder in a slow circle. "Gotta warm up my voting arm."

"Wake me up when it's over," said Becky, sprawling on a flat rock.

Beneath the iridium statue of Jalasu Jhuk stood the Xotonian Council. In addition to Loghoz and Kalac, there were Glyac, Dyves, and, of course, the dimwitted and outspoken Sheln. At the moment it was whispering something to Loghoz. Loghoz blinked uncertainly.

"By special request," said Loghoz, "the first to speak will be Council Member Sheln."

Sheln stepped forward, its thol'grazes folded humbly. There were hisses from the crowd, a few outright boos. The preceding months had not been kind to Sheln, politically or physically. By all accounts it had spent most of its time shut up in the municipal archives, reading over arcane laws and statutes. Perhaps it was trying to shed its public image as a complete moron.

"Greetings, Xotonian people," said Sheln. Its voice sounded uncharacteristically reedy and weak. Sheln had lost weight since the great battle. Its once overstuffed physique now looked saggy and deflated. Sheln had been caught on the wrong side of history: Blinded by its hatred for humans, it had opposed the efforts to fight the Vorem in favor of attacking the human miners. In hindsight, that position looked ridiculous.

"Allow me to extend my warmest welcome to our newest citizens," said Sheln, fooling no one. It was well known that it blamed the Earth children for its waning fortunes. In fact, most assumed this would be Sheln's last term of office on the Council.

"Power," said Sheln, "or the lack thereof. That is what we came here to discuss. Our reactor is failing, and we don't know how to fix it. We've lost our Stealth Shield. The Observatory barely functions. Agriculture, air circulation, and sanitation are crippled. Life in Core-of-Rock is becoming unbearable. And if the Vorem return, simply put, we are in trouble. This situation cannot stand."

I was confused. Sheln was summarizing the problem accurately and without a stupid or self-serving agenda. Perhaps the wormhole had taken us to some alternate universe where Sheln wasn't an utter mold-brain?

"But there is hope!" cried Sheln. "And once again it comes from young Chorkle here. What a prodigy, folks. And a hero of the great battle too! Let's hear it for Chorkle. What would we do without this little one? I have always said that the offspring are our future."

A few in the audience clapped uncertainly. The lack of applause wasn't a reflection on my personal popularity—though I noticed that Zenyk kept its thol'grazes folded. It was just that anyone was leery of agreeing with Sheln. I too wondered what it was getting at.

"You see, Chorkle has identified our new planet. And apparently it is home to an advanced and friendly civilization that was an ally back in the Time of Legends! It's possible that they can now help us fix the reactor."

A murmur ran through the crowd. The idea of more contact with outsiders didn't sit well with a lot of Xotonians. A few started to tear up preemptively. Yet still, a chance at solving our problems had a strong appeal.

"Therefore, for the good of the Xotonian species, I propose that we immediately launch a mission to the surface of this new planet, Kyral," said Sheln.

My gul'orp dropped open. Sheln had put forth the exact proposal that Kalac had intended to!

Someone called out, "Hey, over here. I'm a hero too!" Of course, it was Hudka. My grand-originator obviously couldn't let a public speaking appearance by Sheln pass without interruption.

"Hudka," sighed Loghoz, "while the Council recognizes your valiant service, we simply don't have time for—"

"No, please, let the ancient one speak," said Sheln, trying to sound deferential. "Hudka reminds us that history is still alive."

"Thanks," said Hudka. "Sheln, I was all set to call you a fat, self-serving, mold-brained creep, a toxic blight on the very political process itself. But I'm not going to do that. I will give credit where credit is due. For the first time in your life, you have made perfect sense." Then to the crowd, "Let this be a lesson, folks: Stupidity is not an incurable disease!"

A ripple of laughter swept across the plaza. Sheln forced a grotesque smile onto its face and tried to look like everything was in good fun. Its eyes weren't smiling though.

"The next to address the Conclave," cried Loghoz, "shall be Chief of Council Kalac!"

Kalac stepped forward.

"Greetings," said my originator. "In fact, I had intended to put forward exactly the same proposal. Thank you, Sheln, for stating the case so well."

Sheln nodded respectfully, its face still a pained smile.

Kalac continued. "The reason I felt this matter should be brought before the Grand Conclave, however, are the risks. It is only fair that they be addressed in public."

"If we undertake a mission to Kyral, we may end up drawing more attention to ourselves. We believe the Aeaki who inhabit the planet are friendly, but our information is hundreds of years out of date. The data we've gotten from the Observatory is limited. And, as we all know, our recent luck with alien encounters has been *mixed* at best. The truth is that we don't honestly know what we'll find down there. And to compound that risk, it appears there is already a Vorem trireme somewhere on the surface of the planet."

The crowd shuddered. A few of the more easily frightened Xotonians clutched each other for support.

"Still," continued Kalac, "I believe that a mission to Kyral is our best hope to bring the reactor and the Stealth Shield back online. And maybe even to help our young human friends return to their families. So I encourage you all to vote in favor of Sheln's plan." Kalac concluded its speech. The crowd seemed persuaded.

"If there are no further proposals," cried Loghoz, "then let us vote—"

"Pardon me, Custodian," said Sheln humbly, "but I wish to make one small amendment."

Loghoz looked around. Dyves seemed uncertain. Glyac seemed asleep. Kalac was unreadable.

"Go ahead, Sheln," said Loghoz.

"I propose," said Sheln, "that Kalac lead this vital mission to Kyral. It is an honor that our esteemed Chief of Council has earned many times over. And I can imagine no better leader for such a crucial endeavor."

I was thunderstruck. I had figured that Sheln only wanted to go ahead with the mission to screw it up or somehow turn the situation to its own advantage. Maybe even start a new war with the Aeaki, if we could find them. But with Kalac in charge, Sheln wouldn't get the chance.

"Very well," said Loghoz. "An amendment to the proposal: Kalac shall lead the mission to Kyral. Any objections?" There were none.

The proposal passed overwhelmingly, by a vote of 5,664 to 82. And one of the nay votes shouldn't have counted, since it was cast by a confused Hollins.

After the Conclave, the crowd slowly dispersed, perhaps a little more hopeful than when they had left their darkened homes. A few Xotonians were even shaking Sheln's thol'graz as it lingered by Jhuk's statue.

"So what was that about?" asked Nicki. "Voting the same way as Sheln makes my skin crawl."

"Yeah, what *was* that about?" asked Hollins. "Seriously. I'm asking. I only understood, like, twenty percent of what they were saying. Sheln wants to open a juice bar, but Kalac thinks it should serve packing tape instead?"

"What? No," I said. And I explained how Sheln had co-opted Kalac's idea and even suggested that my originator should lead the mission.

"Oh, that is pretty good," said Hollins, smiling. "Same old Sheln."

"What do you mean?" I asked.

"See, Sheln doesn't want to get caught on the wrong side again," said Hollins. "So it stole Kalac's idea. If the plan works, Sheln at least gets some credit for coming up with it. But if it doesn't—and this is what Sheln is hoping for—Kalac, the leader of the mission, will take the blame. It's all upside for Sheln. Not as dumb as you think, that one."

"Heh," said Becky. "I bet you that Sheln's hoping that Kalac doesn't come back from Kyral at all." Hollins nudged her hard with his elbow.

"Sorry," said Becky. "I mean—I'm sure that won't happen, Chorkle."

I hadn't really considered it before, but who knew what dangers my originator might encounter down on the planet's surface? "Kalac will definitely come back," I said. I hoped it was true.

• • • •

The four humans and I formally volunteered for the Kyral mission as well. After all, there were no better pilots on all of Gelo than Becky and Hollins. And Nicki and I were pretty handy with a blaster turret. And Little Gus, well . . . he could cook. Sort of. How could the five of us possibly pass up the chance to have an adventure on a strange new world?

"Absolutely not," said Kalac.

"But we fought in the great battle," I said. "Not to brag, but we're, you know, heroes." I only threw this term around on rare occasions, like when it might win an argument or get me something for free.

"You did, and you are," said Kalac. "Your courage meant the difference between victory and defeat. Gelo owes you a debt that will never be repaid."

"Here comes Kalac's famous 'but,'" said Hudka from its battered chair across the room.

"But you're still just children," said Kalac. "I couldn't bear it if something happened to you, Chorkle. Or any of the humans, either."

"So just because we're young, you won't let us help?" I asked. Kalac shook its head.

"Well, if age is all that matters, then I should be in charge of this whole asteroid," said Hudka, who was happy to jump into any argument against Kalac. "I hereby decree that all citizens must rub my aching fel'grazes no fewer than three times a day. And let them not be shy, but really get *in* there—"

"The fact is," said Kalac, cutting Hudka off. "You already have helped enough, Chorkle. You found the cyclopaedia entry. You and the humans have repaired the starfighters and even trained other pilots to fly them. Pilots who are grown-ups and fully understand the risks of undertaking a mission like this. They don't have their whole lives ahead of them. Trust me. When you have your own offspring, you'll understand."

All my arguments were futile. Kalac would not be persuaded. And unlike a Grand Conclave proposal, this matter wasn't up for a vote.

"Eh, look on the bright side, kid," said Hudka, placing a thol'graz on my i'arda. "With Kalac gone, none of us have to bathe."

"Wait. Everyone else has been bathing this whole time?" said Little Gus.

The next day, Ornim and Chayl boarded one of the Xotonian starfighters, the one we called *Phryxus II*. The ship was powered and ready for flight.

"Keep three eyes on everything around here while I'm gone," said Kalac to me.

"I will," I said.

"If you see any nacho cheese down there," said Little Gus, "try to bring back a sample."

Kalac smiled and nodded. "I love you, Chorkle," it said. "And I love you humans too." Then it turned and followed the others aboard.

The ship's engines fired, and they took off for Kyral.

CHAPTER FOUR

A sense of hope pervaded Core-of-Rock. With Kalac and the others gone, the Xotonian people felt that their leaders were working toward a solution to the problem. Surely the reactor would be repaired, and then everything would return to the way it had been for ages. All the lights and computers would blink back to life. No more cold food or piles of uncollected garbage rotting in the streets. The darkness would be lifted.

Few seemed to worry when the ship didn't radio back to the Observatory—temporarily fully powered, just for this purpose—to confirm their safe landing. I worried though. I worried a lot.

"Atmospheric conditions can certainly disrupt transmissions. There's probably an electrical dust storm down there. We've seen many since we began observing the new—

er, Kyral," said Ydar to me. "I'm sure all is going according to plan. Kalac is a very brave and capable leader." Did I hear a tinge of nervousness in the High Observer's voice?

All that day, we heard nothing. And the next day as well. The days turned into weeks. Still there was no message from Kyral's surface. I began to think about Kalac all the time. I pestered Ydar daily for information. There was none.

I realized now how my originator must have felt when I had seemingly disappeared in the days after the asteroid quake. I regretted putting Kalac through such pain. Even Hudka, who always made jabs at Kalac when it wasn't around, was strangely quiet.

The lack of mission contact was an open secret in Core-of-Rock. Soon tensions were running higher than ever. Neighbor began to turn against neighbor. Accusations—that certain citizens were using more than their allotted share of power or were hoarding food or other supplies—ran rampant. Several fights broke out in the marketplace. There were even a few cases of houses getting robbed—something unheard of in our small, tight-knit society. Beneath it all was the underlying fear that the Vorem—perhaps a whole new legion from their distant homeworld—could arrive at any moment to destroy us. After all, we had no Stealth Shield to conceal us from their long-range scanners.

More and more often, the human children and I took refuge in the hangar. We spent our time tinkering with the two remaining Xotonian starfighters, the *Roosevelt* and the *T'utzuxe*. We'd made a lot of progress on both ships, which were now mission-ready. While we worked, I often activated the ship's communicators, hoping for any sign from Kalac. Operating under such limited power, I worried that the Observatory might miss a transmission from the *Phryxus II*. It was no use though. Each time, I just heard radio silence. Still, I listened.

When the twins' birthday arrived, it provided a much-needed distraction. We gathered in the hangar to celebrate on Yshoj 7th (August 23rd), a date that coincidentally fell just five days before our Xotonian Feast of Zhavend, the most important holiday on Gelo.

I resolved not to bring the others down, so I tried to put aside my Kalac anxiety for the duration of the party. To start things off, Gus, Hollins, and I serenaded the twins with a traditional human birthday song. Even Pizza yowled along. The children took great pleasure, because this particular song was legally restricted on their home planet.

"But how can someone own a song?" I asked. Among all the aspects of human culture that baffled me, this one was the hardest to grasp.

63

"I dunno," said Little Gus, "but if you sing it back home and word gets out, you have to pay some super-old dude, like, six hundred dollars in royalty fees."

"It's actually probably our best bet at getting rescued," said Becky. "Let the copyright lawyers track us down to deliver a cease-and-desist letter."

Based upon my understanding of human traditions, I presented the twins with my gift: two precious Feeney's Original Astronaut Ice Cream bars, mushed together into a vaguely squarish shape. In the center, I had placed a large, burning mushroom.

"Um, wow. . . . Thank you, I think?" said Nicki.

"I hope you enjoy the birthday cake! Congratulations on being born several years ago," I said. "It took me a long time to get the mushroom burning. Somebody lost the welding torch." I squinted at Hollins, who just shrugged.

"Sure, yeah, it's, uh, really great," said Nicki as she flung the mushroom onto the ground and tried in vain to stamp out the fire. For some reason, open flames were required at every human birthday.

We each ate a tiny sliver of Feeney's Original Astronaut "birthday cake." Actually, I ate three. Five, at the most. I tried to savor the oversweetened, artificial goodness. There were, after all, only a few bars left in this entire star cluster.

I wished I had rationed them more carefully. Perhaps Kalac would return with the advanced Aeaki technology required to synthesize new Feeney's Originals. A Xotonian could dream.

After cake, it was time for more presents. Nicki and Becky presented each other with a gift. Nicki gave Becky a well-worn book called *Advanced Concepts in Astrophysics*. Becky gave Nicki her copy of *Vampire Band Camp: The Complete Ninth Season*. Neither one of them looked too thrilled, so they decided to swap.

There were two more wrapped gifts for Becky sitting on the ping-pong table. Both had cards that said they came from a "Secret Admirer."

The first was a gaudy necklace of big pink and purple jewels. The second was an old sock full of stink-pods, a horrifically pungent variety of Gelo fungus. As predicted, Becky gagged when she opened it. Instantly, the whole hangar smelled like hard-boiled feet.

"Ha ha. Super funny," said Becky to Hollins, who was doubled over with laughter. "Honestly, I think one gag gift would have been sufficient, you jerk." He just managed to duck out of the way as she whipped the ridiculous pink necklace at his head. It clattered across the floor, and Pizza ran to chase it. From the corner of my third and fourth eyes,

I noticed that Little Gus was frowning.

Next, Nicki unwrapped her gift from Hollins. It was a small, intricate x'yzoth crystal carving of a human female holding a round shield and a spear. A few days earlier, I had gone to the market to help Hollins commission it from Layiz the jeweler.

"It's Athena," said Hollins. "The Greek goddess of wisdom."

"Huh," said Nicki. "Thanks." She seemed less than impressed.

"You know, because you're the smart one," laughed Hollins.

"The smart one?" asked Nicki.

"I mean, you know how—I mean," said Hollins, "how I'm the 'brave leader' or whatever, and Becky is the rebellious one—"

"So you don't think Nicki's brave?" asked Becky with an evil grin. After the stink-pods, it seemed she was out for revenge.

"What? No," said Hollins, "I just mean that each of us is extra *good* at something different. That's all."

"Maybe I'm capable of more than you know," said Nicki, looking unhappy. "And maybe I would be brave if other people gave me the chance once in a while. Instead you think you're 'extra *good*' at telling other people what to do. But sometimes it can be a bit much, Hollins. Ordering everyone around in the fire, even though your Xotonian is *terrible*. Trying to protect me from a bunch of stupid rockbats . . ."

Hollins tried to defend himself but only succeeded in digging himself deeper the more he talked.

And so the birthday party ended on a glum note. Nicki was insulted. Becky was annoyed. Hollins was defensive and frustrated. Once more I descended into my own private concern for Kalac's well-being. Little Gus was the saddest of all. He sat alone, a sour expression on his face, while Pizza snored at his feet. At least the thyss-cat seemed happy.

"What's wrong?" I asked Little Gus once I was out of earshot from the others. "Are you jealous we're not celebrating your birth for no real reason?"

"No," he said. "Becky hated the necklace."

"Yes, pretty funny. We Xotonians don't really have the concept of 'gag gifts,' but I'm definitely starting to see the appeal. I was thinking I could give Hudka a new hat, except it's really a hibernating woolrat—"

"No, you don't understand," said Gus. "I got the necklace for her."

"Oh," I said. "Good one. She hated it worse than the stink-pods."

"Chorkle, I didn't give it to her as a joke!"

"But . . . the gift said it was from a 'secret admirer.' And the necklace was just so . . ." I trailed off as Little Gus stared at me. "Oh," I said.

He sighed and nodded. "I can't believe I blew it so bad," said Little Gus. "It's pink. It's a necklace. It's expensive. Those are three things that girls are supposed to like, right?"

I shrugged. I was truly out of my depth here. In my experience, girls seemed to like holodrive programming and piloting starships and playing extremely aggressive ping-pong. In short, I could see no particular pattern. Plus, I already found the dynamic between Hollins and Nicki hard enough to fathom. Now Little Gus was supposed to be Becky's "secret admirer"? It was just too much.

So I offered him my advice: "Just a thought, but it seems like this might cause a lot of trouble and confusion," I said. I was thinking of the tortured, tangled romances of *Vampire Band Camp*; I didn't want any of my human friends to get an oboe through the heart. "Perhaps you should stop," I added.

"Stop?"

"You know. Forget about it. Choose to focus on something else that humans enjoy. Like flossing your teeth."

"Chorkle," said Little Gus pitifully, "I can't just forget about it."

I left him to his misery and joined Hollins inside the *Roosevelt*. He was angrily attempting to recalibrate its flight controls.

"Where are the stupid adjustable micro-tongs?" he snapped, flinging tools out of the chest and over his shoulder.

"Are 'adjustable micro-tongs' a real thing?" I asked.

"They used to be. Now they're gone. We really need to treat this workspace with a little more respect!"

I could tell he was in no mood for friendly conversation. So I left him in the cockpit and set about trying to fix the hydraulics of the starfighter's blaster turret. They had been jittery and unreliable ever since the great battle. As usual, I turned on the ship's com to listen while I worked. And as usual, I heard only the quiet hum of static.

I'd been fiddling with the turret for the better part of an hour when I finally found the problem: a fluid leak near the main actuator. I sat up to get some polymer to patch the seal, when the ship's com crackled strangely.

I listened more closely. There was a faint noise, barely audible: a rhythmic chime. There was no mistaking it: a Xotonian distress beacon!

"Hollins," I said.

I heard him grumbling from the cockpit as he pounded on something metal. "Stupid statue . . . last gift I ever buy for anyone . . . ungrateful . . ."

"Hollins!" I cried again. "Turn on the cockpit communicator com."

"Huh? Okay, hold on a sec," he called back. "What am I listening for?"

"Do you hear a chime?"

"Nothing," he said.

I scrambled down into the cockpit. Hollins had his ear cocked toward the ship's main communicator. It was quiet.

"I'm not hearing anything," he said.

"There's a distress beacon," I said, flooding with panic. "It's got to be the *Phryxus II*. Down on the surface of Kyral. I heard it!"

We both returned to the com station in the blaster turret to listen. Again the signal was just a faint static. The chime was gone.

"I heard it," I said, adjusting the frequency back and forth across the spectrum. "It was Kalac's ship." Hollins nodded uncertainly.

"Hey," said Becky, stepping onto the *Roosevelt*. "We've got a visitor."

It turned out to be Eromu, the guard captain.

"Eromu, I just heard a distress beacon from the surface!" I cried as I exited the ship. "It's got to be Kalac and the others!"

"Kalac's in danger?" said Eromu. "I'll be sure to notify the Chief of Council."

"But Kalac is the Chief. What are you talking about?" I asked. "What's going on?"

The guard captain looked extremely put out. "I'm sorry," said Eromu, "but I've come to escort all of you back to the city."

"But we need to listen for more transmissions," I said. "We can't leave!"

Eromu shook its head. "No one is allowed outside of Core-of-Rock anymore. For safety's sake."

"What?" asked Nicki, speaking in Xotonian. "Since when?"

"Since the . . . Chief of Council has officially declared a state of emergency," said Eromu.

"Why do you keep saying 'Chief of Council'?" I cried. "Kalac is down on the surface—"

"Not Kalac," Eromu sighed. "I'm talking about Sheln."

CHAPTER FIVE

"**W**hat in the name of Morool are you saying?" I cried.

"Maybe you forgot your own language because you speak so much hoo-min now," said Sheln, reverting to its old mispronunciation of the word, "but I'll repeat it one last time: I am now the Chief of the Xotonian Council."

We stood in a small, cramped office in a public building that had no name. With the Hall of Wonok occupied by Vorem prisoners, this had become the temporary seat of government.

Upon returning from the hangar to Core-of-Rock, I'd proceeded directly here with just one quick detour. I had to tell Hudka about the distress beacon. Plus, if Sheln was attempting some sort of coup, I was going to need my grand-originator to help me stop it. Hudka was a Sheln-buster without equal.

Now Hudka, the humans, and I stood on one side of a raised stone bench. On the other side sat the four remaining members of the Xotonian Council. Behind us stood several members of the city guard, including Eromu. The only person in the room who seemed to be pleased with the situation was Sheln.

"You can't just declare yourself the Chief!" I cried. "We have laws! Kalac's not dead! My originator is on the surface of the new planet! I just heard a distress beacon—"

"Exactly!" said Sheln, interrupting me. "Kalac is absent from Gelo, and we have laws. Loghoz, you're the Custodian of the Council. Please explain."

Loghoz winced, then unrolled a yellowing sheaf, a page from our ancient legal code. Loghoz read aloud, "If the Chief of the Xotonian Council is absent for an extended period of time, the Provost-General of the Council shall be temporarily elevated to the rank and shall assume all duties and responsibilities as such."

"And guess who the Provost-General is," said Sheln, grinning.

"Guano!" cried Hudka. "Kalac beat the ish'kuts off you in the last election for Chief! 'Provost-General' is just the stupid ceremonial title we give to the loser so that they don't weep themselves to death."

73

"I wasn't crying! That was allergies!" snapped Sheln. "And as it turns out, the title of Provost-General is not *completely* ceremonial. You see, for the past few months, I've had a lot of time on my thol'grazes. Time to study the finer points of the Xotonian legal code. I learned some very interesting things. For one, an 'extended period of time' is defined as three weeks under our law. Can someone refresh my memory: How long has dear Kalac been gone?"

"Three weeks today," said Dyves glumly.

"But you're the one who wanted Kalac to go down to the surface," I yelled. "My originator could die down there, you treacherous bag of—" Hollins placed a firm hand on my i'arda to calm me.

"Does meeting. Does of Kalac. Forty-five red sponges? Fat pudding," said Hollins in Xotonian. The room was silent for a moment.

Sheln continued as if Hollins hadn't spoken. "If Kalac were to perish, Chorkle, we would hold a new election for the position of Chief of Council. But your originator isn't dead. Kalac has merely been 'absent for an extended period of time.' And that means I'm in charge. And as Eromu has already informed you, my first order of business was to officially declare a state of emergency for all of Core-of-Rock."

"Shouldn't the rest of the Council vote on something like that?" said Nicki.

"We are at war with the Vorem, are we not?" asked Sheln.

"Oh, I don't know, they seem all right to me," said Becky, her voice thick with sarcasm.

"Quiet, hoo-min!" said Sheln.

"Look, of course we're at war, mold-brain," said Hudka. "What's your point, Sheln?"

"Well, I think you will find that, again, according to the law, the Chief of Council may declare a state of emergency *at will* during a time of war. It is one of just two actions that the Chief may take without any imput from the rest of the Council."

"So you can declare a state of emergency?" said Hudka. "So what?"

"Well, during a state of emergency," said Sheln, "the Chief of Council has much *broader* powers than usual. It's all in the legal code." It was practically giggling.

Loghoz sighed. "We've been arguing for hours, Hudka. Believe me, Sheln, er"—here Loghoz looked thoroughly nauseated—"I mean, Chief of the Council seems to have the law on its side. Our thol'grazes are tied until Kalac returns. Or we have . . . another election."

Loghoz was obliquely referring to the possible death of Kalac.

Becky spoke in Xotonian. "Well, what if something were to happen to Sheln?" she said, cracking her knuckles. "Something bad."

"Very good conjugation," said Loghoz primly, "but remember to roll your *h*'s." It had momentarily reverted to its role as the humans' XSL teacher.

"What? Don't you correct this duplicate's grammar while she's threatening my life!" shrieked Sheln. "Commissioner of the Guards, please remove the unruly hoo-min from the Council chamber."

Eromu gave Sheln a confused look. "I don't understand, Chief. I am a captain of the guard. There is no such title as Commissioner."

"During a state of emergency," said Sheln, "the Chief of Council may make certain temporary appointments for the greater good. And I have created a leadership position within your force. Allow me to introduce the new Commissioner of the Guards!"

I had a sinking feeling in my z'iuk. Somehow, I already knew who it was going to be. From the back of the room, a huge young Xotonian stepped forward, wearing a look of epic smugness on its ugly face. It was Sheln's offspring,

Zenyk, clad in a ridiculous pseudo-military uniform: ill-fitting, brightly colored, and ornate. Practically every centimeter was encrusted with buttons and badges and crystal medals. Did they give out medals for flunking math? Maybe for picking your vel'doc and eating it?

At the sight of Zenyk, Little Gus burst out laughing. Zenyk turned and scowled.

"What?" said Little Gus, speaking Xotonian. "I'm sorry, but you look like a Christmas tree threw up."

"Careful what you say to me now, hoo-min," snarled Zenyk.

"Doesn't . . . of punchings," said Hollins, stepping toward Zenyk.

"That's it," said Sheln. "All of the hoo-mins must go. They simply can't be controlled. Bunch of filthy two-eyed barbarians."

"You heard the Chief, Eromu," snapped Zenyk. "Get them out of here. Now!"

Eromu gave the Council a pained look. It had served under many Councils, and disloyalty and disobedience were against its nature. Still, this was almost too much. "Zenyk," said Eromu at last, "is just a—a youngling." There were far worse words that I might have chosen to describe our new Commissioner.

"And haven't younglings proved they are capable of so much recently?" said Sheln with sarcasm. "I believe Zenyk is ready for this responsibility."

Eromu sighed, then did as it was told, gently leading the human children from the room.

"Hey, what did I do?" asked Nicki.

"You look just like the other one," said Sheln. And then she was gone. Now there were only Xotonians left in the chamber.

"That's better. No more foreign elements corrupting the political process," said Sheln. "Of course the state of emergency also means that no one leaves the city without my permission. So your little hoo-min clubhouse is over, Chorkle. Those two-eyed freaks shouldn't be fiddling with our Xotonian starfighters anyway. They're probably sabotaging them—"

"They saved your worthless *butt* with those starfighters!" yelled Hudka, using a human anatomical word for emphasis.

"Worthless *butt*?" repeated Sheln. "Worthless *butt*! I am the Chief of the Council now! I think you will find that my *butt* is quite valuable these days!"

"What?" said Hudka. "Gross."

"Fine," I said, struggling to remain calm. "I will grant

that my originator has been gone for a while. But that's exactly why we need the starfighters in good working order. I just heard a distress beacon coming from the surface of Kyral. We need to undertake a rescue mission. Kalac, Ornim, Chayl—they could all be in grave danger!"

"Hmm," said Sheln. "That sounds like a pretty big decision. I think we would need to hold a Grand Conclave to debate something so important. It doesn't seem like a matter that should be decided behind closed doors by the political elite. Everyone should have a chance to weigh in."

"So then let's have a Grand Conclave already!" I cried.

"Ah," said Sheln, "you may remember there is a second unilateral power of my new office. Loghoz?"

The Council looked at one another in despair. Loghoz spoke faintly. "Only the Chief of the Council may call a Grand Conclave."

Now Sheln really did burst out giggling. Everyone stared in silence as its flabby body shook with laughter. I had been struck speechless. In an accomplished lifetime of political dirty tricks, this was Sheln's dirtiest.

"Come on," said Hudka quietly. "We don't have to listen to this nonsense anymore. Let's go home, Chorkle." It placed a thol'graz on my i'arda.

"Not so fast," said Sheln. "I'm afraid the two of you have something I need."

"Okay, Sheln," said Hudka, "you can borrow some soap. Honestly, I've been wondering when you were going to ask."

"Shut your wrinkled gul'orp, or I'll have you jailed for sedition," snapped Sheln. "From the time of Jalasu Jhuk, each Chief of the Council has been passed down an eight-digit numeric code. I think you know what I'm talking about."

Indeed, I knew exactly what Sheln was talking about. The code was 9-1-5-6-7-2-3-4. I had memorized it when I saw Kalac punch it into the keypad to open the door of the Vault, the ancient structure where Jalasu Jhuk placed the Q-sik for safekeeping.

"I'm the Chief now, so that means I get the code," said Sheln. It was speaking very quietly, but there was a crazed look in its eyes. Sheln wanted the Q-sik, our ancient weapon of mass destruction, a device capable of destroying ships, planets, even stars.

"Sorry," said Hudka. "Don't know where the code is. Wouldn't tell you if I did. Furthermore, might I respectfully suggest that you go jump in a hot pile of slime eels?"

"One more word and I'll throw you in the Hall of Wonok with the Vorem," said Sheln. Then it turned to me and stared hard. "What about you, Chorkle? Do you know where your originator left the code? Did Kalac give it to you? What is it?"

"Don't know either," I lied. "But I will confess to being mildly curious as to why you want it. What with Jalasu Jhuk forbidding us from ever opening the Vault and all."

"Huh," said Sheln, looking around the room. "Do you see Jalasu Jhuk anywhere around here? Because I don't. And I don't see Kalac either. I run Gelo now, Chorkle. And I want the Q-sik!"

The rest of the Xotonian Council looked horrified.

"To keep it safe, of course," Sheln added, smiling once more.

"Pretty sure it's safe in the Vault," I said. And with that I turned and walked out of the Council Chamber.

"I'll get that code," said Sheln behind me. "One way or another, I'll get that code."

Sheln proved to be a creature of its word. It had already secretly ordered members of the city guard to search our home for the code during the meeting. By the time we returned through the pitch-black streets of Core-of-Rock, two guards, Nar and Ydevi, were already ransacking the place. They opened drawers, flipped furniture, and rifled through documents. We had to wait outside until they finished. By the end, Hudka really did look ready to do something that would be worthy of jail time.

Thankfully their search came up empty. Kalac kept the code (scrawled on an ancient bit of parchment) hidden on its person at all times. This meant that—for the time being, at least—I was the only Xotonian on Gelo who could open the Vault.

Now we sat in grim silence—the four young humans, Hudka, and I—in the living room of my dwelling. Books, furniture, cookware, all of my family's belongings were strewn about the floor. It was dark, save for the glow of human flashlights.

"Well, that was awesome," said Becky.

"Dude, I think your government needs more checks and balances," said Little Gus.

"Is there any way we can change Sheln's mind?" Nicki asked me. "Convince it to call a Grand Conclave after all? If you really did hear the beacon, it means Kalac and the others need our help. Maybe we could appeal to Sheln's conscience?"

At the idea of Sheln's "conscience," Hudka laughed bitterly. It sometimes understood more human-ese than it let on.

"Sheln won't back down," said Hollins. "The last thing it wants is for Kalac to return. It would probably rather blow up Gelo than relinquish control."

"So what choice do we have?" asked Little Gus. "Just wait for Kalac to find a way back to Gelo on its own?"

"No," I said, staring out into the dark city of Core-of-Rock, the sound of that faint, staticky chime replaying in my head. "There's no time to wait." I turned back toward the others. "I'm going to Kyral myself."

The humans looked at one another. Hollins grinned. "Chorkle, I was hoping you'd say that," he said, rising to his feet.

"I can't ask you to come," I said, feeling a swell of the familiar guilt. "It's my fault you're here instead of back on Earth. And Kalac is my originator. I can't ask you all to risk your lives again on my account. I . . ."

"So don't ask, Chorkle," said Becky, patting me on the thol'graz. "We're coming."

"I'd help bring Kalac back to Gelo just to see the look on Sheln's face," said Hollins.

"Yeah," said Little Gus. "You think we're just going to sit here in the dark while you explore Gusworld VII without us? Pretty selfish, Chorkle."

"It's not going to be easy," I said.

"We don't expect it to be," said Nicki. "Even if we manage to escape from Gelo, we don't know what we'll find on Kyral. Environmental hazards, hostile life forms, diseases. Heck, the air down there could be full of toxic spores!" she chuckled. The rest of us didn't see the humor. She cleared her throat. "Sorry. Thinking out loud. My point is: We're going to need a plan."

CHAPTER SIX

"Wow, it's beautiful," said Nicki.

She referred to the traditional green lights of the Feast of Zhavend, now draped from every dwelling and coiled around every stalactite we passed on our way to Rhyzz Plaza.

"Who knows what damage using all this extra power is doing to the reactor, though," she added.

The Feast of Zhavend is a Xotonian celebration of our shared history and culture. It's Gelo's most important holiday, a day the young and old alike look forward to all year. Normally it is a joyous occasion to spend with friends and family.

Not this time though. Even if Kalac hadn't been missing, this Feast of Zhavend would have been miserable.

On the surface it looked like a normal holiday. Against Ydar's recommendation, Sheln had insisted on hanging the lights. The customary crowds had gathered in the street—in smaller numbers than usual—for the public component of the festival. There were oog-ball matches to be played (by far the worst aspect of the Feast—why mar a perfectly good holiday with contact sports?) and fatty foods to be eaten in mass quantities.

Despite the lights, the mood was dark. Sheln's power grab didn't sit well with the city. Its coup was brilliantly executed, but—as anyone might have predicted—Sheln had no talent for actually running the government. It had angered many by imposing a curfew and posting armed city guards at every entrance to the Unclaimed Tunnels. It had even banned the Observers from their own Observatory. Gelo was currently flying blind.

Two city guards, Nar and Ydevi, had been specifical-ly assigned to watch me and the humans to make sure we didn't make any trouble for the new Chief. All day long, they stood outside the door of my dwelling. If anyone left, one of them would trail behind at a distance. Occasionally, I offered them food, but they always refused.

A new nickname for the Chief of Council had already come into common use around Core-of-Rock. Surprisingly,

it wasn't a swear word. Everyone simply called it Imperator Sheln, "Imperator" being the title of the supreme dictator
who ruled the Vorem Dominion.

But Sheln's worst mistake in the eyes of the public—
even more than its subversion of the democratic process—
was how it dealt with the Jalasad.

The central feature of the Feast of Zhavend (aside from
the much, *much* more important presents) is a tradition
called the Jalasad. The Jalasad is a public performance in
which the great deeds of the hero Jalasu Jhuk are commem-
orated. One lucky Xotonian gets to dress up like the Great
Progenitor and reenact such heroic exploits as the Battle of
Three Suns and the Escape from Quyl. Another, perhaps
even luckier Xotonian dresses up as Morool, the ancient
Vorem imperator who pursued Great Jalasu Jhuk across the
universe. Everyone knows these old stories by heart, yet
each year we thrill to see them performed onstage.

In the Jalasad, Morool is a buffoon—a ridiculous villain
that the crowd loves to hate—whom Jhuk repeatedly and
humorously outwits. Crafting a revolting Morool costume
is very important to the Feast of Zhavend. And each year
the Jalasad performers—Linod's originator, Lhoy, was one
of them—somehow manage to outdo themselves in terms
of Morool's hideousness.

This year, though, the jowly mask of the Morool costume bore an unmistakable resemblance to a certain public figure. All agreed that this was the ugliest Morool to date.

When Sheln saw the mask, it flew into a rage. By its decree, the Jalasad was officially canceled. Instead, Sheln itself would personally deliver a two-hour public lecture to the festival audience. The topic: the importance of not criticizing our leaders during a time of war.

It was shaping up to be the worst Zhavend on record (at least since the Great Giant Spider Gift Exchange Debacle of '26). But it couldn't have been a more perfect opportunity to execute our plan.

The human children and I had spent the preceding days making preparations and gathering supplies. Becky had even put on Nicki's glasses once or twice to throw the guards off their trail. Now everything was in place. We had food, water, a hundred meters of nylon rope, five human thermal blankets, and the cyclopaedia volume that described Kyral packed away. It was almost time. We had only one chance to pull this off.

A rowdy crowd gathered at Ryzz Plaza for Sheln's speech. Dozens of city guards surrounded the stage to keep the audience back. Already, several angry and anti-Sheln chants were competing with one another. Some repeated "Sheln's the worst!" at the top of their b'hueys. Others yelled the marginally more positive "Bring back Kalac!" A third contingent offered a simple "Stink head!" over and over again. This last chant was my personal favorite, possibly because I started it.

Hollins, Nicki, Becky, and I stood on the edge of the crowd. As always, Ydevi and Nar were nearby, watching. A tiny Xotonian hunched beside me, leaning on a gnarled cane, the hood of a ratty old cloak pulled up over its head. It would have been incredibly suspicious for my grand-originator not to show for a Sheln-heckling opportunity.

The Chief of the Council took the stage to a hearty chorus of boos. I was glad to see the general malaise in Core-of-Rock finally focused on a worthy target.

"All right, all right!" yelled Sheln over the din. "Everybody shut your gul'orps! It's speech time! Happy Zhavend, you pack of dirty ingrates!"

"Where's Kalac?" cried someone.

"Not here!" Sheln yelled back.

"Sheln ate the Chief!" called someone else. The crowd snickered.

"Enough!" cried Zenyk, standing among the guards in its ridiculous Commissioner's uniform. "The first one of you who throws something is going straight to jail!" Ze-

nyk was young but, like its originator, physically imposing—bigger and stronger than many adult Xotonians. Its
threat managed to quiet the hecklers down a little. Sheln
continued.

"Respect," said Sheln. "It's something that has been sadly lacking on this asteroid of late. When participating in the
public discourse, I have *always* treated others with respect."

At this, the crowd roared in anger and surged forward,
and the guards shoved them back.

"The next one of you who disrespects my office is going
to face dire consequences!" cried Sheln. "You will listen to
my whole speech about being nice, or I'll have you executed!" A few of the guards turned back toward Sheln, their
faces confused, horrified. This was not how they wanted to
spend their holiday.

The crowd murmured darkly but made no further attempt to rush the stage. Meanwhile, across the city, a faint
noise was growing louder by the second. I gave a subtle nod
to the humans. They nodded back.

Sheln continued. "I believe it was Jalasu Jhuk's famous
lieutenant, Wonok, who once said, 'Always do as you're
told and you need never think for yourself.' Wise words.
Folks, this is why you have leaders. So you don't have to
waste time and energy worrying your little microbrains

over things that shouldn't concern you . . ." Sheln trailed off as the sound—now a whining roar—had begun to drown out its misinterpretation of the famous quote. The crowd looked around uncertainly.

"What is that noise?" bellowed Sheln. "I'm giving a historical speech here! This is one for the ages—what? What in the name of Morool are you all looking at?"

The collective gaze of the crowd had drifted to a point high above and behind Sheln. Indeed, as the Chief of the Council turned, it was the last to see what they were all staring at.

A lone masked figure sailed over Ryzz Plaza on a frightfully loud alien vehicle—those who attended "human school" might have recognized it as the rocket-bike they had reassembled in class. The Xotonian who steered it—shakily and uncertainly, it must be said—wore a hideous mask, indeed this year's Morool. Behind the rocket-bike there trailed a huge flapping banner, phosphorescent human letters glowing on black parchment: "Sheln Sucks!"

"What?" shrieked Sheln. "What does that banner say?"

And at this, the crowd exploded in laughter. Sheln had deliberately avoided learning any human language at all. Most of the crowd, on the other thol'graz, attended human school and understood perfectly well.

The rocket-bike began to fly in low, dangerous figure eights above the plaza, just a few meters over the crowd. The Xotonian people cheered with each roaring flyby.

"Shoot! Shoot! Shoot that traitor!" commanded Sheln. "This is ruining my otherwise perfect speech!" None of the guards responded. When push came to shove, even Zenyk wasn't prepared to actually vaporize another Xotonian for no good reason.

At last, Sheln leaped off the stage and yanked one of the blasters from a guard's holster. The Chief of the Council only got off two shots—blazing bolts of green energy, well wide of their target—before another guard wrestled the blaster from its thol'graz.

"You need to practice your Xenostryfe III, O Glorious Imperator!" taunted the rocket-biker from above. And it whipped the rubbery mask off its face.

Sheln cried out in rage and anguish, audible above the bedlam: "Huuuuuuuuudkaaaaaaaaaa!"

Indeed, it was my grand-originator, doing flips and barrel rolls and other difficult maneuvers that I worried might exceed the eye-thol'graz coordination of one so old. The crowd surged forward toward the stage once more. The guards, while unwilling to vaporize their unruly fellow citizens, continued to shove them back. Finally, a unified chant took hold: "Sheln Sucks! Sheln Sucks! Sheln Sucks!"

Pandemonium had broken loose in Ryzz Plaza. Our moment had come.

From the corner of my third and fourth eyes I could see that Nar and Ydevi were thoroughly confused. After all, Hudka was supposed to be right beside them. They had followed the old coot all the way from my dwelling. But by the time they looked back, Linod had already discarded its old cloak and cane and faded back into the crowd. My good friend had played its part admirably.

"Come and get me, you mold-brain!" howled Hudka, and it took off through the city at incredible speed, trailing smoke and flame.

"After it!" shrieked Sheln, its voice close to breaking. "Go after it! Arrest that traitor!"

"Get Hudka!" cried Zenyk. The guards in the plaza looked at one another. Then they took off after the rocket-bike on fel'graz, leaving the stage unguarded. The first rotten mushroom hit Sheln approximately four milliseconds later. Soon the Chief of Council was being pelted with garbage from all sides. Sheln shrieked for the guards to return, but they were already gone. The speech had practically turned into a riot. I regretted that I couldn't stay and enjoy it until the end.

But the humans and I had already made our escape. We ran in five separate directions, leaving Ydevi and Nar behind in the chaos.

The children were to regroup on a deserted side street to gather our supplies. We'd stashed them there, disguised as colorfully wrapped Zhavend presents.

Alone, I ran toward the center of Core-of-Rock. There was one important item I had to obtain before we left. Hollins was right: Sheln would rather blow up Core-of-Rock than give up power, and that had stuck with me.

I rejoined the humans at the nearby usk-lizard stables. Luckily, Ixoby wasn't manning the gate. Presumably, the young guard had joined the others in trying to chase down Hudka's rocket-bike.

On the spur of the moment, Little Gus decided to release all the other usk-lizards from their stables. At first, the big, dumb beasts snuffled uncertainly at the prospect of freedom. Then they plodded off in their separate directions. If any guards were to follow us, they would need to catch their own ride.

Becky, Nicki, and I hopped onto Goar; Hollins and Little Gus took Gec. Unresolved tensions from the twins' birthday party had rearranged the usual riding order.

And then we were galloping through the city. Away in

the distance, we could still hear the whine of Hudka's rocket-bike and the raucous crowd. According to the children, the vehicle had hours of fuel left.

"It looks like we're home free!" cried Hollins.

As we approached the entrance to the Unclaimed Tunnels, though, I heard Becky curse under her breath.

A solitary figure stood in our path. It was Captain Eromu, still guarding its post. Becky slowed Goar to a halt. Gec stopped behind us. Eromu regarded us in silence, its thol'grazes crossed. The guards were under strict orders to allow no one to leave the city. And no one followed orders like Eromu.

I opened my gul'orp to explain. I wanted to tell the captain that we weren't lawbreakers or rebels but that we had to try to save my originator, that I couldn't leave Kalac down on Kyral's surface when I knew it was in danger, that Sheln would drag its fel'grazes, and by the time a rescue mission was finally mounted, it might just be too late. I wanted to tell Eromu that if it felt it had to vaporize me, then so be it. But I would not be dissuaded. I would not give up.

Before I could say anything, though, Eromu simply nodded and stepped aside. The captain already knew where we were going. For the first time in Eromu's life, it set aside the rules.

As we galloped past, Eromu tossed something up to me. I caught it, then stared at Eromu. The guard captain offered a quick salute. It had given me its energy blaster.

I turned the weapon over in my thol'graz: tarnished green metal with an usk-leather grip, surprisingly heavy. One of only 256 on all of Gelo. I'd never held an energy blaster before. I wasn't sure I wanted to. I opened my pack to stow it away.

The frightening truth was that the blaster was far from the most dangerous weapon I carried. From inside my bag came the faint glow of the Q-sik.

CHAPTER SEVEN

We made the trip from Core-of-Rock to Flowing-Stone in record time. In our minds, each stray sound we heard as we raced through the Unclaimed Tunnels became the Xotonian city guards closing in on us. Once Sheln realized that we were gone, it would be easy enough to guess where we were headed. The other guards wouldn't be as sympathetic as Eromu.

By the time we arrived, the usk-lizards had been worked into a lather. As we leaped from the saddles and raced toward the hangar, Gus stopped.

"Hold on," said Gus. "I'll be right behind you guys."

"Dude, there's no time!" cried Hollins. "The guards could be here any minute!"

But Gus had already turned and dashed off into the phi-liddra forest, his flashlight twinkling in the mist.

"We should all agree to pee *before* we do this stuff," said Nicki.

Down in the hangar, we powered up the *T'utzuxe,* the least damaged of the two remaining starfighters.

"No arguments, Becky," said Hollins. "I'm flying."

"One argument, Hollins," said Becky. "I'm flying."

"Ugh, fine!" said Hollins. "But only because you could use the practice."

Becky snorted and took the cockpit. We ran through a quick battery of system tests: power, propulsion, artificial gravity, navigation, communications, weapons, sensors, and life support.

"Well, weapons are still on the fritz, but otherwise everything looks good to go," said Nicki, "more or less."

"What does 'more or less' mean, sis?" asked Becky, adjusting the controls to her preference.

"Well, we've flown these ships in space and around Gelo," said Nicki, "but they took a beating in the battle. Kyral's gravity and atmosphere might very well tear us to pieces when we try to land. Our life support could give out. Or the automated navigation systems could fail while we're trying to—"

"Okay, okay, Nicki. We get it," said Hollins, cutting her off. "No time to worry now."

"Hey, I'm just thinking out loud here," she snapped. "I'm supposed to be 'the smart one,' aren't I?"

Hollins grimaced and said nothing.

"Guys, help!" cried Little Gus from across the hangar.

We saw him struggling toward the ship. He was pulling a big, blue, unwilling shape behind him: Pizza the thyss-cat.

"Dude, what are you doing?" cried Hollins. "Pets aren't allowed in restaurants. What makes you think you can bring one on our interplanetary rescue mission?"

"Pizza wants to come," said Little Gus. "He wants to help us!" All visual evidence contradicted his statement, however. In fact, I'd never seen the thyss-cat like this. The closer the beast got to our ship, the more Pizza whined and growled and resisted Little Gus.

"Let him go, Gus!" cried Hollins. "Seriously, we don't have time for this! I guarantee you that the city guards are on their way here right now."

"Does . . . anybody," wheezed Gus, pulling Pizza as hard as he could, "have . . . like . . . a steak or something?" Now, three meters from the *T'utzuxe*, Pizza wouldn't budge. The thyss-cat stood rigid, facing the ship and wailing pitifully.

"Eh, not everybody likes flying," said Becky, shrugging.

"This wasn't part of the plan, Gus!" said Hollins. "If you don't come aboard right now, we're leaving you!"

"Oh no," said Nicki.

Across the hangar, several Xotonians ran toward the ship, blasters at the ready. Indeed, they were city guards. They had caught up to us.

"Stop!" cried Ydevi. "You are not authorized to be here!"

"It's now or never," said Becky, powering up the thrusters and opening the hangar bay doors. The atmosphere began to rush out of the chamber and into the void beyond.

At last, Little Gus gave up. He let go of Pizza and scampered aboard the *T'utzuxe*. For an instant, Pizza seemed totally confused that he'd been abandoned. It was almost as though the thyss-cat wanted to keep Gus from boarding the ship. Pizza gave one final yelp. Then—an instant before the automated hatch closed—he leaped inside after Gus.

"He likes cutting it close," said Little Gus, rubbing Pizza's neck. "Adds drama." But Pizza was more distressed than ever. The thyss-cat kept trying to position himself between Little Gus and the back of the ship, all the while making a low growl in his throat.

"What, is he sick? That thing better not throw up inside my ship," said Becky as we lifted off the ground. Somehow she never seemed more at ease than in life-threatening situations. "Hey, Hollins, got any inspirational Teddy Roosevelt quotes for us?"

"Uh, 'Believe you can and you're halfway there,'" said Hollins, his face pressed to the viewport. Beneath us, the guards had begun to fire their weapons.

"You learned that one from me," said Nicki curtly.

A few green energy bolts whizzed past us as the *T'utzuxe* rose toward the open hangar doors. Maybe it was wishful thinking, but the shots seemed a tad halfhearted to me. Perhaps, like Eromu, the other guards knew we were trying to save their true Chief.

We blasted out into space. Little blue-gray Gelo shrank away behind us, along with the crippled battle cruiser. Green Kyral grew. Its lopsided planetary ring faded into a cloud of dust as we approached. We could see the fissures and icy canyons on Ithro, its moon.

"Turn the communicator on," I said. "Listen for the *Phryxus II*'s distress beacon."

Becky did. And almost immediately, we heard the telltale chime ringing over the speakers.

"Kalac!" I cried. I hadn't imagined it! And the closer we got to Kyral, the clearer the sound became.

"Okay, I'm getting a read on it," said Nicki, regarding a display projected from her holodrive, now connected to the

T'utzuxe's navigation system. "Looks like it's coming from a land-bound point in the Northern Hemisphere. About eight thousand kilometers north-northeast of that big inland sea. You see the one I'm talking about? It's kind of shaped like a . . . dolphin wearing a sombrero?"

A brief discussion of the sea's true shape ensued—some felt it looked more like a banana playing football. Personally, I thought it resembled a zaeper with two rha'tills, but no one else knew what that was. As Kyral swelled to fill our view, the fuzzy green ball focused itself into distinct plains and mountains and forests and oceans. Kalac was down there somewhere. Hopefully, it was still alive.

With all our attention squarely focused on the new planet, none of us heard the hatch of the cargo hold scrape open. Only Pizza saw the stowaway creep silently from his hiding place. The thyss-cat snarled.

From behind me, there came a voice, somehow familiar. "Turn this ship around," it said, speaking oddly accented Xotonian, "or I will kill you all."

As one, we turned. Standing behind us was a dark figure. Though he spoke Xotonian. he was not one of my people. He was a Vorem. In one hand, he clutched what looked to be some sort of improvised energy weapon.

"I told you so," said Little Gus under his breath.

The Vorem was a young male. He was stripped of his armor and wore a filthy, ill-fitting legionary's uniform. His stringy black hair hung down in his eyes.

"Fly me back to the Vorem battle cruiser *Secutor* immediately," he commanded. I heard a desperate tinge in his voice. He looked wild, half-starved.

"We're not going to do that," said Becky in Xotonian. "And if you hurt anyone, I'll crash this ship. You'll be a little purple stain on that big green planet, tough guy."

The starfighter rattled as we entered Kyral's highest atmosphere.

"Do as I tell you to do, alien female!" the stowaway shrieked.

At that instant, Pizza flew at him. Somehow—quick as a thyss-cat himself—the Vorem dodged out of the way, and Pizza tumbled into the open cargo hold. He quickly slammed the hatch shut behind the beast.

As he turned back to face us, Hollins's fist caught him square in the face. The Vorem stumbled, and Hollins swung again. The second blow never landed, though. The Vorem blocked it with his arm and returned two hard kicks: one to Hollins's stomach, the second to his face. Hollins's head snapped back, and he dropped to the floor, unconscious.

"That's it! What did I tell you, guy?" cried Becky, standing from the pilot's chair, her fists balled. Now the starfighter was shaking and bucking wildly. We were tumbling in an uncontrolled spiral toward Kyral.

The Vorem hesitated. Perhaps he hadn't expected her to carry through on her threat to crash the ship. Suddenly there was a flash. An arc of blue light leaped from his little weapon to Becky. For an instant, she convulsed as though every muscle in her body had contracted at once. Then she too fell to the floor of the ship. The legionary had taken out our two best pilots.

Nicki stood but froze when the Vorem trained the weapon on her. Frantically, he pointed the weapon at each of us in turn: Nicki to Little Gus to me then back to Nicki. He was panting wildly. His plan, such as it was, was in as much of a downward spiral as our ship.

Outside, the blackness of space had become a deep blue. The shade grew lighter with every passing second, as the density of Kyral's atmosphere increased. Through the viewports, I saw flames as bits of debris burned off our hull. Inside, pieces of the ship were knocking themselves loose. Countless warning lights flashed. Our descent was far too rapid. The flight stick vibrated wildly. Somewhere Pizza roared in anguish.

"Take me back to my ship!" he bellowed again. But none of us dared move. "Turn around and—"

The Vorem gave a wordless cry as the shot from my blaster caught him in the arm. He fell back against the hull, and his strange little weapon clattered across the floor. Nicki grabbed it. Perhaps he hadn't considered that we too might be armed.

I held the energy blaster in my thol'graz, trained on him. I hoped he didn't realize that I was terrified to fire the weapon again. If I missed, the shot might damage some vital system—or worse, tear a hole in the hull and depressurize the starfighter.

Little Gus dove for the flight stick. Outside, I could make out the shape of individual rivers, rocks, and trees. But they were coming at us way too fast.

Gus pulled up as hard as he could. I could feel the *T'utzuxe* straining to obey. Straining but failing. Nicki was yelling something I couldn't understand.

"I can't hear you!" I cried.

But she had already folded her head toward her knees. I saw the Vorem slowly close his red eyes in resignation.

We crashed.

CHAPTER EIGHT

The ship hit Kyral. My face hit a sparking instrument panel. There was a continuous deafening roar that seemed like it would never end. I bounced off the floor. Or was it the ceiling? The shaking of the ship slowed and then stopped altogether. I tasted blood and heard the roar of fire. All around me the air was filled with thick black smoke. The warning lights had all gone out.

Now Little Gus and Nicki were dragging Hollins away. And Becky wasn't dead. She was moving, pulling herself up onto unsteady feet. I could hear Pizza mewling like a cub. I fumbled around until I found the latch of the cargo hold, and I released it. The thyss-cat burst out of the hold and scrambled past me through the haze. Instinct told it the way out. My own instincts felt dull and uncertain, so I tried to follow Pizza.

Beside me a valve exploded in flame, and I fell flat on my z'iuk. If I had been human, the flare would have surely caused me to lose all my head-fur. Crouching down low, I found that it was easier to breathe. So I crawled like a cave slug toward the exit.

My thol'graz brushed something. It was rubbery, pointed: a black boot. There was a leg inside it. It was the Vorem. He was pinned between the hull and a heavy support girder. His uniform was slick with amber-colored blood. He'd been killed in the crash.

Another ball of fire bloomed from a snarl of ruptured tubing. The whole ship was burning now. I'd worked with the starfighters enough to know that there were dozens of volatile compounds coursing through the ships' inner workings. When the fire reached them, the *T'utzuxe* would explode.

Over the flames I heard something: a quiet moan. I was wrong; the Vorem was alive! It would serve him right to die, I thought, since he brought this disaster upon us. I fumbled past him toward the exit.

I stopped. I couldn't do it. No matter how evil he was, I couldn't just leave him to burn.

I groped back through the smoke until I found the Vorem again. I wrapped all four of my thol'grazes around

107

his leg and pulled with all my might. He didn't budge. I pulled again. He was stuck fast beneath the girder.

There was even more fire crawling up the inside of the hull. The smoke and the heat made it hard to think. Outside I could hear the human children screaming for me.

I clambered back toward the bulkhead and found Eromu's blaster lying in a sticky pool of coolant. I adjusted the weapon to its maximum power setting and pointed it at the girder that was pinning the Vorem down. Then I fired. A green bolt of energy leaped from the blaster and sheared a white-hot hole through the metal. But it wasn't enough. I aimed and fired again. Finally, the girder shuddered and fell into two pieces with a shower of sparks.

Summoning all my remaining strength, I somehow dragged the Vorem's limp body—he was as tall as Hollins, at least, if not as heavy—across the deck of the burning starfighter and out onto the surface of a new world.

I blinked in the bright sunshine and sucked in a gulp of air.

"What are you doing, Chorkle?" cried Little Gus in disbelief. "Why did you save him? Dude is super, *super* evil!"

"We all need to get away from the ship!" screamed Nicki. "Like, now!"

"Help me," I rasped. Nicki and I hefted the Vorem up between us. Somehow we dragged him about thirty meters before we all collapsed onto the ground. Nearby I saw Becky standing stiffly. Hollins was sprawled on the ground, his eyes still closed.

I turned back just in time to hear a thunderous boom and see the starfighter go up in a twenty-meter-high cloud of flame. A few seconds later, we were showered with little bits of ash and smoking debris.

"Well, that sucks," said Becky. She worked the stiffness from her arms.

It was only as I watched the *T'utzuxe* burn to the ground that I remembered the Q-sik. Where was it? I felt a surge of panic until I realized that it was still safely inside my pack, which—thank Great Jalasu Jhuk of the Stars—had somehow stayed on my i'ardas through the crash. I shuddered to think what would have happened if the Q-sik had been aboard that exploding starship. Jhuk had warned that any damage to the device might release the incredible energy it contained all at once, with devastating consequences.

Hollins was sitting up now, rubbing his face. One of his eyes was ringed with a dark purple bruise, courtesy of the Vorem's boot.

The Vorem was still unconscious, lying in the grass and breathing shallowly. In the bright sun, he looked frail and gaunt.

"So what do we do with him now, Chorkle?" asked Hollins, frowning. I had no answer for his question.

"I think I have an idea," said Becky, taking the blaster from my thol'graz. She scowled and pointed it at the Vorem. I closed my eyes. After a long moment, I opened them again. She had lowered the weapon.

"Okay, fine. I'm not going to just shoot him while he's unconscious," she said at last.

Nicki knelt beside him and began to check his vitals.

"Well, I think I feel a steady pulse," she said. "Are they, uh, supposed to have pulses? Or is that a bad thing?" I shrugged. None of us knew any more about Vorem anatomy than she did. She started to dress his wounds—a big gash across his chest and the blaster burn on his arm. She was operating under the assumption that human first aid was better than nothing.

"Man, you've sure got a soft spot for aliens, don't you, Chorkle?" said Hollins.

"I couldn't just leave him there to die," I said. "I shot him once already. Doesn't that count for something?"

Little Gus prodded the Vorem with his toe. "So I get why we can't just vaporize the creep now, without due process or whatever," said Gus, "but couldn't we just slap some bandages on him and leave before he wakes up?"

"Nope," said Hollins. "He's way too dangerous to be left alone."

"Well, he sure laid you out," laughed Becky.

"Yeah. And he lit you up like Times Square with his little zapper thingie," said Hollins as he searched the Vorem for more weapons.

"That must be where all the missing tools from the hangar went," said Nicki. "He was using them to build this." She turned the strange little device over in her hand.

"He was probably stealing food too," said Hollins.

"Hey! My phui-chips!" cried Becky, suddenly remembering. "Okay, I changed my mind. Let's kill him."

"What do you think this is?" asked Hollins as he pulled a small circular token out of the legionary's pocket. It bore General Ridian's crest on it—three black suns—and looked to be made of gold.

"Hey, I, uh, think that's mine," said Little Gus. "Can you believe he stole Becky's chips and my, uh, special gold medallion that's probably worth thousands of dollars?"

Hollins shook his head. "We're not murderers, and we're not thieves either, Gus," said Hollins, shoving the token back into the legionary's pocket. "Guy can keep his oversized commemorative coin or whatever it is."

Just then, the Vorem startled us all by crying out in his sleep. "I . . . failed you. . . . ," he murmured. "Sorry I'm weak . . . Sorry . . . General. . . ." And once more he was silent. The humans and I looked at one another, speechless.

Little Gus was the first to break the silence. "Ahem. Some of you may have missed it, since we were crashing at the time, but I just want to take this opportunity to offer another resounding I-told-you-so. This is the dude I saw running around Core-of-Rock in the fire! Maybe now you'll believe me when I tell you important stuff. . . ."

I lost the thread of what Little Gus was saying as I noticed something curious about the Vorem. A little object was attached to his belt. Not a weapon. It looked like a featureless black screen a few centimeters in diameter. I knelt and examined it, then tried for the better part of a minute to activate it. No matter what I did, though, it wouldn't turn on. At last, I figured it had been damaged in the crash, so I gave up.

"Okay, okay, okay," Hollins was saying to Gus, "just spit it out. What other important information do we need to know?"

"Like I told you guys before, Pizza can say 'hamburger'!" cried Little Gus.

"Wait, where is Pizza?" asked Nicki.

The thyss-cat was nowhere to be seen. We decided to survey our surroundings and search for Pizza. Hollins stayed behind with the blaster trained on our new prisoner and a grim expression on his face.

For the first time, I really took in the landscape. Somehow, this world was even greener than it appeared from space. In one direction, a sunny plain extended for thirty kilometers, toward a colossal mountain range just a shade purpler than Kyral's lavender sky.

In the other direction, there stretched a dark forest of woody treelike plants. They had deep blue trunks and pale green leaves of oddly geometric shapes—pentagons and hexagons and sharply pointed stars. High above us, three black specks wheeled in between the clouds: birds (or the local equivalent).

Little Gus sniffed the fresh Kyral air (thankfully it was breathable; in my experience, breathing is one of the most important things). "Weird as this place is," he said, "it somehow kind of looks like Earth. . . . I mean, it would if there were more parking lots and stuff."

"The moons are kind of a giveaway," said Nicki, pointing to the sky. I could just make out two faint circular outlines.

"Wait. Kyral only has one moon!" I said, suddenly terrified that I'd misidentified this planet completely.

Nicki smiled. "Chorkle, the little one is Gelo," she said. I looked up again. She was right. It is an odd feeling to realize that your home is just someone else's moon.

We found Pizza crouching in the tall grass nearby, yellow eyes peering off into the forest. The thyss-cat seemed to perceive something out there that the rest of us couldn't. This time, of course, we heeded his concern.

Gus hung back with Pizza, while Nicki, Becky, and I ventured farther into the forest to take a look. Many trees were huge, a hundred meters tall with trunks as wide as a Core-of-Rock street. Their thick canopy nearly blocked out the sky. Only scattered patches of sunlight managed to find their way to the forest floor. My eyes, used to the subterranean environment of Gelo's tunnels, found the dimness more agreeable. The occasional rustle of foliage or snap of a twig told us there were more than just plants here. We were surrounded by life. Once, I saw a little lizardlike creature flit among the branches on a pair of leathery wings.

"I'm sorry," said Nicki, "I know that we're supposed to be looking for danger right now, and I'm actively resisting the urge to be nerdy, but . . . I really just have to do this!" And she dashed over to a small—and to my eyes utterly unremarkable—shrub and snipped off a blue branch. "Don't tell Hollins," she said, and she placed the branch into a plastic bag and scribbled something on the label. Nicki had collected her first sample.

"Great," sighed Becky. "And so it begins." When Nicki had arrived on Gelo, she'd acquired roughly two tons of similar bags filled with every type of fungus our asteroid could offer.

"Look! Just look at this," said Nicki, holding up the bag. "Look at how regular the branch structure is. It's almost crystalline! So cool."

"I'll take your word for it," said Becky. "But, sis, we really should concentrate on figuring out our location."

"Yeah," I said, "Every minute we wait is a minute Kalac and the others are in danger."

"Well, I have a map of the planet on my holodrive, courtesy of the ship's sensors," said Nicki patting her pack. "The problem is figuring out where exactly on the map we are. Do you see any landmarks?"

We looked around. The forest spread out ahead of us as far as the eye could see.

"Do blue trees count?" I asked.

Nicki didn't answer. She was already distracted, taking a cutting from another Kyral plant. This time her target was a hairy teal vine that wound its way up the trunk of a massive tree.

"Oh, come on, Nicki," said Becky. "That's probably space poison ivy."

Just then I saw something sparkle in a distant pool of sunlight. I blinked and nudged Becky.

"Wow," said Nicki, still distracted by her vine, "it does actually seem to be giving me a rash. Utterly fascinating—"

"Hush," I hissed.

We all crept toward the glint. In the quiet, our footfalls suddenly sounded far too loud. Each crunch echoed off the surrounding tree trunks.

Ten meters away, we realized that we were looking at a piece of rusty metal. It sat atop a pile of vines and foliage in a small clearing. On its surface was a symbol painted in orange: a triangle with three dots over it. Intelligent life! It had to be the Aeaki.

On the ground in front of the scrap of metal, we saw something else. It was a strip of what appeared to be leather. In the center of it sat a pile of electric yellow berries, each of them a perfect little decahedron. While the metal could have been any age, these berries looked ripe and couldn't have been more than a few days old. Someone had been here recently.

"Maybe it's an offering?" said Nicki.

"Check this out," whispered Becky. On the ground beside the path were several tracks: four clawed toes, several centimeters deep. "Whatever made these was big. Like, apex-predator big," said Becky. "Is 'splitting up to explore the mysterious forest' starting to seem like a bad idea to anyone else?"

"Let me just collect one of those berries before we go," said Nicki as she started toward them.

"Nicki, stop!" I cried. She froze.

Creeping forward, I found what I was looking for: a thin cord strung taut a few centimeters above the forest floor. A shadow passed across the ground of the clearing.

"What was that?" asked Becky, looking up. But the sky was just an empty patch of lavender. However, suspended above the edge of the clearing, we saw a net of heavy vines. It was a trap. The twins and I looked at one another.

At that instant, we heard Little Gus cry out. We turned and ran the way we had come, back toward the edge of the forest.

"Help me!" he screamed. As we approached, we saw him standing alone on the grassy plain. He was looking up in terror.

"What's wrong?" cried Nicki.

Suddenly, a big shape fell out of the sky and darted toward Gus. He dove to the ground as it swooped past. It was a huge, winged alien creature covered in red and orange feathers.

The creature shrieked and dove again. This time Pizza leaped out of the grass at it. The thyss-cat wrapped its front paws around the flying alien and pulled it down to the ground. They rolled in the grass until the alien flapped its massive wings hard enough to throw Pizza off.

"Get it, boy!" cried Gus. "Get the giant space bird!"

A bolt of energy hit the ground near Pizza's feet. I turned and saw another one of the avian creatures—practically identical to the first—crouched behind a rock. It was shooting at Pizza. The thyss-cat yelped in pain as one of the bursts of energy seared its shoulder.

"No!" screamed Little Gus. He charged the new attacker just as Pizza raced off into the brush.

The second avian squawked and shoved Gus back with the butt of its blaster weapon as he tried to pound it with his fists. "Ver'sald! Ver'sald!" it screamed over and over again. It was using the Xotonian word for "stop."

"You speak Xotonian?" I cried in astonishment.

"You speak Aeaki?" it said, sounding no less astonished. Gus slowly stopped hitting it.

For the first time, I got a good look at the creature. It was nearly two meters tall, yet slender, so light on its feet that it seemed to weigh less than me. The body of the alien was covered with orange-and-red plumage so bright it even put Little Gus's brilliant orange head-fur to shame. It had two broad wings—articulated at the ends for grasping—and a long neck that ended in a beaked head. It wore a simple tunic woven of dried brown grass. Two beady golden eyes darted around nervously.

"You shot Pizza!" said Little Gus, now speaking Xotonian.

"*Pizza*," said the avian, lingering on the human word for a moment, "tried to eat Ikuna." It raised its blaster again. "You are space aliens?"

Nicki, Becky, and I looked at one another. We shrugged and nodded.

"You have come to blow us up and rob our hunting traps?"

"No," said Nicki. "We mean you no harm. Are you Aeaki?"

"Yes, I am Hisuda of the Oru," said the Aeaki proudly. "Are you allied with the Uji or Esu?"

"No," I said, "we're not allied with anyone."

"What about the Abi?"

I shook my head.

"Good," said Hisuda, lowering the blaster, apparently satisfied. "We will crush them all."

The second Aeaki—Ikuna, I presumed—walk-hopped toward us and cocked its head. To my eyes, the two of them were indistinguishable. Ikuna, though, seemed to defer to Hisuda.

"The blue monster-beast is still running free," said Ikuna, glaring at Little Gus. "We should find it and kill it and take its hide."

"No!" cried Little Gus. "Don't hurt Pizza. He doesn't mean you any harm. He just got scared and wanted to protect me. Why'd you fly at me like that, anyway?"

"Why were you touching our hunting traps?" snapped Ikuna, gesturing back toward the forest. I could see now that Pizza had taken a bite out of the feathers of its wing, leaving a bald spot.

"Sorry," I said. "We didn't know that trap was yours."

At this, Ikuna snorted incredulously. "The Oru symbol is painted right on it!" cried Hisuda.

"We didn't know that was the Oru symbol," said Nicki. Hisuda shook its head in disbelief.

It was as though our ignorance of who owned which traps was the most incredible thing they'd ever heard. This garnered a much bigger reaction than, say, the fact that we had come to their planet from another world.

"We heard a great racket, and we came here to investigate," said Hisuda. "Why did you burn up your starship?" The Aeaki pointed toward the plume of black smoke billowing into the air.

"It wasn't exactly a choice," sighed Becky.

"And if you are not thieves and raiders, what are you?" asked Hisuda.

"We came from up there," I said pointing to Gelo in the sky, "to find three aliens. They look like me."

"So . . . very ugly?" said Ikuna.

I sighed. "I guess. Here, let me show you something."

I made a move for my pack, and again Hisuda pointed its blaster at me. I froze.

"I'm not reaching for a weapon. I want to show you a book," I said. Hisuda nodded uncertainly. I slowly pulled the cyclopaedia out of my pack and opened it to Kyral's entry. I pointed to the writing. "This is about your planet. Kyral."

Ikuna squinted at the book. "Magic spells," said Hisuda dismissively. This Aeaki might speak my language, but apparently it couldn't read it.

"Not spells," I said, closing the book. "They're just

words that say the Aeaki and the Xotonians are friends. That's what I am: a Xotonian. So maybe—maybe you can help me?"

Before either could reply, a third Aeaki joined us. It was virtually identical to the others.

"Two more outlanders," said the new one. In one hand-wing it held an Aeaki blaster; in the other it clutched Eromu's smaller one. Hollins trailed behind, his hands in the air.

"Hi, guys," said Hollins to us. "Looks like we found the mysterious Aeaki, huh? And guess who woke up."

The Vorem legionary stood beside him. He glared silently, clutching his wounded chest.

"Thank you, Aloro," said Hisuda. Then it stared at the Vorem for a long time, cocking its head this way and that, before it spoke. "Do you all come from the new moon?" It waved toward the ghost of Gelo up in the sky.

"No," said the Vorem. "I am Taius Sovyrius Ridian, son of Stentorus Sovyrius Ridian, legate of the Vorem Dominion. Humble servant of His Majesty Phaebus Onesius Aetox XXIII, the most glorious imperator of a thousand worlds."

My mind was reeling. I didn't understand. He called himself Ridian! But how could this legionary be General

Ridian's son? Ridian's son was killed during the invasion, and I'd seen the legate buried myself. This Vorem had to be lying . . . didn't he?

The humans gaped at me in disbelief, and I noticed that the Aeaki were no less upset than we were.

"Vorem," snarled Ikuna. And both Ikuna and Aloro raised their blasters as though to vaporize Taius Ridian.

"Stop," said Hisuda quietly. The other Aeaki lowered their weapons. Then Hisuda sighed and gave a bow. "Welcome, honorable Legate Ridian, to the Dominion world of Kyral."

CHAPTER NINE

"Aloro, go and tell the Raefec whom we have found," said Hisuda. Without another word, Aloro took off and flew away over the forest. The rest of us sat in the sun and waited.

Only the Vorem remained standing. The humans and I stared at him, and he glowered off into the middle distance. I was glad that two remaining Aeaki were armed.

At last Becky broke the silence. "So you're General Ridian's son," she said to him. "Taius, was it?"

His eyes flicked toward her for an instant, then back to staring at nothing. He didn't reply.

"Well, if you ever see your old man again," she said, "tell him he can bill me for the battle cruiser."

"You'll pay the price, alien," said Taius.

"Both of you, be quiet," said Hisuda, raising her weapon. "The Raefec will decide."

Yes, Hisuda was female. As we waited for Aloro to return, we learned that all three of these Aeaki were female. Indeed, all the hunters in their society were women. If circumstances had been different, I would have been fascinated to learn more about the culture of an alien race. But as it was, all I could think about was the fact that we were standing on a world ruled by the Vorem Dominion—with the son of General Ridian.

After that initial exchange, though, Taius spoke no more. Twenty minutes later, Nicki noticed a black speck in the distance. It grew larger and larger until Aloro landed beside us.

"The Raefec says we are to fly to Oru immediately!" she squawked.

"Very well," said Hisuda.

"Hang on," said Becky. "What's a Raefec, anyway?"

"The Raefec leads us in battle," said Hisuda. "She guides us with her wisdom."

"So basically it's like your society's equivalent of a Little Gus," said Little Gus.

Hisuda shrugged. "Her word is law," she said. "If she says we fly to Oru, then we fly to Oru." The three Aaeki took off and flapped in tight circles over our heads, apparently expecting us to join them in the air.

"Um, no disrespect to your culture, but . . . we can't actually fly," said Nicki.

The three Aeaki landed and squawked in contempt. "But you flew here from the new moon," said Hisuda, waving at the sky.

Hollins stepped forward and tried to explain in Xotonian. "Hello. Of Gelo, we doing of spaceship. Now, today, spaceship is hot dinner. Fire. Hot dinner. Doesn't flying. Goodbye!"

Now Hisuda was more confused than ever.

"Thanks for taking charge of the situation, brave leader," whispered Nicki in human. "Super helpful."

"Long story short: We have no ride," said Becky to Hisuda, "thanks to Junior here." She threw a thumb toward Taius Ridian. Taius opened his mouth as though to reply, but instead he just glared dangerously and said nothing. He looked like he wanted to murder everyone present.

"But the ground on Kyral is not safe for travel," said Ikuna, hopping from foot to foot and glancing about nervously. "Many things want to eat the Aeaki."

"Well, then, maybe we could, like, ride on your backs," suggested Little Gus.

At this, all of the Aeaki hooted with pure derision.

"You cannot! The aerodynamics are all wrong. Aeaki cannot fly carrying a bunch of stupid *dead weight*!" said Hisuda, meaning all of us. Becky was on the verge of taking offense at this description, but Nicki calmed her.

As we gathered our belongings to leave, I turned toward the *T'utzuxe*. Its wreckage still smoldered.

"Cheer up, Chorkle," said Hollins, patting my i'arda. "She's up in spaceship heaven now."

"But without the ship's sensors," I said, "we have no way to track Kalac's distress beacon."

"Enough talking!" chided Hisuda. "We cannot waste any more time. Walking will take long enough as it is."

"No. We can't leave without Pizza," whined Little Gus, scanning the horizon.

"Gus," I said, eyeing the Aeaki's blasters, "I'm not sure we have a choice."

And so we set out through the forest toward the Aeaki's home, a city they called Oru. A breeze rattled the odd geometric leaves as we walked.

According to Hisuda, Oru was the capital of a mighty nation of the same name. Our Observers had seen only scattered signs of civilization on the surface, but just as Core-of-Rock was concealed, perhaps their great city would be too. If Kyral was a world of the Dominion, though, I worried what would happen to us when we got there. Would we be turned over to the Vorem?

Hisuda took the lead, and I walked behind her. Next came Taius, a scowl locked on his sharp face. He didn't talk, and the Aeaki asked him no questions. In fact, I got the distinct impression that they wanted as little to do with him as possible.

From time to time, I saw him check the small technological device attached to his belt, which now appeared to be working just fine. I cursed myself for not taking it from him when he was unconscious. Once he caught me looking at him and turned away in disgust.

Becky and Hollins walked right behind Taius, watching his every move. Next came Nicki, who kept stopping to discretely bag and tag specimens near the path. Little Gus somehow managed to be even slower than her. He kept lingering to gaze out among the trees, hoping for a glimpse of Pizza. Ikuna took up the rear, repeatedly prodding Gus and Nicki to go faster.

I jogged ahead so that I could speak to Hisusda out of Taius's earshot. Her weird hopping gait meant that in order to keep pace with her, I had to alternately run and then stop and wait.

"Hisuda, are there other Vorem on this planet?" I asked her.

"Sometimes," she answered cryptically.

"Do you think your 'Raefec' will hand us over to them?"

"She keeps her own council. I have no idea what the Raefec will decide. Now stop asking me questions—it is causing you to walk even slower."

Behind me, Little Gus thought he saw something in the forest. "Piiiiiiiizzaaaaaa!" he called out.

"Be quiet!" scolded Ikuna.

"But he's out there somewhere," said Gus pitifully.

"Yes, and worse things too. The ground is not safe," squawked Ikuna. "Not safe!"

"Please, can't we just go look for him?" asked Gus. Ikuna shook her head. She was not swayed by his emotional appeals. I joined Little Gus as he lagged behind the others.

"Don't worry," I said, trying to comfort him. "Thysscats are tough, wily creatures. They're survivors. Pizza can always follow our scent."

"I'm worried he'll have nightmares," said Little Gus. "Before he goes to sleep, I like to sing to him. Jazz standards mostly. A few show tunes." Then he added quickly, "Please don't tell anybody I told you that." I nodded and kept on walking.

A sheer bluff now rose from the forest floor ahead. Up close it was composed of crumbling gray stone covered with tangled clumps of blue vines. I could see now that its face was practically hollow, completely riddled with caves. It stretched upward a hundred meters into the sky, just above the tallest tops of the trees.

"Behold Oru," announced Hisuda. She puffed her bright plumage with pride. The humans and I looked at each other. Had we arrived? None of us saw a city anywhere.

"Oh, it's really beautiful," said Nicki, trying to be polite. Inasmuch as Hisuda's beaked face could express any discernible emotion, she seemed to frown.

Little Gus kicked a little rodentlike skull—the ground all around us was littered with the bleached bones of tiny animals and what looked like guano. "You guys remodeling or something?"

"Oru is not *here*," said Hisuda with disgust. "Up. Above." And she took off from the ground, beating her great wings up to the top of the bluff. She circled once and then landed beside us.

"Yeah. As my sister already said, we can't fly," said Becky.

"But you Aeaki probably don't have roller coasters," said Little Gus. "So let's call it even."

"In fact, it doesn't look like they have much of anything," whispered Hollins in human. He had articulated exactly what had begun to worry me. Still, there was a chance the other Oru or their "Raefec" might know something about Kalac and the others—if they didn't turn us over to the Dominion, that is.

"I think I can get us up there," I said. I took the coil of human rope, then sprang three meters into the air and grabbed hold of a clump of vines. There are many things that I am not particularly good at: oog-ball, geology worksheets, telling all the *Vampire Band Camp* characters with similar haircuts apart. But like most Xotonians, I am an excellent climber. So I started to scramble up the side of the gray cliff.

I'm not sure what I was expecting from great Oru. Perhaps I'd unconsciously focused on the phrases "urbanized" and "cultural mecca" from the cyclopaedia (now heavy as brick in my pack as I climbed). But I had seen the pride with which Hisuda beheld her home. If not a bustling society full of flying cars and robot housekeepers, I will admit I was at least imagining . . . a city.

Instead, the totality of Oru was a few dozen huts—made of grass and garbage—surrounding a big central fire pit. It was no more than a village, and a humble one at that. The population—barely fifty Aeaki, as far as I could see—walk-hopped and flitted about on top of the table-flat mesa I had just scaled. Half of them looked virtually identical to Hisuda, Ikuda, and Aloro, with the same blazing-red plumage. The other half were smaller. Their feathers were as drab as dead leaves, with just a few fiery highlights at the tips of their wings and around the throat. I saw the same orange triangle-and-three-dots motif from the hunting trap repeated throughout the community. Oru's logo, I supposed.

As I stood on the edge of the cliff and observed the huts, a few of the locals cocked their heads to stare at me.

"Don't mind them," said Hisuda, landing on the ledge beside me. "They have never seen anyone like you before . . . so ugly, I mean."

"Right, I get it," I said, gritting my ish'kuts.

Just then I noticed a little Aeaki child, all alone, peeping out from behind one of the huts with genuine curiosity. This one's feathers were neither blazing orange and red nor brown, but instead pure white.

"Who's that?" I asked Hisuda.

"Don't mind her," said Hisuda with contempt in her voice. "She is not an Oru." I turned back, but the young Aeaki was gone.

"Now that you have had the time to take it all in," said

Hisuda, sweeping her wing dramatically, "what do you think?" I could tell that she wanted me to be impressed.

"It's great," I said, trying to keep the disappointment from my voice. "That's a nice tall pile of, um, garbage you've got there." Maybe it was all some sort of elaborate cover, but the place didn't look like it had any starships to speak of. Without ships, rescuing Kalac and the other Xotonians—much less getting back to Gelo—was going to be a real problem.

"Oru is a very great city," said Hisuda. "Only Hykaro Roost is greater."

"I've heard of Hykaro Roost," I said. "It's the Aeaki capital, right?"

She shook her head yes. "It was built by the gods."

I tied the human rope to an outcropping and tossed the other end down. Slowly, one by one, the humans ascended the bluff. We had to haul up Nicki's samples separately since her pack already seemed to weigh more than she did. Once, when it bumped the cliff wall, a single sample bag fell all the way back down to the ground.

"Come on, guys, be careful!" said Nicki. "That bag was full of important dirt! I mean—whatever."

At last, the humans all made it to the top. Taius still stood with Aloro and Ikuna, thirty meters below. He ignored the rope and started to climb, hand over hand, up the cliff. Becky and Hollins watched him the whole time.

"Anybody got a big rock?" Hollins asked quietly when Taius was about halfway up.

Becky looked around at Oru. "Well, Chorkle, I owe the Xotonian race an apology," she said. "This place makes Core-of-Rock look like way less of a dump."

"Thanks?" I said.

"I'm excited we're finally in the big city now," said Little Gus, examining a heap of wet rags on the edge of the village. "I can't wait to take in the art museums. Go to the theater. How late do you think the restaurants stay open?"

"Stop making fun," said Nicki. "It's important to be sensitive. This is our first contact with an alien culture."

"Come on. Lighten up, Nicki," said Little Gus. "A couple of jokes aren't going to destroy the Aeaki civilization."

"Yeah," said Becky, "destroying their civilization would take a strong gust of wind, at least."

Again, everyone but Nicki laughed. Little Gus kept laughing though, too loudly and for too long. It was something he'd been doing a lot of recently when Becky told a joke.

"Good one, Becky," said Little Gus. "You're super funny. Humor is a gift."

"Did anyone check Little Gus for traumatic brain injury after the crash?" Becky asked the rest of us. Little Gus frowned.

"What are they saying?" Hisuda asked me.

"They were saying that they've never seen a place like Oru," I replied truthfully. This pleased Hisuda, as well as Ikuna and Aloro, who had landed beside her.

Just then, a purple hand clawed its way over the edge of the cliff, startling us all.

"Ugh. Just like a horror movie," muttered Hollins as Taius heaved himself over the top. He lay on the ground for a moment, panting from the effort. Then he noticed that all of us were staring at him.

He suddenly reached into the pocket of his threadbare uniform. We all froze, except Little Gus, who scrambled behind the wet rag heap. Had Taius concealed some weapon that Hollins hadn't found?

Instead, he pulled out Nicki's sample bag filled with dirt. He tossed it to her, and she caught it.

"You dropped your dirt," said Taius. For a minute, none of us knew what to say.

"Enough chatter," said Hisuda. "All of you outlanders must be presented to the Raefec."

Taius strode past me. As he did, I could have sworn I

saw him grin for a second, before his face reverted to its normal scowl. Strangely, I much preferred the scowl.

As we walked, I did notice that the citizens of Oru were openly gawping at him and whispering among themselves. They looked less than thrilled to have a Vorem in their village.

"This is the Raefec's great house," said Hisuda, indicating a longer hut adjacent to the central fire pit. Instead of grass and refuse, it was made of more permanent stuff: planks of bluish wood and mismatched sheets of corrugated plastic. "It is the most beautiful structure in all of Oru," said Hisuda. "Please take a moment to appreciate it."

Inside, the long hut was dim and smelled of rotting meat. The only light came from the glowing coals of two braziers. The walls were painted with intricately detailed murals in bright colors: battle scenes of orange-and-red Aeaki warriors conquering other Aeaki with purple and gold feathers, green and black feathers, and many other color combinations as well. To my surprise, the artwork really was quite beautiful.

Two real-life courtiers—their plumage dust-colored with red and orange highlights, marking them as males— stood behind a carved wooden chair. In it hunched an old female Aeaki, her once-bright feathers faded with age, a blanket over her lap. In one wing she clutched a staff—a piece of metal rebar with frayed electrical wires braided around it. Feeble as her body was, her eyes still appeared sharp.

"Raefec Azusu," said Hisuda. She, Aloro, and Ikuna bowed. Hisuda prodded me with a wing, and I bowed too. The humans quickly followed. Only Taius remained upright.

"Greetings," said Azusu, "and welcome to Oru." Her tone was not welcoming.

"A most sublime and amazing metropolis," said Nicki, laying it on a little thick, in my opinion.

"Oh, please," said Azusu. "What are you supposed to be anyway? No feathers. No beaks. You all look ridiculous."

Nicki looked a little put out. "Uh. We're *Homo sapiens*."

"Never heard of 'em," said Azusu. "And what about you, Ugly?" She was looking at me now.

"I'm Chorkle. I am a Xotonian," I said. I thought I saw something flash in her eyes, some hint of recognition. But in an instant it was gone. "I'm searching for three others like me."

"Haven't seen 'em," she said. Immediately, my is'pog sank. She turned to Taius. "And you. I know what you are. Mighty Vorem. No armor, though. How come?"

"I lost it," he said. Was there a note of shame in his voice?

"Too bad," said Azusu. "You boys look much scarier with it on." She sized him up. "Right now you remind me of . . . an egg without a shell."

Little Gus stifled a laugh, and Azusu glared at him before turning back to Taius. "So, young Vorem, what brings you to Kyral?" she asked.

"I understand that this is a world of the Dominion," said Taius. Odd phrasing. Did that mean that he'd never heard of Kyral himself, I wondered? How big was the Vorem Dominion that they'd lost track of all the planets they'd conquered?

"You *understand* correctly," said Azusu.

"I request a meeting with the local Dominion administrator," he said, "to explain my situation."

"Local Dominion administrator? You're looking at her," said Azusu. She reached into the folds of her blanket and pulled out a little black ring the same size as the medallion in Taius's pocket. She tossed it to him.

He examined the intricate carvings on the ring's surface. "You're the Dominion praefectus for this region?" he said with disbelief.

"Sure am. Most folks around here just shorten 'praefectus' to 'Raefec,' though," said Azusu. "The fact is, I don't do too much 'administrating' for the great Imperator these days." At this, all the Aeaki in the room laughed, a shrill, unpleasant squawking sound.

"Very well, Praefectus," said Taius. "Then I command you to take me to the nearest Vorem military outpost."

Azusu glared at him. "You command me, do you?" she said. "You *command* me." There was something dangerous in her tone. One of the brown-feathered courtiers placed a wing on her shoulder. "Don't try to calm me, down, Un-uro!" she snapped.

Taius paused. "I do command you," he said. "I am a legate of the Vorem legion. I outrank a praefectus." He reached into his pocket and showed her his own gold token.

Azusu glared at him. "Kyral is technically a Dominion world, boy. But you may find that here, your fancy rank doesn't matter as much as you'd like. In fact, you may find that very few Aeaki have fond feelings for our absentee landlords, the Vorem."

This time, the brown-feathered Aeaki—apparently called Unuro—spoke to Taius. "That is not to say that we ourselves have anything but the purest loyalty to the great Vorem Dominion. Praise the great Imperator . . . er who is it these days?"

"Aetox XXIII," said Taius.

"By the gods, you're already at twenty-three? Congratulations!" screeched the other drab-feathered Aeaki.

Azusu shot him a look. "Leave politics to the grown-ups, Biji." She turned back to Taius. "But, as my servants say," she croaked, "praise the Dominion." Her words dripped with venom.

"Praise the Dominion," repeated Taius. "I also require that you take these four"—he indicated the four humans—"into custody, for questioning. I believe they were involved in an earlier attack upon a Vorem ship." Curiously, he didn't point to me.

"Hang on just a second," said Becky. "This purple creep stowed away aboard our starfighter and made us crash-land it on Kyral. If anyone should go to jail, it's him! Attempted murder. Destruction of property. Endangering a minor." She pointed to Little Gus. Gus nodded.

"You crashed the ship, you crazed female!" cried Taius, losing his cool. "I asked you to take me back."

"And you were so polite about it too," said Nicki.

"Enough," shrieked Azusu. "First off, do you see any prisons around here? No one is going into 'custody.' As for Vorem military outposts, there aren't any. Odd how little you seem to know about this valuable Dominion holding, Legate."

I could see the hope draining from Taius's face. "If there isn't a permanent Vorem military presence on Kyral," he said, "then I will require the use of a starship. I need to return to my father's battle cruiser as soon as possible."

"Do we *look* like we have starships? Sounds like you just wrecked your only way off this planet!" laughed Azusu. "Look, I'll tell you what Kyral has in ample supply. Grass, garbage, and death. If you need any of those three things, we'll be happy to oblige.

"But you—" said Taius.

"Pardon me, Raefec," I interrupted. "Are you absolutely sure there are no ships here?"

"No, you got me. There are plenty of ships! I'm holding out on you," she said sarcastically. "In fact, I've got ten of them. I just *choose* to live in a trash hut surrounded by idiots." Unuro and Biji fluffed their feathers indignantly.

There it was. The Aeaki—so far, less friendly than the cyclopaedia promised—wouldn't be able help us after all. The humans looked crestfallen, except for Hollins. He merely looked confused.

"But from what I've read of Kyral," I said, "it is supposed to be a very technologically advanced world."

"Then you must have some very old books, Chorkle the Xotonian," she said.

141

I nodded. She was right. "So what happened?" I asked.

"*They* happened," she said, pointing ominously to Taius. "Look, I'll show you something." Slowly and with great difficulty, she extricated herself from the old wooden chair. When her two servants attempted to help her up, she swatted at them with her wings. At last, she stood, and she led us to a dark corner of the long hut.

"We don't have books anymore, these days," said Azusu. "All we can manage are pictures." She indicated a set of three murals with different subject matter from the others.

The first showed Aeaki of all colors cowering together in a city as fire rained from the skies. In the next scene, black armored figures marched in orderly lines through a charred wasteland, driving the Aeaki before them. A few resisted, but the Vorem tore them apart with blaster fire. The third scene in the triptych showed a handful of Aeaki bowing to the victorious Vorem legion. The ground was littered with the corpses of their comrades.

"Long ago, Kyral was a wondrous place," said Azusu. "A beautiful, idyllic world. Billions of Aeaki lived in peace. Cities, commerce, science—you name it, we had it!"

"Did you have roller coasters?" asked Little Gus.

"Probably," said Azusu, nodding. "Everyone says that Hykaro Roost was built by the gods, but it wasn't. It was built by us. We could fly to other planets on our own ships! They were much better than the Vorem junkers. And they could travel faster than light! We traded with distant worlds. Explored the universe."

She paused. "But we had something the Vorem wanted. The crust of Kyral was rich with phanium. That's a mineral ore that's used in making hyperdrives, the engines that allow for interplanetary space travel. So the Dominion attacked us. We fought, of course. Even joined an alliance against them. The League of Free Civilizations, it was called. Ha!" She laughed joylessly. "Fat lot of good it did. Free? Civilization? Thanks to the Vorem, the Aeaki are neither anymore."

"I've heard of the League of Free Civilizations," I said. Jalasu Jhuk's hologram had mentioned it when we had discovered the hidden hangar. General Ridian mentioned it too, just before he'd attempted his invasion of Gelo.

"Yes, it makes sense you'd know of it, because the Xotonians were members," said Azusu. "The Aeaki and the league held the Vorem off for awhile. But at last, they breached our defenses. Hit us with their nuclear weapons. They burned everything."

"That's what created Kyral's planetary ring," said Nicki. "Debris from the explosions."

Azusu nodded. "In a matter of hours, our civilization

was a memory. A few Aeaki survived. Half of them refused to give up, and they kept on fighting. I guess they're fighting still. The other half surrendered to the Vorem, including my brave ancestors." She chuckled darkly. "That's how my praefectus badge was passed down to me. We bowed to those who had burned our world and became part of the Dominion."

"But if you're part of the Dominion," I asked, "where are all the Vorem?"

"Gone," she said. "The Vorem did stay for a few years. They stamped out the last of the underground resistance left in Hykaro Roost. Stripped the planet of all its phanium. Took anything else of value that wasn't nailed down or burned. Then they left."

"So they've forgotten about you," said Becky.

"Not exactly," said Azusu. "Every few years the Vorem Dominon lands a big, impressive-looking starship somewhere near Hykaro Roost to keep us cowed. They frighten the locals and toss a shiny medal on whichever nearby warlord can show them one of these." She held up her praefectus badge. "Then they take off again for the stars."

She sighed. "But not before making sure the Aeaki have a few more energy blasters," she said, patting the one at her hip. "It might sound strange for conquerors to arm the conquered. But they're not here, and they know we'll just use them on one another. Let us conquer ourselves." She laughed again, but this time no one joined her.

I looked around the hut. The tale of Kyral's fall had Ikuna and Aloro seething with rage. Azusu's male servants looked very nervous indeed. Taius was unreadable

"Maybe Kyral could come back," I said. "Maybe the Aeaki can rebuild. You can't give up hope."

"Enough. The only thing I find more tiresome than Vorem is pointless optimism," said Azusu. She turned to Taius. "But speaking of Vorem, you still haven't explained why you're here."

Taius swallowed. "I have come here on a routine reconnaissance mission to—"

"Pshaw. He's not supposed to be on Kyral," said Nicki. "We all came here by accident. We warped into this galaxy through a wormhole from the other side of the universe, along with the asteroid where the Xotonians live. It's actually super interesting. The wormhole opened after we—"

"All ate a big lunch!" I said, shooting Nicki a look. She had almost accidentally mentioned the Q-sik.

"You lot came with the new moon?" asked Azusu.

We nodded.

Azusu stared directly into Taius's eyes now. "So, Legate,

now that you know the tale of how the great Dominion destroyed our civilization and pillaged our world, what do you have to say for yourself?"

There was a long silence before he spoke. "The Aeaki shouldn't have fought back," said Taius. "If you had simply surrendered, your civilization would have survived."

Ikuna couldn't handle it anymore. "Let's kill the Vorem scum, Raefec Azusu!" she screeched from behind me. "Toss him from the top of Oru and be done with it. He can't even fly."

"No, no, no," cried Unuro. "We are loyal Vorem subjects! We love the Vorem. Raefec, remember, your own claim to power is a Dominion title. You are their local representative!"

"You heard the *Homo sapiens*," said Ikuna. "No one even knows this Vorem worm is on Oru."

"It could be a test!" said Unuro. "If we help him, maybe the Imperator will reward us. With more weapons, perhaps! Or even some of these 'roller coasters' I've been hearing so much about! In fact maybe the *real* enemies are these other five. I bet they're in league with the Uji. Perhaps the Dominion wants them—"

"The Dominion doesn't even remember that Kyral exists," said Ikuna.

"Wrong," said Taius. "My father's battle cruiser, *Secutor*, is orbiting this planet as we speak. If you help me, *he* will reward you."

"Yeah. More like *half* his father's battle cruiser," Little Gus corrected him. "And not the good half either. No weapons. No communications. It can't even move. Also, his dad's a huge wad."

"What? My father is not a 'wad'!" snapped Taius.

"We can't take this little red alien's word for it, Raefec!" squawked Unuro. "If we harm a Vorem legate, then the Dominion will rain fire from the skies again. We'll all be burned!"

"If General Ridian actually wanted Junior back," said Becky, "he probably would have contacted us about it sometime in the last three months. He didn't. You know why? He doesn't care."

At this, Taius turned and glared at her with pure hatred. His fists were balled, and his teeth were bared in a snarl. He opened his mouth to yell something, but Azusu cut him off.

"All of you, shut up," said Azusu. Her little black ring caught the firelight as she turned it over in her wing. "I need time to think about this. Everyone out." She bowed her head sarcastically to Taius. "With your permission, of course, *honorable Legate*."

Taius said nothing, but he turned to leave.

Unuro and Biji remained behind the throne, looking concerned for their aged Raefec. Asuzu turned to them. "I said *everyone*!" she squawked. Her two servants hung their heads and followed us out of the hut.

For an instant, I spied the small, white-feathered Aeaki peeping around the edge of the doorjamb. Eavesdropping? At once, she disappeared again.

"Raefec Azusu," I said, stopping. I turned to face her. "May I ask one more question?"

"Make it quick," said Asuzu. She rubbed her temples as though she had a terrible headache.

"Why do you all speak Xotonian?" she said.

"Around here we call it Aeaki," she snapped. But then she softened. "You're right: It isn't our native language. If we ever had our own, it died in the nuclear fire." She gestured toward the mural.

I nodded and stepped out into the sunlight. The whole village of Oru had gathered outside the Raefec's hut.

"So what just happened in there?" asked Hollins. "I definitely caught something about roller coasters."

CHAPTER TEN

Night had fallen on the village of Oru, and the fire pit was blazing. The crowd of villagers had not dispersed for two hours. The Aeaki gave all of us aliens a wide berth, though, as we sat on the ground and waited.

On one side of our three-meter bubble of space, Taius Ridian rested, legs crossed, eyes closed. I huddled with the humans on the other side.

"Now I think I understand how you all must have felt when you first came to Core-of-Rock," I whispered. "Everyone here hates us."

"Yup. 'Oru'?" said Little Gus. "More like 'O-ruce.'"

We all stared at him. No one laughed.

"What?" he said. "They can't all be winners."

"Hey, I wonder what that one did," said Hollins. "They treat her even worse than us." He pointed across the fire to another patch of empty space. At the center of it sat the small, white-feathered Aeaki. She was playing in the dirt and talking to herself. Around her neck she wore a shiny necklace of nuts and bolts.

I stood, and the crowd parted before me as I walked toward her. "Hi," I said. "What are you doing?"

The little Aeaki looked around nervously. She didn't seem to realize that I was talking to her.

"Just watching," she said at last. "Watching and listening."

"What's your name?" I asked.

"Eyf," she said.

"My name's Chorkle," I said.

"I'm—I'm not an Oru," she said as though confessing to some grave sin. Then she turned away in embarrassment.

"Yeah. I'm not either," I said. "And I'm glad too. With a few exceptions, the Oru seem to be jerks. And the exceptions all seem to be mold-brains."

Eyf stared at me. Then she laughed, a high chirping sound. A few nearby Aeaki gave us disdainful looks.

"You are a space alien," she said, dropping her voice to a whisper.

"Yup," I said, "I can even do this." And I changed my skin color to the mottled orange and red of the Oru Aeaki plumage. Eyf gasped.

"I wish I could do that," she said. "But my feathers just stay white." She regarded her own wing. "I'm not an Oru," she repeated glumly.

I was about to ask her what was so great about being an Oru anyway when the crowd started to murmur. I shifted to see what they were looking at.

At last, Azusu had emerged from her long hut. She cleared her throat and addressed the crowd.

"As you all now know," said Azusu, "we have outlanders here in Oru. They came all the way from outer space to our little village. Few of you have ever seen one in person, but that purple fellow there is a Vorem."

Some squawked in disapproval. Taius stood and faced the crowd, defiant.

"Some say we should kill him," said Azusu, "after what his species did to this planet, to the Aeaki. Maybe he deserves it?" About half the crowd cheered at this. Azusu quieted them and continued. "Others say we shouldn't court trouble. That we should bow down to this little Vorem legate. Arrest his enemies"—she waved at the humans—"maybe even toss them off Oru and watch them splatter." She glared at Unuro, but he appeared unapologetic. No one actually cheered for the second option, but I could tell that some were open to it. The humans all looked sick with worry.

151

"Well," said Azusu, "you all know your Raefec. If half the Oru want one thing and half the Oru want another, old Azusu will pick a third thing just to spite everyone." A light chuckle came from the crowd.

Azusu turned toward us. "All of you aliens: Vorem, *Homo sapiens*, Xotonian," she said, waving her wing dismissively, "we of the Oru clan will do you no harm. But neither will we help you. Tomorrow you must leave this village. You can take as much food and water as you can carry. But I won't have a Vorem living here among us, trying to pull rank with me. And I won't give aid to wanted fugitives either. Not while I'm still a Dominion praefectus."

The crowd grumbled, but they seemed to accept the verdict. The humans smiled with relief. I, for one, didn't mind exile. One day was quite enough time in the village of Oru for me. If they couldn't help us find Kalac, they were wasting our time.

"Um, excuse me," a tiny voice called out.

"What?" said Azusu, looking around in annoyance. "Who is that?"

Little Eyf stood and stepped forward. "It's me, um, Eyf?" she said, as though unsure of her own name. Her voice was trembling.

Azusu squinted at her. "But you're not an Oru."

"I—I know I never spoke up before, but I just wanted to say that, um, these aliens can't fly like we can, Raefec."

"Yes, we all know that, genius," snapped Azusu, getting a big, mean laugh from the crowd. "With insights like this, no wonder nobody listens to you!"

"Right, um, well, what I mean is that if they leave the village, they'll have to walk. Across the ground."

"So?" said Azusu.

"But on the ground," squeaked Eyf, "there are crells and stalking yost-leopards and even great rahks hungry for flesh. There is the cursed Glass Desert, where nothing lives. And the sickly marshes full of creeping sleem. On the ground, they will be easy targets for the Uji, Esu, Abi, and all the other clans we haven't even heard of. Praefec, to walk across Kyral—that's almost a death sentence."

"Almost. But not quite," said Azusu with a shrug.

"But Raefec, the Xotonian"—Eyf pointed to me—"is just looking for others of its kind who might be in trouble." So she had been eavesdropping. "Without help from one who knows Kyral's dangers, then there is no hope of ever finding them."

"Aye, and who's to help them?" asked Azusu.

"Um . . . I could?" said Eyf.

"You're making me repeat myself, you ignorant hatchling," snapped Azusu in a dangerous tone. "As I said before: None of the Oru will help these aliens!"

Eyf took a deep breath. "Well . . . I'm not an Oru."

The crowd gasped. Azusu considered Eyf's words for a moment. "You're right," she said at last, "you're not. You've lived in the village. You've eaten our food. But you're not an Oru. Never were. You may do as you wish."

Eyf looked taken aback. It was as though this was the first time in her life that she'd actually gotten what she wanted.

"But," continued Azusu, "if you leave here with these aliens, don't you ever expect to come back."

Eyf's beak fell open. Azusu had already turned to hobble back into her long hut. The crowd dispersed, and before long we were alone. Only, Hisuda, Ikuna, and Aloro remained. Since they had found us, it was the three hunters' responsibility to watch us until we left the village. Eyf too remained. She seemed to be in a daze. The humans and I approached her.

"Eyf," I said to her, "thanks for the offer. But you don't have to help us if it means losing your home. What's wrong with your Raefec, anyway? She's as hard as an usktusk."

"Azusu's not that bad. Kyral is a dangerous place, so she

has to be dangerous too," said Eyf. "I want to help you. I'm not sure why, but I want to."

"You don't even know us," said Nicki. "We could all be serial killers."

"We're not though," said Becky. "Except Hollins."

Hollins, hearing his name, spoke up. "Because saying hello. Of hello, tiny bird-face!" He extended his hand in a friendly greeting.

Eyf cringed, though, and buried her face in her wing. She looked mortified.

"Don't mind him," I said. "'Tiny bird-face' is, uh, a great compliment where we come from. If we really like something, we might say it's, uh, very 'tiny bird-face.' Right, everyone?" The humans nodded.

"No . . . I'm not upset," whispered Eyf from behind her white feathers. "It's just . . . I'm . . . not used to so much *conversation*."

"The fact is," I said, "we do talk all the time. Sometimes we even argue."

"Do not," said Little Gus.

"But if that makes you uncomfortable, Eyf, all the more reason not to leave Oru," I said.

"No, no, no," said Eyf, still hiding her face. "I like it. I think—I think I might have a lot to say. . . ." After this statement, though, she was quiet for the rest of the night.

No one offered us lodging in a garbage hut, so we slept under Kyral's stars beside the dying firepit—the humans, Eyf, and myself on one side; Taius on the other. I didn't ask where Eyf normally slept, but it was presumably no more comfortable than the hard ground. Hisuda, Ikuna, and Aloro roosted nearby, blasters at their sides.

While the others drifted to sleep, I laid awake, head on my pack, thinking of Kalac. Somewhere, it might be looking up at the same glittering sky. Or not, I suddenly realized. My originator might have already passed to the Nebula Beyond. I felt a pang of terror. I almost wanted to leap to my fel'grazes and leave Oru that instant.

Instead, I shifted and saw two red eyes glittering at me from across the embers. Taius Ridian was awake and staring at me. I rolled over to face the other way.

In my dreams, I saw Taius looming over me, holding something in his clawed hand. It was the Q-sik, glowing with fearsome power. He leveled it at me and—

I awoke suddenly in the night. The fire was totally dead. Someone was standing over me. Not Taius, but Ikuna the hunter. She quickly hushed me before I could say anything.

"Don't believe the Raefec or her coward servants," whispered Ikuna. "We Oru hate the Vorem."

I nodded.

"We have been forbidden from giving this one what he truly deserves"—she threw a wing in Taius's direction—"but that doesn't mean that you can't."

In explanation, she handed me something. It was cold and heavy, made of metal: Eromu's blaster.

CHAPTER ELEVEN

I could tell Nicki was getting frustrated. "See, it looks like a *dolphin* wearing a *sombrero*," she said to the Aeaki. They stared back blankly. Even if Kyral had either of these two things (it didn't), they couldn't understand the human words.

"Pardon my friend," said Little Gus, "but it actually looks like a *banana* playing *football*." This did nothing to clarify the shape of the drawing in the dirt for Hisuda, Aloro, and Ikuna.

To figure out where we were going, we needed to know where we were. Based upon our flight path when we crashed, Nicki determined that we were anywhere from two hundred to a thousand kilometers from the distress beacon.

At first Nicki had pulled out her holodrive and brought up a spinning three-dimensional projection of Kyral. It wasn't detailed, but it showed the big features (such as the aforementioned dolphin/banana sea). The map even showed a general radius from which the distress beacon of the *Phryxus II* had emanated—a dishearteningly large circle, several thousand square kilometers wide. Still, it was better than nothing.

Eyf was fascinated, but holographic projections proved too much for the other Aeaki to comprehend. Hisuda kept waving her wing through the hologram to disrupt it. When she couldn't, she ultimately declared the device to be "magic spells." Ikuna and Aloro agreed that they wanted nothing to do with it. Privately, I suspected that they didn't even understand they were looking at a map. They probably thought Kyral was flat.

So Nicki put away the holodrive and resorted to drawing the geography in the dirt with a stick. This garnered scarcely better results.

"Have any of you been to the sea?" asked Nicki. "The sea? It's like a very big lake. With lots of water." The Aeaki shook their heads. Despite the mobility of flight, none had apparently ranged far from their home.

"I have been to Hykaro Roost," said Ikuna unhelpfully.

To aid Nicki's presentation, Hollins even tried pulling out a simple instrument called a "compass" that he'd somehow carried with him all the way from Earth. As I understood it, the needle of the compass was a magnet. On Earth, it would always point toward the northern pole of the planet. Here, though, it was useless. The needle spun wildly, sometimes lingering in one direction or another before spinning again. Kyral's magnetic fields were simply different.

Hisuda also declared the malfunctioning compass to be "magic spells." She took it from Hollins and smashed it against a rock before he could stop her. Then she handed it back as though she had solved a very pressing problem.

"Does broken," said Hollins sadly.

At last the Aeaki gave up and wished us good luck in a manner that indicated they were glad to be rid of us.

"Be careful with that one," whispered Hisuda as she pointed to Eyf. "She's not an Oru."

"Oh, really? I hadn't heard!" I yelled, startling her. Hisuda shrugged at our folly, and the three hunters took off, flapping back to the village high above.

And so we all stood together in the forest at the base of Oru's cliff. Our packs were filled with Aeaki food, such as it was. Mostly it consisted of little packets of seeds and nuts wrapped in leaves. Each of us had been given one fire-charred creature on a stick, presumably to eat (or maybe just to to ruin our appetites so we wouldn't get hungry at all). Whether it was rodent, lizard, or other, none could say.

We were free to continue our search for Kalac and the others. I, especially, was eager to start. But we had no idea which way to go. We were at a loss.

"Okay, I'm going to throw a stick up," said Little Gus, "and when it lands, whichever way it's pointing, that's the direction we start walking."

He picked a stick up off the ground and tossed it high into the air. We watched as it hung for a moment, then fell back to the ground and landed right on Hollins's head.

"Ow!" cried Hollins, and he followed that with several of the expletives the humans had forbidden me from using.

"And it seemed like such a foolproof plan," said Becky.

"Okay, sorry, Hollins," said Little Gus. "Obviously, this navigation system needs some fine-tuning. Let me try it again." He stooped to pick up the stick, but Hollins kicked it away from him, at which point Nicki grabbed it, bagged it, and labeled it "stick."

I sighed. So far we were off to a great start.

"You," said a voice from behind me, "Xotonian." I turned. It was, of course, Taius Ridian. Again, he'd climbed down the sheer cliff without the aid of any rope.

"What do you want?" asked Hollins in human-ese, stepping forward. "Are you trying to start something now that we're not in the village anymore? No zapper now, tough guy. You really think you can win in a fair fight?"

When they stood nose to nose, it was clear Hollins was a few centimeters taller and several kilograms heavier. Still, I remembered how deadly quick Taius had been in the fight aboard the *T'utzuxe*.

"I don't know what you're saying, alien," said Taius. "Your language sounds like barking grybbs to me."

Beside me, Nicki and Little Gus were trying to look tough (with mixed results). Becky had a thick branch in her hands. She was ready to fight. Eyf had already alighted in a tree too high for Taius to easily reach. I had one thol'graz in my pack, gripping Eromu's blaster. I felt the weight of the Q-sik beside it.

"But *Homo sapiens* don't interest me at the moment," hissed Taius in Hollins's face. "I want to speak to you. *Chorkle*."

It gave me a chill to hear him utter my name. "I don't think we have anything to say. You should leave us in peace," I said. "It's best that you go your way and we go ours."

"And which way would you be going?"

"I . . . we're going to . . . see, there's this dolphin-sombrero sea and . . ." I trailed off. He had me, and he knew it.

"I thought so," he said, stepping past Hollins. "Let's talk. Alone."

"Ha ha. Good one, Junior," laughed Becky at Taius. "You might be a creep, but at least you've got a sense of humor."

"I'm unarmed," said Taius, ignoring her and speaking only to me. "You may keep your energy blaster. If that makes you feel safe."

He'd either guessed what was in my pack or had seen Ikuna give it to me in the night. I pulled the weapon out and stepped toward him. "Okay," I said, "I'll hear what you have to say. But it won't make a difference."

"What? Are you nuts?" said Little Gus.

"Chorkle, he's dangerous," whispered Nicki. "I mean, not that I'm scared."

"It's okay," I said. "Come on. Follow me." And Taius did. We walked a few dozen meters into the forest, just far enough to be out of earshot but not out of sight of the others. They all looked on with grave concern, ready for action. I could see Eyf flitting nervously from branch to branch.

"So?" I said to Taius. I aimed the energy blaster at a point between his eyes, with my frib on the trigger.

"So," said Taius, "your Xotonian ruler is somewhere on

this planet. In danger. You're trying to follow the distress beacon from its ship." They were all statements, not questions.

I didn't want to give him any information he could use against us, but he already knew. So I nodded. "Not 'ruler,'" I said. "'Leader.'" Did he also know that Kalac was my originator, I wondered?

"Without your starfighter's sensors, you have no way to locate the beacon," he continued.

Here, I said nothing. Again, he was right, and he knew it. "Well, I do," he said.

"What do you mean?" I asked.

He reached to his belt and unclasped the little black square. "Is this the beacon you follow?" He held it close to my ear. I instantly recognized the staticky Xotonian chime! Kalac's chime!

"Yes, that's it!" I cried, unable to contain my excitement.

He quickly palmed the device. "This is a zowul, a Vorem emergency tracker," he said. "But I recalibrated it to pick up your beacon instead. Your rul—your *leader's* ship is not far from here, really. A few hundred kilometers at most. But you'll never locate it on your own."

"So why are you telling me this?" I asked. "Just to taunt me?"

"No," said Taius. "I offer to help you."

"Oh, and why would you do that?" I asked. "Just out of the goodness of your is'pog—I mean heart—I mean whatever gross organ pumps gross Vorem blood?"

He looked momentarily confused by the metaphor. "No," he said. "Kindness is weakness. I would do it to serve myself."

"What are you talking about?"

He looked around and sighed. "I'm trapped on this world. No Vorem legion behind me. The Aeaki are worse than useless. I have no way to contact my father. No way home. I'm in a worse position now than when I was hiding like a vermin in your asteroid's tunnels." He sounded truly pathetic as he spoke.

"It's a little late for sob stories, Taius," I said. "Maybe you should have tried for sympathy before you wrecked our only starship."

"I didn't mean to crash the ship. And I don't ask for *sympathy*." He spit the word out with disgust. "I ask for a promise: If I locate your leader, you must do everything in your power to get me back to my—to General Ridian. Believe me, if there was some other way, I would try it."

"You know," I said, leveling the energy blaster at him,

"we *could* just take that tracker from you. Use it to locate the ship ourselves."

"You could try," he said ominously. "But even if you succeeded in obtaining it from me, the zowul wouldn't work."

"What are you talking about?"

"Here, try it," he said. And he tossed me the little device. I caught it. Once again it went dead. And once again there was no way for me to turn it on.

"The zowul is keyed to my biometrics," said Taius. "A highly advanced security feature. I have to be holding it for it to function. This way our enemies cannot use our own trackers against us."

I tossed it back to him. "You know," I said, "I find it hard to believe that you suddenly want to help us. Considering you just asked Azusu to lock us up."

"I only wanted the humans arrested," he said, truly confused. "Not you."

"But they're my friends!" I cried. He looked back at me blankly as though he didn't understand the concept at all.

"Fine. Whatever you say," he said with a shrug. "The fact is that you need me."

I hated to admit it, but he was right. As far as I could see, the only way to find Kalac and the others was with his little tracker, his "zowul." Still, some bargains aren't worth making.

"No," I said, "we'll find our own way."

"Please," he said, all the remaining arrogance draining from his voice. "Your Xotonian leader's ship is the only way off this backwater planet. I have to get back to the Vorem legion. I can't fail my father again." Good, I thought. Apparently, Taius didn't know that there might still be a Vorem trireme somewhere on Kyral. I wanted to keep it that way.

"The answer is still no," I repeated, "and if you don't leave us alone, I really will shoot you. Again. And I won't aim for your arm this time!" I neglected to mention that I hadn't been aiming for his arm the first time.

Taius stared at me. I turned to rejoin the others.

"Wait!" he cried. I turned back. He'd lost every bit of his icy confidence now; he looked totally desperate.

"What?" I asked.

"There's something else," he said, his voice barely a whisper. "You—back in the ship you . . ." He trailed off.

"Spit it out," I said. "This is your last chance, Taius."

He took a deep breath. "I don't know how your society works. You live in tunnels. You hide in the dark. You seem weak and cowardly. . . ." I frowned, and he could tell he wasn't off to a strong start. "I mean, the rules of your world are different from mine, I guess. But among the Vorem, to owe anything to someone is humiliating. But to owe another your life, especially an inferior—a non-Vorem—it's *disgraceful*." He hissed the last word.

It started to dawn on me what Taius was getting at.

"Back on the starfighter," he said, "you dragged me out before it exploded. You saved me from dying. I owe you my life."

"You do," I admitted.

"I have to repay that debt," he said, "or else I am weak." He was looking at the ground now. Tears were rolling down his cheeks. It was unsettling to see a Vorem weep.

I stared at him in silence. "Okay, Taius," I said, lowering the energy blaster. "If you lead me to Kalac, I'll help you back to your father. And you can consider your debt to me paid."

He looked up at me, and I could see something different in his red eyes.

"But if you try to pull anything," I said, "I swear to Morool I'll vaporize you."

"I won't," he said, wiping his nose. "Just promise me you won't tell anyone that I cried."

I nodded.

. . . .

"Absolutely not!" cried Becky. "He electrocuted me. He destroyed our ship. And he ate my phui-chips!"

"*You* destroyed your own ship," said Taius. It was like his emotional meltdown had never happened. He was back to full-on sneering villain mode. Needless to say, he wasn't endearing himself to the others. Becky, in particular, looked like she wanted to choke him until his red eyes popped out of his head.

Hollins stepped forward and poked Taius in the chest. "Does telling," he said in Xotonian. "Of Vorem did flying to space car called Ridan space car. When does asking?"

"Very good point," said Taius mockingly. "Should I be writing this down for posterity?"

"What Hollins means," said Nicki, "is that if we *had* flown you back to the battle cruiser when you told us to, what would have happened to us? And be honest."

Taius thought for a moment, then he answered. "You all would have been interrogated. If you had any value as hostages, you would have been imprisoned."

"And if we had no value as hostages?" I asked.

"You would have been executed," he said. Nicki, Becky, and Little Gus shook their heads in amazement.

"Um," said Eyf from above.

Taius looked confused. "This is what happens when weaker species choose to battle the Dominion," he said with a shrug. "Everyone knows it."

"Stop explaining," I said to Taius. "You're not helping your case." His mouth twisted into a snarl, but he heeded my advice and said nothing. The Vorem might be good at conquering planets, but their people skills needed a lot of work.

The humans and I huddled and spoke to one another in their language so that Taius wouldn't understand.

Eyf circled overhead. She seemed particularly agitated by all our arguing. "Um," she said again.

"Taius is a creep," said Becky, "plain and simple."

"Yeah, I don't know about this, Chorkle," said Hollins. "Is he up to something?"

"Honestly, I don't think so," I said. "I believe he's desperate." It might have helped to tell them I'd just seen him blubbering like a larvae, but I had given Taius my word I wouldn't tell. And the humans probably wouldn't have believed me anyway.

"Then as much as I hate to say it, it seems like using his tracker—his zowul thingie—is the only way," said Nicki. "For now, Taius's goal happens to align with ours. It makes sense."

"Come on," said Little Gus. "We're really going to trust somebody with red eyes? Seriously? *Red eyes?*"

"I don't like it either," said Hollins, "but what other choice do we have? How else do we find Kalac and the others?"

"We could do Gus's stick thing again," grumbled Becky.

"You liked the stick thing?" asked Little Gus. "I call it Little Gus-ing which way to go!"

"No," said Becky. "I don't like the stick thing. I'm being sarcastic. You're acting super weird, dude."

"What?" cried Little Gus. "Nothing. Not me. Weird? No. What?"

Becky squinted at him before speaking to the rest of us. "Trusting Taius Ridian is a mistake," she said.

"Teddy Roosevelt once said, 'The only man who never makes mistakes is the man who never does anything,'" said Hollins.

"Little Gus once said: 'People with red eyes are bad news,'" said Little Gus.

"Look, it might not be a good option, but at this moment it happens to be our best. We have to do it," said Hollins as though this was the final word on the matter.

"What are you? The boss? Shouldn't we vote on it?" asked Nicki with a hint of irritation in her voice.

"Yeah, fine," said Hollins. "Let's do that."

"Eyf, do you want to vote?" I asked.

"No," she said, "but um . . ."

We voted. It was three to two. Nicki, Hollins, and I voted in favor of following Taius. Little Gus and Becky voted against. Of course, I hadn't told them that I'd already given Taius my word. All the while, he watched us with a look of contempt on his face.

"Um, look, excuse me Chorkle and *Homo sapiens*," said Eyf, landing nearby. "But soon it will be nightfall." It was true. We'd wasted half the day looking at maps and debating. It was time to get moving. Every minute we dallied might make all the difference.

I approached Taius. He sat on a flat rock, legs crossed, eyes narrowed. His pack was on the ground beside him. "Okay, Taius," I said, "lead the way."

Hollins stepped up from behind, holding Eromu's blaster in his hand. "Nice. Or does zapping," he said to Taius in poorly accented Xotonian. For once, though, his meaning was utterly clear.

Taius stood and picked up a walking stick—about as tall as his shoulders—off the ground. Then he smiled with a flash of pointed white teeth. "Good," he said. "I thought you were going to stand around blathering all day."

"Watch it," said Little Gus. "Blathering is what makes humanity great."

Taius eyed the little device in his palm, and I heard the faint chime of the *Phryxus II*'s beacon. Then he started off through the forest. The rest of us followed behind: four on foot, one on fel'graz, and one flying through the air.

I turned back for one last look at Oru. The mesa on which it sat rose straight up from the forest floor. The sheer walls of its cliffs were riddled with rectangular caves and choked with creeping vines. I suddenly realized that the bluff I was looking at wasn't a natural landform at all. It was an ancient skyscraper.

CHAPTER TWELVE

As we traveled, a very curious thing began to happen. With every kilometer we put between ourselves and Oru, Eyf opened up a little bit more. At first it was an unprompted statement here or there. Then the occasional personal anecdote. By sundown she couldn't stop talking.

"And one time I was flying, and I saw a cloud, and the cloud looked like a foot, but I knew it wasn't because obviously it was just a cloud. . . ." She kept up a continuous stream of chatter as she glided through the blue branches above our heads.

"Good story," said Little Gus wearily.

"It seems like nobody's ever talked to her before," whispered Nicki.

"She's trying to fit a lifetime of conversation into one single day," said Becky, rubbing her forehead.

"And I was just looking at it, because how often do you see a cloud that looks like a foot?" Eyf continued. "And the answer is: sort of often. Maybe once every three days? But there's no guarantee—"

"Can you just be quiet!" snapped Taius. "For one minute!"

Eyf whimpered from the branches and was silent.

"Hey," yelled Becky. "She can talk as much as she wants!"

Taius glared at her.

"Eyf, keep telling us about the foot," said Becky.

"First off," said Eyf, "it wasn't a foot. It was a cloud that looked like a foot. . . ."

We were an odd polyglot group. When the humans and I spoke among ourselves, it was in their language—to the total exclusion of Eyf and Taius. When Eyf or Taius needed to communicate, it was all in Xotonian, which meant that Hollins couldn't always follow. We were four species speaking two languages. Somehow, though, we seemed to manage.

Now the sun had dropped below the horizon, and the sky—when we could see it peeping through the forest canopy—was a far deeper shade of purple streaked with bands of crimson. By my chronometer, we'd been walking for more than four hours.

"And then another time I saw a cloud, and it wasn't really shaped like anything, but I didn't—um, we should stop," said Eyf, actually interrupting herself as she alighted on a rock ahead of us. "For the night. This is a good place. A very good place." She waved toward a massive tree behind her. It was the biggest I'd seen yet on Kyral—one hundred twenty meters tall and probably forty meters around the trunk. It was covered in knotty bark—so blue it was practically black—and lined with branches as thick as usk-lizard tails.

"If by 'stop,' you mean 'stop telling that boring story,' then I'm all for it," snapped Taius as he checked his zowul. "But we still have more than three hundred kilometers to go, and we wasted too much time today. We should keep walking through the night to make up for lost time."

His direct attention startled Eyf. "But Kyral is a very dangerous place in the darkness," she squeaked.

"Maybe you're just a coward," said Taius, moving toward her. She cringed backward.

"Funny you should call *her* a coward," said Becky, stepping between them, "since you're the one who's been hiding for the last three months."

"That wasn't because I was afraid!" he cried. "It was part of my plan. To get back to my battle cruiser!"

"I see," said Becky as she looked around at the dark forest. "So how *did* that plan work out for you?" she asked. Little Gus snickered. Taius scowled.

"I'm as eager as anyone to keep going," I said. "But Eyf is the only one of us who knows anything about this world. If she says we should stop, then we should listen to her."

"Well, this looks like as good a place as any to camp," said Nicki. "I can start collecting wood for a fire—"

"No, no, no, no," said Eyf, hopping up and down with panic. "No fires in this forest!"

We all looked at her. Hollins approached and spoke to her gently and semi-correctly in Xotonian: "Of no fire. Having why this, tiny bird-face? Of."

She took a deep breath. "Uji, Esu, Abi, and all the other clans," she said with a fearful wave toward the sky. "If they saw, they would swoop in and attack us on sight. Take us prisoner or worse."

"But the Aeaki sleep at night, don't they?" I asked.

"Yes, mostly," she admitted, "but we should not take chances. I am more worried about the other things that a fire would attract. Hungry, creeping things. Beastly things."

"Sounds like a load of garbage to me," said Taius.

"Good thing nobody asked you," said Becky.

"Okay, so we pitch a camp with no fire," said Nicki,

shrugging and tossing her pack down. "We have our thermal blankets. If we get too cold, we can just do jumping jacks." Nicki started to push a mound of dried leaves together for a bed.

"No, no, no," said Eyf, "not on the ground." She pointed to the huge tree that towered over us. "Up there. We roost."

"I'm a legate of the Vorem Dominion," said Taius. "I don't 'roost.'" He dropped his walking stick to the ground and slumped down at the base of the trunk.

"I wanted to say the same thing," whispered Becky to me, "but I can't agree with *him*."

So the rest of us scaled the massive trunk. The bark provided handholds that even the clumsy humans could grasp. About ten meters up, Eyf deemed it safe to stop.

"Interesting," said Nicki, looking down. "Just high enough for the fall to kill us. We might crack our skulls open. Or injure our spinal—"

"Good night, everyone!" said Hollins, loudly cutting her off.

We each picked one of the tree's massive branches to sleep on. Taius remained on the ground, occasionally looking up at us and shaking his head.

I shifted and found that ultimately there was no comfortable way to sleep in a tree. In fact, I worried that I would stay awake all night. I rolled over again. Below me I heard Little Gus's voice. Very quietly, at almost a whisper, he was singing an old human song called "Georgia on My Mind." Perhaps he hoped that Pizza might hear? I settled in for a long and sleepless night.

I was awakened by a bloodcurdling wail from somewhere out in the forest. My eyes, well adapted to darkness, saw nothing. I stayed put, too afraid to investigate the sound.

When morning came, we all found that Taius Ridian had joined us in the tree. He never spoke of it, and even Becky resisted the urge to taunt him. I guessed that all of us had heard that same awful noise.

Away from the others, I asked Eyf about it. "What was that scream last night?"

"A rahk," she said with a shudder, and she pointed to the soft loam at the trunk of the tree. All around it were the same deep, clawed tracks that we'd seen near the Oru hunting trap. Each was as big as any five human footprints. Whatever a "rahk" was, one had been sniffing around the base of the very tree where we slept. As a courtesy, I didn't mention this to the others. I figured I was already scared enough for all of us.

We walked onward through the forest, following Taius. Every so often he would stop and listen to the faint chime, take a reading, and make a few adjustments. He reckoned that if we kept up a good pace, we could reach the beacon in eight days. He also expressed extreme doubt that we would keep a good pace.

The morning mist burned off, and by midday the air of the forest was warm and humid. Once, we rounded a bend and disturbed several winged reptilian creatures as they ate. Ugly as the little gray-skinned scavengers were, their meal proved more disturbing: decaying Aeaki remains. On wooden stakes were three of their skulls, mostly picked clean. The bare white bone gleamed in the sunlight.

Eyf picked up a faded gold feather from the ground. Then she found a purple one and held the two together. "Uji," she whispered. "We are in their territory."

"Who did this to them?" I asked.

Eyf shrugged. "Esu? Abi? Yko? Even Oru, maybe. We should get away from here. Quick." Not even Taius disagreed.

Once we'd put a few kilometers between us and the clearing, we stopped for a break. We sat on a little hillock in the sun to rest our legs and fel'grazes, respectively. All around us pieces of rusted metal and broken chunks of concrete poked up through the foliage.

I touched my own thol'graz and yelped. My whole skin hurt!

"Wow, Chorkle, you're roasting," said Nicki as she looked at me.

"I guess living in a cave your whole life, you didn't get the chance to work much on your base tan," said Becky. "You've got a sunburn, pal."

I looked at my i'ardas. They were now approximately the color of a Feeney's Original Astronaut Ice Cream bar.

"How do I unburn myself?" I asked. I tried camouflaging myself a number of different colors, but each one still had a distinct rosy tinge. And my skin still hurt.

"You can't. All you can do is cover up," said Hollins. "Here, use this." He reached in his pack and handed me a spare human thermal blanket.

"Ow! Ow! Ow!" I squealed as I tried to wrap it around my i'ardas. "That's making it worse!"

"I know it hurts, but you have to keep the sun off. Otherwise you'll be the color of Little Gus's hair by the end of the day," said Hollins.

"I say go for it, Chorkle," said Little Gus. "It's pretty much the best color. I call it 'flaming marinara.'" He took

181

a bite of his charred creature on a stick, chewed once, then spit it out.

As the rest of us ate our seeds and nuts, Eyf happily regaled us with more stories from her life.

"And I looked in the hollow log, and the only thing that was in there was just moss!" she said with a big laugh. Believe it or not, she had already told this thrilling tale once before.

"Eyf," I asked her, thinking of the three skulls, "why do the Aeaki seem to distrust each other and fight among themselves so much?"

"I don't know," she shrugged. "Aeaki always fight. Kill those with different feathers. Sometimes there are alliances between clans, but they always break up real quick. Then it's fight, fight, fight again. Only in Hykaro Roost do they not fight, because it is a holy place."

"The Aeaki might be a bunch of savages," said Taius, "but at least they've figured out the truth of the universe. It's kill or be killed. Strength or weakness."

"If you think that's the truth of the universe," I said to him, "then I feel sorry for you."

"When the Vorem Dominion attacked your asteroid," he said, "what did you Xotonians do?"

"We fought back," I admitted.

"Then you've proven my point."

"But the Vorem Dominion didn't have to attack!" I cried. "The Aeaki don't have to kill each other just because they have different feathers! It's a choice."

"It is?" said Eyf.

"Tell it to those three lucky Uji we saw earlier," said Taius, ignoring her. "Ask them what choice they had."

We sat in silence for a while until Nicki spoke. "Eyf," she said, "if you're not an Oru, what are you?"

Here, for the first time in a day, Eyf seemed reticent. "Nobody knows," she said at last. "Before I hatched, there was a big battle. All the clans nearby fought each other for many days. Nobody remembers why they were fighting, or maybe they don't tell me. The Oru and the Uji won, though—they were allies then. Many, many, many Aeaki died. When it was done, among the bodies they found an egg. But nobody knew whom it belonged to.

"Azusu decided to wait for the egg to hatch. If it had green and black feathers or yellow and tan or any other colors but Oru orange and red, she would have killed the chick inside."

"That's horrible," said Nicki.

Eyf shrugged. "But the egg was me," she said. "And my feathers have no color. Just white." She held up a little wing

183

as proof. "So Azusu didn't know what to do. I was not Esu, Abi, Yko, or any other clan anyone had ever heard of. So she decided to let me live with the Oru in their village, even though I am not one of them. She is not so bad."

"But they treated you like garbage!" said Becky.

Again, Eyf shrugged. "Better than being dead," she said.

That night we made camp in another tall tree. This time, Taius made no argument.

"We should keep watch," he said. "We don't want to get caught unawares."

"Yeah, I don't like the thought of you being awake while I'm not," said Becky.

"Fine with me," said Taius. "The rest of you can take shifts while I sleep. As long as someone is keeping a lookout." And he rolled over and went to sleep.

Becky grumbled, but in fact she had gotten exactly what she wanted. So Eyf, the humans, and I divided the night into six one-hour shifts, one for each of us.

I took the first watch. It was uneventful, and I found my mind wandering. I thought of Kalac's beacon chiming away somewhere in the darkness. I looked up at Gelo, glowing brightly beside Ithro in the night sky. Had Hudka been arrested by the glorious Imperator Sheln? Was my grand-originator languishing in prison with the captured

Vorem legionaries? I thought of Azusu and bands of colored Aeaki clashing in battle and then finding an egg in the aftermath, a new life on a field of death. I thought of Vorem fire raining from the heavens. I thought of Taius, crying in the woods.

There came a gentle tap on my i'arda that—due to my sunburn—hurt like Morool. I swallowed a whimper and turned to see Becky. My watch was over.

"Hey, Chorkle," she whispered. "Can you keep a lookout for a minute? Nature calls."

"Nature calls what?" I asked. She frowned and tactfully explained the situation.

We climbed down the tree to the ground. Becky walked a few meters into a thicket of bushes, and I wandered off to give her privacy. I took in a big breath of cool night air and listened to the rhythmic drone of alien insects.

That's when I heard it: a snuffling grunt somewhere nearby. I looked at the back of my thol'grazes. My sunburnt skin had camouflaged itself automatically. There was a crashing sound, and I felt the ground shake.

Something was galloping toward me. Something huge. On pure instinct, I crouched and sprang high into the air an instant before it came barreling through the underbrush. At the very height of my jump, one of my scrambling thol' grazes caught a tree limb. I hung there as the thin branch bobbed up and down under my weight.

Below me, I could see the beast. It was a massive creature, bigger than an usk-lizard. It galloped on four clawed feet. It was covered in feathers, though it had no wings and looked too heavy to climb. This creature—a rahk, I now assumed—must find its meals on the ground, I realized. And its long, razor-sharp beak left no doubt as to what those meals must be.

The rahk glanced up at me with one angry orange eye. I discharged my stink gland, but a breeze carried the spray past the beast. It had already charged off in Becky's direction.

"Chorkle?" she cried as she heard the noise. The rahk was making no effort to move silently now.

I dropped to the ground and followed the swathe of crushed bushes and broken saplings that it had torn through the forest. Despite the rahk's bulk, the beast was much quicker than me.

"Becky, run!" I cried.

"What?"

"Run!"

The rahk burst through the bushes and went right for her. Becky ducked out of the way just as a clawed foot swiped for her head and took a chunk out of the tree behind her. Then she turned on her heels and ran as fast as she could. The rahk whirled and followed.

Something—a rock or a root—caught Becky's foot, and she tripped and sprawled onto the ground. She flipped over on her back as the rahk bore down on her with all its weight.

Just then, a dark figure leaped forward. It whipped something through the darkness and bashed the beast across the forehead. *Crack!* The dazed rahk stopped in its tracks and made what must have been the least frightening noise of which it was capable: a high-pitched, confused squawk.

Taius Ridian had brained it with his walking stick. The rahk blinked at him for a moment and then let loose a long, murderous wail—the same sound I had heard from the forest the night before. Standing so close, the noise was terrifying. I had to fight the urge to turn and flee.

Taius grasped his stick in both hands and shifted into a defensive position. With amazing speed, the rahk began to slash at him with its front claws. By shifting his position and twirling the stick, he deflected three swipes that looked like they could have knocked down a house. The fourth snapped his stick clean down the middle and left him holding the two halves.

Before the rahk could finish Taius off, a stone bounced off the side of its beak, snapping its head to one side. It turned to see Becky, up on her feet now. She'd already scooped up another rock to throw. The rahk hesitated for a moment as it tried to decide which of the two of them to kill and devour first.

Suddenly, the forest was lit in a flash of green. A bolt of energy ripped through the rahk's hind leg. Hollins fired Eromu's blaster again. The second shot left a smoking stripe across the beast's back. The rahk gave one last hellish wail. Then it galloped off into the forest, shaking the ground like a minor earthquake.

All of us stood, looking at one another and panting. At last, Becky spoke. "Thanks, Hollins."

"Don't mention it."

Then she mumbled something under her breath to Taius.

"What?" Taius asked, dropping the two half sticks to the ground.

"Thank you," she said quietly. "And I'm seriously not saying it again."

Instead of smug or arrogant, Taius looked mortified. "*Thank* me?" he whispered. Perhaps the Vorem were allergic to gratitude.

Hollins stepped toward Taius. He looked at the broken walking stick, then looked right in Taius's face and nodded in approval. "Good," he said in Xotonian. But he lifted Eromu's blaster and tapped it for emphasis. "Still. I of looking." He pointed to his eyes and then to Taius. "Pudding feet," he added for some reason. Taius looked deeply confused.

Eyf alighted on a branch near me. "I can't believe it!" she squeaked. "I saw the whole thing! You defeated a rahk! You defeated a vicious, hungry rahk!"

"'Defeated' is a little strong," I said, "Maybe 'dissuaded.' 'Discouraged'?" I was afraid that the beast might return at any moment.

"Yes, it is best to be careful," agreed Eyf emphatically. "That baby rahk's mother may be somewhere nearby."

"Mother?!" I cried. But Eyf had already flown off.

None of us slept the rest of the night.

CHAPTER THIRTEEN

"The Glass Desert," said Eyf.

From the edge of the forest, we gazed out across the sparkling plain. As far as I could see, the ground was flat, glittering, and utterly lifeless. I guessed this was one of the barren patches of Kyral's surface that the Observers had seen from space.

"It's beautiful," said Hollins, picking up a chunk of the crumbly pale-green mineral. It shimmered in the afternoon sun.

"It's trinitite," said Nicki, "the glass residue that's created by the heat of a nuclear explosion." Unconsciously, she glanced at Taius. He said nothing.

"Is it radioactive?" asked Becky. "If I grow another arm, I'm going to need new clothes."

"Maybe a little," said Nicki. "But I wouldn't worry

about it, sis. We've spent so much time in space, we've already absorbed a ton of radiation. A little more isn't going to make a difference."

"Thank you for setting my mind at ease with your comforting words," said Becky with a sigh.

"Well, whatever this place is called, we need to cross it," said Taius, checking his zowul. "Trying to go around it will take us hundreds of kilometers out of the way."

"The Glass Desert is a bad place," said Eyf. "A very, very, very bad place."

"There's nothing to conceal us. We would be out in the open," I said, looking skyward. "Any passing Aeaki would be able to spot us from the air." Indeed, the day before, we had seen several black specks wheeling above the forest. Eyf had forced us to hide until they passed. Crossing the desert would mean no cover.

"Yes, other Aeaki could see us," said Eyf. "But also the Glass Desert is cursed! Very cursed! Extremely cursed! One of the most cursed places!"

Taius frowned. I could tell that part of him wanted to say something snide about superstition and cowardice. But he held his tongue. It may have been my imagination, but little by little, he seemed to be softening. After four days together, he wasn't as quick with his jibes or his contempt.

He was more willing to pitch in and lend a hand when it was needed.

"Kalac is still in danger. We don't have the time to go around it," I said. "I think we should cross."

"No," said Hollins, speaking in Xotonian for Eyf and Taius's benefit. "Big risky." Eyf agreed heartily.

"All right," said Becky. "I guess we take another vote."

"Vote again?" asked Eyf. "How does vote work?"

"We all pick the choice we like," said Nicki. "Then we raise our hands or wings—"

I cleared my gul'orp.

"Or thol'grazes," added Nicki. "And whichever choice has more *votes* is what we all agree to do." Nicki raised her hand to demonstrate.

Eyf was fascinated by the idea. I guessed that no one in Oru had ever asked for her opinion on anything.

I sighed. "You, uh . . . you get a vote too, Taius," I said. Becky huffed and held her hands out to me in exasperation. I shot her a look, and she stopped. Taius himself looked supremely uncomfortable. But in the end, he did vote.

The final count was five-to-two in favor of crossing the Glass Desert.

Eyf was personally wounded by the result. "Everyone voted against me," she said. "Except this big, simple one."

She waved toward Hollins. "Do all of you . . . hate me too?" she whispered.

"No, it's just democracy," I said. "We can disagree without enmity."

"Sort of," added Becky.

"It's a way that groups can make choices together," said Nicki.

"So you do this all the time?" asked Taius. "Whenever it is time for a decision, you all have to stop and raise your hands? It's . . . inefficient."

"It's not a perfect system," I admitted. "But on Gelo, we do vote on matters of great importance."

"But then the smartest gets equal say to the most foolish!" cried Taius in disbelief. "The strongest is made equal to the weakest!"

"Yup, that's kind of the point, dude," said Little Gus.

"And what if your ruler disagrees with the vote?" asked Taius.

"As I said, on Gelo we don't really have a ruler. We vote for those who would represent us. And if we don't like what they've done, we can vote them out of office."

"And then the leader just steps down? Because a bunch of common rabble *voted* for it?" asked Taius.

I hesitated as I remembered Sheln's unprecedented power grab. "Under normal circumstances," I sighed.

"It is the same on your planet?" Taius asked Nicki.

"Mostly," she said. "Though not everywhere."

Taius couldn't believe what he was hearing. "It would never work on Voryx Prime," he said. "If a Vorem seizes power, he never relinquishes it. Not until it is pried from his claws. And while he has power, he does as he pleases. He crushes those who oppose him to gather more power for himself. In our whole history, not a single imperator has ever abdicated. Perhaps this drive is the reason our world rules a vast empire and your worlds don't!"

We were silent. Taius suddenly looked around, perhaps conscious that his words might have offended the rest of us. In fact, the humans looked at him with pity.

"Of maybe," said Hollins. "But . . . why?"

"Why *what*?" asked Taius.

"Why . . . empire?" said Hollins, shrugging.

"Because," said Taius. "Because we—because by conquering other worlds, we gain wealth and glory."

"But the Vorem already *have* wealth and glory," I said.

"Of course we do!" said Taius. "And we want more."

"But you have more than anyone," said Becky. "How much more do you need?"

Taius threw his hands up. "I don't know!" he said. "Just—just *more*."

"So when does it end?" I asked.

Taius shook his head as though the question was ridiculous. But he didn't offer an answer.

Ultimately, Eyf accepted the result of our vote to cross through the Glass Desert, but she begged that we travel at night to avoid being seen from above.

I called for another vote on Eyf's idea, just so she might win one. She was thrilled at the unanimous result in her favor. So we waited among the trees for the sun to drop below the horizon. In the meantime, Eyf wanted us to vote on all matters, great and small. We humored her for a while, but when she finally asked us to vote on which of six blue pinecones was the prettiest, we had to call an end to it.

"I'm starting to come around to the Vorem way of thinking on democracy," whispered Little Gus.

The reds and golds of the sunset were doubly brilliant as they bounced off the trinitite. Soon, the Glass Desert gleamed silver with moonlight. We set out, and before long, we'd left the little noises of the forest behind us. The only sounds were the faint chime from Taius's tracker and the crunching of brittle green glass underfoot. The desert didn't feel cursed to me, but there was something somber about it. I think that the others felt it too, for no one spoke. Not even Eyf.

We didn't make it across before the sun rose again. The morning came, and we found ourselves in a vast wasteland, a sparkling green infinity in every direction. Above us, the sky was crisp and cloudless. If we didn't know where we were going, I might have panicked. Xotonians understand the world by the twists and turns of caverns, but here there were no turns. Or maybe the Glass Desert was all turns?

After a night of walking, we were all tired. In fact, Eyf admitted she had almost fallen asleep on the wing.

"It's okay," she said. "I would have woken up when I hit the ground."

"We should keep going," said Taius. "We only have about twelve kilometers until we're across." He looked haggard though, and I could see dark circles under his eyes. "Or wait, maybe it's twenty." He slapped the side of the zowul. It was more static than chime now.

"Is there something wrong with that thing?" I asked.

"No," he said. "Maybe." But he put up no further argument as the rest of us flopped onto the brittle ground in exhaustion.

"One of us needs to . . . " said Taius, trailing off.

"What?" asked Nicki.

Taius snapped awake. "What?" he said, "I mean, we should keep a watch. . . . I'll take the first one."

"Okay," said Nicki, rolling over.

. . . .

"Wake up," hissed Hollins.

The sky above us was dark and ominous. The sun was just a slightly brighter patch of hazy air.

"Did we—did we sleep the whole day?" I asked. I was sore and groggy, and my gul'orp felt as dry as the desert itself.

"No," said Hollins. He was standing and looking off into the distance. Great brownish-green clouds were rolling toward us from the horizon. The other humans were pulling themselves up off the ground. Only Taius still snored.

"Taius!" cried Hollins.

The Vorem awakened with a start. He looked around for a moment. "I fell asleep," he admitted.

"We go," said Hollins in Xotonian. "Go. Go. Now."

"What is that?" asked Becky, eyeing the churning clouds.

"Dust storm," said Nicki. "We sometimes saw them

197

when we observed Kyral from space. It looks like a big one."

In the distance, I could see little flashes of lightning now. The storm was moving toward us fast.

"The Glass Desert is cursed!" squeaked Eyf. "Cursed! Cursed! Cursed!"

"We need to . . . " said Taius, fiddling with the tracker. "We should go. . . . We . . . The storm is causing interference. I don't know where to go!"

Hollins grabbed Taius's shoulder. He pointed to the only landmark in sight: our own tracks. Then he pointed in the direction that they were headed and nodded. Taius nodded back. We would try to keep going the way they pointed.

"Don't wait for us!" I cried to Eyf. She nodded and took off. She stood a better chance of outpacing the storm if she flew.

The rest of us jogged—then ran—in single file: Hollins, Nicki, Little Gus, me, Becky, and Taius. Little cyclones of dust appeared before us. We tried our best to keep our tracks in a straight line behind us, but the storm was erasing them fast. The cyclones grew larger. The wind had picked up, and it was howling now. I could feel the dust against my skin, in my eyes, everywhere. The sun was gone from the sky.

Soon I started to to have trouble keeping track of Little Gus. He would fade away and then suddenly reappear. I worried I might lose him permanently. I realized that I was running with my eyes closed. The dust made it hard to breathe and even harder to see.

"Wait!" cried someone up ahead. It was Hollins. He'd stopped. Thankfully Nicki and Gus stood beside him.

"Can't keep going," yelled Nicki over the howl. Gus tried to say something, but he only coughed.

"Blankets!" yelled Hollins, pointing to me.

I was confused for a moment, until I remembered the crinkly human thermal blanket that I'd been wearing as a cloak to keep the sun off. Hollins had already pulled his out of his pack. The humans had five, one for each of them, plus the spare I'd been given. Gus and Nicki unfurled theirs.

"Where are Becky and Taius?" I cried. But no one could hear me over the scream of the wind. The dust was a searing sting now—I guessed it was made of tiny glass particles. I couldn't see two meters ahead of me, and that was when I could bear to open my eyes. I coughed every time I inhaled.

Lighting flashed somewhere nearby, followed by a deafening crash of thunder. Without thinking about it, I hit the ground. I opened an eye the barest width and saw no one around me.

So I wrapped the blanket over as much of my body as I could and tried to lie as flat as possible. All around I heard thunder and the hissing scrape of flying sand. Even the blanket was not enough to keep out the fine, choking dust. I coughed continuously. The wind tore at the edges of the blanket. At times it felt like I would be picked up bodily by the storm and carried away—like an Aeaki on the wing.

I waited. And waited. Gradually, the thunder came less frequently. The pitch of the wind lowered, and the dust storm seemed to die down. At last, I was startled by the prodding of something outside the blanket. I opened my eyes—gummy with dirt—for the first time in hours.

The air had cleared some, and I could see the sun once more. Nicki was standing above me. She was completely coated in fine dust.

"Well that was *fascinating*!" she said, and then she coughed up a big glob of greenish spit.

We found Hollins and Little Gus nearby, both as dusty as Nicki and myself.

"Are we dead?" asked Little Gus, trying to brush himself off. It was futile.

"Good idea with the blankets," I said to Hollins. he wiped the snot from his runny nose and gave me two thumbs up.

"Are you all dead?" came a faint cry from above.

"I don't know! No one will tell me!" replied Little Gus.

Eyf landed nearby. She looked like she'd escaped the worst of it. "The edge of the Glass Desert is that way!" she said, pointing, "I saw it! Not far! Not far at all!"

Two dark shapes stumbled toward us through the settling dust. Taius was trying to spit, but his mouth was too dry. Becky's hair looked like some sort of deranged animal clinging to her head. She was refolding her own thermal blanket. Luckily she'd had the same idea.

"Wait," said Little Gus, doing some quick mental math. "You two only had one blanket."

Neither one of them spoke.

"We only have five blankets," said Little Gus quietly. "Did you two share a blanket . . . through the whole storm?"

"I don't want to talk about it," said Becky.

Taius didn't either. He pulled out the zowul, no longer disrupted by the weather. Thank Jalasu Jhuk I heard the telltale chime once more.

CHAPTER FOURTEEN

On the far side of the desert, we followed the beacon into a mountain range that had no Aeaki name that Eyf knew. The trees became smaller and farther between as we climbed up into the scrubby hills.

I caught Little Gus staring back the way we'd come. The lifeless green of the Glass Desert spread out behind us.

"Do you think he'll be able to follow our scent across *that*?" he asked. He was talking about Pizza.

"Yes," I lied. In fact, I worried that the dust storm had scoured away all trace of our passing.

We made camp on a high ledge deemed inaccessible to most "beastly things" by Eyf. She felt reasonably sure we were out of rahk country for now. The big predators on Kyral were forest dwellers.

Our Oru provisions had run low, so Eyf helped forage

for more edible things. This meant seeds and grasses and herbs, mostly. Once, she flipped a rock and found dozens of squealing yellow grubs underneath. She offered to share, but the rest of us politely declined. So she ate them herself.

"Can you imagine eating something like that?" asked Hollins as he watched Eyf peck the little grubs out of the dirt.

"Yuck," I said. "I wish we had some normal food, like a freeze-dried ice cream bar or a nice fried cave slug."

Eyf even deemed it safe for us to make a fire. We were beneath a rocky overhang, so the flames would be hidden from any Aeaki who might be flying overhead.

With a heat source and some fresh ingredients, Little Gus resumed his long-standing role as the group's cook. He really outdid himself, too. He used several red tubers to make a delicious savory soup. The only unappetizing aspect was that it was exactly the color of human blood. Slurping it down, I felt a bit like one of the *Vampire Band Camp* undead.

"What do you call this stuff?" I asked him, finishing my second bowl.

"Oh, I think you know," said Little Gus.

I sighed. "Little Gus Soup?"

"What? No," he said, scratching his head. "It's actually called borscht. But 'Little Gus Soup' does have a nice ring to it. Plus, nobody on this planet can argue."

"It tastes like wryv," said Taius, unbidden. We all turned to stare at him.

"The Vorem one said a not-mad thing!" whispered Eyf. Taius turned away.

"What's 'wryv'?" I asked.

"Nothing. It's just a dish we have on my world," he said. "But usually it has meat in it. Raw meat."

The humans and I looked at one another. Taius had been less hostile in the recent days, but he'd been far from forthcoming. This was the first bit of personal information that he'd offered up. Only Little Gus rolled his eyes. Since the dust storm, he'd been quite rude to Taius at every turn. I suspected it had something to do with the fact that he'd shared Becky's blanket.

"What's it like on your world?" I asked.

Taius hesitated. "Voryx Prime is a harsh, barren planet. We live in fortified cities, always ready for attack."

"Sounds really nice," said Little Gus. "Very welcoming. How are the beaches?"

"You're all making fun of me," he said.

"No, we're not," I said. "Do you miss it?"

Taius squinted at me. "What do you mean, 'miss it'?" he asked with a hint of his old sneer.

"Chorkle means: Is it fun? Or interesting?" said Nicki. "Are there people there you'd like to see again? TV shows you need to catch up on?"

"*Fun?*" he said as though he'd never heard the word before. "No, it's not fun. . . . I suppose Voryx Prime is interesting. Our culture is very . . . complicated."

"How?" asked Hollins.

"Well," said Taius, "Vorem society is divided into castes. Lowest are the alien slaves. Then the Vorem slaves. Then the plebeians and the soldiers. And above all are the patricians. The patricians are the great houses that built the Vorem Dominion."

"Huh. You sure the *slaves* didn't do some of that?" asked Becky.

Taius opened his mouth to respond, but then he closed it. Perhaps he hadn't considered the idea before. "Well . . . you might have a point," he said at last. "But those with power are all patricians."

"So I guess we can assume you're one too, huh?" asked Little Gus.

"Yes," said Taius proudly. "Ridian is an ancient house. We have imperial blood. In fact, my grandfather could have been imperator. But he was betrayed and executed. The current imperator is my cousin."

"Wow," said Little Gus. "I knew you were a fancypants, but I didn't know we had actual *royalty* here with us. A real 'Prince Charming'!"

Taius stared at him blankly.

"It's from a fairy tale we have on Earth," cried Little Gus in exasperation. "Read a book once in a while!"

Taius shrugged. "I do read books. Military history, mostly."

"Of course you do," said Little Gus.

"Speaking of the military," I said, "you're a patrician, but you're also a legate in the Vorem legion, right? Which is sort of like a general or something?"

"Legate is an officer's rank that is lower than a general," said Taius. "My father's a general."

"But you can't be much older than us," I said. "Aren't you a little young to be leading troops into battle?"

Here, he tensed. "Vorem war training begins early. When we are children."

"Yeah, well. Seems like you could have used a little more training," said Little Gus.

Taius's eyes flashed. "What?" he cried, suddenly as enraged as I'd ever seen him. "How dare you—I should've—I mean, the battle on Gelo was not a foregone conclusion! If we'd done more reconnaissance, I wouldn't have failed! The legion I was given, they were a pack of cowards! And even Imperator Rhado lost a battle. It's not . . . It wasn't my . . . I should have won!"

The rest of us stared at him in silence. Taius was panting. A strand of spittle hung from his lips.

"Well, it's a good thing you didn't," said Becky simply, and she stood to leave. The rest of the humans followed her—Little Gus with a click of his tongue. Even Eyf, who loved conversation more than anyone, walk-hopped away to her own bedroll.

And so I sat alone by the dying fire with Taius. Both of us were quiet for a long time.

"My father is not the forgiving type," he said, startling me. "If I ever return to General Ridian, he may well put me to death."

"What?" I said. "Why?"

"For losing the battle," he said. "He's always believed I am weak and foolish and incompetent. He gave me command of the Gelo invasion to prove myself. But all I proved was that he was right about me."

I was torn. I was obviously glad that we'd beaten back the Vorem legion and kept the Q-sik from General Ridian. At the same time, death seemed a harsh penalty for anyone, even Taius. And deep down, some part of me remembered the times when I felt I couldn't measure up to Kalac's standards.

"There was no way to know we had starfighters," I said, shrugging. It was an odd position to be comforting someone who had tried to conquer your civilization.

"Forget the space battle; I should have won in the tunnels!" he said. "By the formulas of the Dominion War College, I had more than enough troops and firepower to beat a bunch of untrained cave dwellers."

I frowned at him. "No offense," he added halfheartedly. "I just . . . I don't know what happened. I lost."

This brought us to something I'd been wondering about for a while. "How *did* you survive the battle?" I asked him. "We thought we buried you."

"There was a legionary about my size who'd been killed in the fighting," said Taius. "I dressed his body in my armor. I even left my blaster with his corpse, though I realize now how useful it would have been in the months that followed. I didn't want to leave any clues of my existence."

"Perhaps only one in a million could survive in the Unclaimed Tunnels for that long," I said. "It would have been almost impossible, even for a Xotonian."

"I've had survival training," said Taius. "But it wasn't easy. I practically starved. Once, I was so hungry, I ate this glowing red slime I found under a rock. Just shoved it down my throat by the handful, even though it tasted awful. After that, I started smelling colors. I thought my legs were lasers for a full week." And he laughed.

Taius Ridian actually laughed! It wasn't a sinister muah-ha-ha-ha cackle either. It was just a wry, lighthearted chuckle. I laughed along with him.

"After weeks, maybe months of stumbling around in the caverns," he continued, "I heard a group of Xotonians, and I followed them all the way to your hangar. I hid nearby and observed. And little by little, I took tools and small quantities of food, undetected."

"Not totally undetected," I said, thinking of the missing phui-chips.

"I realized that you occasionally sent your starfighters out for test flights."

"Yes," I said. "The humans were training Xotonians to fly them." Taius cocked his head. I realized that I'd let it slip that, by and large, my people didn't know how to fly our own starships. "I mean the humans were training young Xotonians, like me, to fly them," I said, trying to cover. "Because the elders had no time to do it themselves."

He nodded. "In fact, when I decided to stow away aboard your starfighter, I assumed it was one of those

short training flights, with only one or two Xotonians aboard. I hadn't counted on trying to overpower
five of you, plus whatever you call that blue predator."

"Thyss-cat," I said. "'Pizza' to his friends."

"I don't think I'm among those," he said. "Anyway, my
improvised static gun wasn't up to the task. So the great
Taius Ridian failed once more." He laughed again. This time
there was no joy in it.

Something Hudka once said sprang to mind. "Well, if
things always worked out," I quoted, "just imagine how
boring life would be."

He considered this for a while. "I have a question for
you," he said.

"I know what you're going to ask," I said somberly.

"You do?"

I nodded. "You want to know what it's like to be the
best Xenostryfe III player, perhaps of all time," I said. "All
I can say is that it feels good. Really good."

"What?" Taius asked, staring at me like I'd gone completely insane. I grinned. And he laughed for a third time.

"That's not what I was going to ask," he said. "You
think I'm too young for the responsibility I was given—
commanding the invasion—but I could say the same for

you. Why did the Xotonians send a group of children to save their stranded leader?"

I sighed. Part of me didn't want to tell him. But another part of me felt empathy for Taius. "Well, Kalac is my originator," I said. "It's like a mother or a father, but we only have one. That's why I'm here."

"So rescuing Kalac would increase your respect and prestige in its eyes?"

"I guess," I said, shrugging. "But more than that, I don't want my originator to come to any harm. I love Kalac."

"Does Kalac love you?" he asked.

"Yes," I said.

"Then Kalac is not like my father," he said.

I wanted to comfort him somehow. I wanted to assure him that he was wrong and that even though it might not feel like it sometimes, his father loved him. But I'd spoken to General Ridian. I remembered the casual way he'd threatened to destroy Gelo and everyone on it. It made my blood run cold just to think of his voice when he'd said it. Ridian was a monster. Why would someone like that love their own offspring? Why would they love anyone? For all I knew, Taius was right.

So I didn't try to comfort him. Instead I said, "I'm sorry."

Taius nodded. Then he turned away and spoke no more.

I rolled over too, suddenly struck by how much more comfortable the hard rocky ground was than a tree limb.

On the edge of the darkness, I saw a figure silhouetted against the sky. It was Becky. She hadn't left after all. Had she heard the whole conversation? I opened my gul'orp to say something. Before I could, she was gone.

CHAPTER FIFTEEN

"We're close now," said Taius. The chime of the beacon came through his tracker, loud and clear. "Just ten kilometers to go!"

On the other side of the mountains, the landscape changed again. It was forested, but a lower, thicker, wetter forest than before. In the distance, more ruined skyscrapers poked out of the mist.

As we descended, Nicki tried to tell us all something about the windward and leeward sides of mountains having different levels of precipitation. When Hollins said this was interesting, she thought he was mocking her, and the two of them started arguing. I couldn't listen to any of it.

My mind was racing. We were about to reach the *Phryxus II*! We were about to find Kalac! I pressed onward. Several times I accidentally outpaced Taius and then had to wait for him to catch up when I realized that I didn't know where we were supposed to go.

Once, I turned and saw the humans whispering to one another.

"What?" I asked.

"Chorkle," said Nicki gently, "we haven't discussed the possibility, but there's a chance we could find the *Phryxus II* and Kalac might be . . ." She trailed off.

I knew what she was getting at, but I couldn't allow myself to think about it. I only knew that I had to keep going. I wouldn't stop for any reason.

"Look at that!" said Hollins. He pointed to a nearby tree. It had been sheared off at a height of about forty meters, like something huge had collided with it. The top of the trunk was charred black.

We saw another, and another. There were dozens, stretching away into the distance. They were snapped lower and lower as we went. The beacon rang from the tracker, but we didn't need it anymore. We could follow the swathe that had been cut through the forest. Something had definitely landed nearby, smashing through the trees as it went.

I realized that I was running now. I'd left the others behind, but I didn't care. Over the next rise it looked as though we would find the Xotonian starship.

"Wait!" hissed Eyf, landing in front of me and nearly causing me to crash into her. "I think I see someone ahead." Her Aeaki eyes were far sharper than any of ours.

"Maybe it's Kalac!" I whispered.

Taius and the others caught up to me, and we all crept forward through the brush toward the low hill. There, in a clearing ahead of us, was the *Phryxus II*. The sun glinted off its windshield. It had clearly crash-landed here. The star-fighter was damaged but intact, unlike the poor *T'utzuxe*. This gave me hope. It meant that the passengers might have survived.

I heard a clanging sound. Eyf was right. Someone was here. I wanted to call out to Kalac and the others. But I held my gul'orp.

From behind the *Phryxus II* stepped three Aeaki hunt-ers. Their plumage was a brilliant combination of cyan and pink. They somehow seemed even more warlike than the Oru. They were clad in hide and bone armor, and each of them wore a colorful yet grotesque mask over her face. I looked to Eyf. She shrugged nervously. She didn't know the clans on this side of the mountains.

We watched as two of the Aeaki set about trying to pry off a big piece of the *Phryxus II*'s hull while the third kept a lazy watch. Though it was damaged, that starfighter was our best chance of getting off Kyral. We couldn't let these scavengers dismantle it. We had to stop them. Hollins poked me. He held up Eromu's blaster with a questioning look in his eyes.

I shook my head. The three of them had their own energy blasters slung at their sides. We would be outgunned in a fight. But Kalac, Ornim, and Chayl might still be inside the ship or somewhere nearby. Or maybe this new clan had taken them prisoner. The Oru had given us a reasonably friendly welcome, all things considered. Perhaps these three Aeaki would do the same. Something about their frightening masks made me doubt it though. I had no idea what to do.

Taius tapped me on the i'arda and nodded. Then he stepped forward into the clearing. The three Aeaki froze and turned their blasters on him. What in the name of Morool was he doing, I wondered? Eyf and the humans looked frantic.

"Halt," he said to them.

"What are you supposed to be, outlander?" squawked one of them.

"My name is Taius Sovyrius Ridian," he said. "I am a legate of the Vorem Dominion." He flashed his golden insignia.

216

The hunters looked at one another. It was hard to read an Aeaki to begin with, but under the masks it was impossible.

"Well, you happen to be standing in Eka territory," said the leader.

"Last I checked," said Taius as he waved expansively, "all of this was *Vorem* territory. Kyral is a Dominion world. That means all of you are Dominion subjects. And I demand you stop dismantling that starship right now."

I held my breath. He was coming on awfully strong. Revealing his rank had saved him once before with Hisuda. But didn't he understand that even the Aeaki who professed loyalty to the Dominion on Kyral still hated his kind?

At last, the Eka leader looked to her companions and then bowed low. His gambit had worked!

Then she laughed. "How about we dismantle you instead?" she said, standing. "The Eka never surrendered to the Dominion, and we're not about to start now. We're not your subjects."

Taius blinked. He hadn't expected this. "But," he said, "this is—Kyral is a—"

"In fact, being a Vorem in Eka territory is a very serious condition." She cocked her blaster rifle and leveled it at his head. "Probably fatal."

"Wait," cried Becky, leaping forward. "Don't shoot him!"

This startled the three hunters. They looked about uncertainly, considering the possibility that the whole jungle might be full of strange outlanders.

"What are you?" asked the Eka leader, now aiming at Becky. "Another alien?"

"I'm his . . . " she sighed. "We're his prisoners." She waved toward us. We looked at one another and stepped out of the brush.

"He conquered our worlds," said Becky. "Isn't that right, guys?"

We nodded. I got the sense that this was probably the strangest day of these three Eka's lives.

"Well," said the Eka leader, "after we vaporize him, I guess you'll be *our* prisoners." All three laughed again.

"Don't shoot him," said Becky. "Or . . . or . . ."

The Eka looked less than impressed. "Or what?" asked the leader. Becky had no answer. Her eyes darted around frantically.

"Or he'll rain fire from the skies," said Nicki.

"Yeah. That's it!" said Becky, nudging Taius hard with her elbow. "Isn't that right, Taius—uh, Legate Ridian?"

"What?" he said. "Oh. Yup. Rain fire."

"His ship is standing by in high orbit," said Nicki. "Nuclear missiles armed and ready to launch."

"See it?" said Little Gus, pointing at the sky. "It's just behind that cloud." The Eka squinted upward. They no longer looked so confident.

"They're watching from space," said Becky, "waiting for his signal. Or for something to happen to him. Because if it does—"

"Ka-boom!" yelled Hollins. All three Eka jumped into the air, reflexively flapping up a meter or two before landing again.

The Eka leader chastened the other two hunters (though she had jumped just as high). Then she turned to Eyf. "What about you?" said the leader to Eyf. "You're no alien. Why are your feathers white? What are you?"

"I was an Oru from across the mountains," said Eyf sadly, "but this Vorem one drained the color from my feathers. All he had to do was wave that little black box toward me." She pointed to Taius's zowul and whimpered in faux despair.

Taius looked around, then held the device up ominously. The distress beacon chimed, and the three Eka hunters moaned in terror. The thought of white feathers—of losing their own clan identity—was even more frightening than a nuclear strike.

"Now I repeat," said Taius, "don't touch that starship."

"Okay, okay, Vorem!" said the Eka leader, now bowing in earnest. "No need to be hasty! Praise the Dominion."

Taius looked to the rest of us.

"Praise the Dominion," we repeated in unison. He nodded.

"Let us just be going back to Eka," said the leader. "No need for you to bother with us anymore, mighty Vorem lord." She screeched up toward the sky as though they could hear her in Taius's imaginary ship. "Praise the Dominion!"

The three Eka hunters spread their wings as though to fly away. I was close enough now to see that the *Phryxus II* was empty. Did that mean that Kalac, Ornim, and Chayl had survived the crash?

"Wait!" I cried. "If you want to stay in the legate's good graces, you need to help him with his secret mission." Taius stared at me, confused.

"He is searching for three fugitives," I continued. "They look like me, only taller. They're, uh, escaped prisoners!"

The three Eka glanced at one another. The leader spoke. "Yes, some of the Eka saw them. More strange little outlanders running through the forest weeks ago.

We shot at them a few times, but we missed."

"Where were they going?" I cried.

The Eka leader squinted at me. Perhaps I was overstepping my bounds as a humble prisoner. Taius could sense that I was on the verge of blowing our ruse.

"Quiet . . . knave," said Taius to me. Oddly, when he actually tried to sound like a villain, he was totally unconvincing. "I'll, uh, ask the questions around here," he said, clearing his throat. "So, yeah, where were they going?"

"Toward Hykaro Roost," said the Eka leader, pointing out into the jungle. "That way. Fifty kilometers."

"Very good," said Taius, nodding. "Now leave here at once. And I trust we shall encounter no further hassles while we are in 'Eka territory.'" He slathered the last two words with contempt. The Eka assured us that we would not. They bowed and nodded, nodded and bowed, and then took flight.

We watched them as they dwindled to nothing more than black specks in the sky. When they were finally gone, we breathed a collective sigh of relief. Immediately, we all started talking in an excited mix of human-ese and Xotonian.

"Good show, Becky!" cried Hollins, cuffing her on the back. "You just jumped right in there and saved his purple butt." He threw a thumb toward Taius, who still looked completely dazed.

"Yeah, Becky, bold move!" said Little Gus. "Side note: Your hair looks really nice today."

"No it doesn't," she said. "And when I saw Taius flopping around like a fish out of water, I just knew I had to jump in there"

"Yeah, real smooth, Taius," said Little Gus to Taius in Xotonian. "That Aeaki called your bluff, and suddenly you got quieter than a library full of rocks."

"What?" said Taius, snapping back to reality. "Oh yeah. After they weren't impressed by my badge, I had absolutely nothing. Without Becky, I was done for," he admitted with a laugh. His laughter startled the others (as it had startled me before). Taius frowned. "Eyf!" he said sharply, spooking the little Aeaki.

"Yes?" she said, cowering behind her wing.

"The whole draining-the-color-from-your-feathers thing?" said Taius, holding up the tracker. "That was pretty smart!"

"And they actually believed it!" squeaked Eyf. "They are very, very, very simple on this side of the mountains!"

"They saw Kalac, Ornim, and Chayl! They're alive!"

said Becky. "I mean, not that they wouldn't be. But they definitely are!"

The others cheered. Hollins clapped me on the back. Even Taius smiled, though I thought there was a touch of melancholy in it.

"It sounds like they're headed for Hykaro Roost," I said. "What do you know about it, Eyf? Lately, I've found my cyclopaedia to be a bit out of date."

"Hykaro was once a great city," said Eyf. "The gods themselves lived there, but they left it empty. But all the clans come to trade. No fighting among Aeaki is allowed. When you visit the Hykaro Roost, it is customary to bring an offering—something from the time before the Vorem— and toss it into the Midden. It is a little ritual to help us remember what was lost."

We were silent. Eyf took two of my thol'grazes in her wings. "I am very, very, very happy that the Xotonian ones you're looking for are still alive," she said.

"Me too," I said. "It's no one's birthday, but I feel like celebrating." I rummaged around in my pack and found what I was looking for. "Hollins, can you use your knife to cut this into seven pieces?" And I tossed him the only Feeney's Original Astronaut Ice Cream bar on the whole planet.

"Sure. Seven pieces," he said, unfolding his pocketknife. "But loath as I am to admit it, I think Becky deserves a little extra."

Hollins cut it up and distributed the tiny slivers. Taius didn't like the taste; he claimed it was so sweet it made his fangs hurt. Meanwhile, Eyf started talking twice as fast as normal. We'd each already had a piece when we noticed that there was one left. Nicki was gone.

I wandered off a little ways and found her alone in the jungle, sitting on a fallen log. She had her holodrive out, and she was playing a very angry game of Xenostryfe III. The way she was blasting those poor flying saucers, I almost pitied them. She snarled as she lost her final life.

"Something wrong?" I asked. "I mean, aside from the fact that you're marooned on a planet full of monsters and hostile bird-people."

"No. Nothing's wrong," she said. "I'm perfectly fine. It's probably the humidity. Look at this weird leaf." She pointed to an octagonal one on the ground beside her. "I'm so into stuff like that. Isn't it *fascinating*?" Her teeth were clenched as she spoke.

"Are you angry about something?" I asked.

She sighed. "Everyone gave Becky credit for stepping in back there," she said. "But she didn't have a plan any more than Taius did. I was the one who thought of saying that his ship was watching."

I hadn't realized it, but she was absolutely right. "That's true!" I said. "It *was* your idea! If you hadn't thought of that, we'd be prisoners. Or worse."

She nodded.

"So you want more credit?" I asked. "I can tell the others—"

"No!" she said. "I'm not some showboat. It's just . . . it's just . . . I was scared. I had the plan, but I was scared."

"So was I," I said. "They were pointing energy blasters at us. It was scary."

"But what if Hollins is right?" she asked. "What if I'm just 'the smart one'? What if I'm not brave? Not a leader?" She pulled out the little carved statue of Athena that Hollins had given her. I had no idea she'd brought it with her.

"Come on," I said. "Hollins didn't mean anything by that. He cares a lot about you. And you are brave."

"Am I?" she asked. "I never just rush into danger like Hollins or Becky. Or you."

"I think there are different kinds of leaders. And different types of courage," I said. "And most of the time, rushing into danger isn't bravery at all, it's stupidity. You have to pick your moments—"

But just at that moment, Hollins burst into the clearing with all the tact of an angry rahk. "Nicki! So here's where you're hiding!" he said, laughing. She frowned. It was the exact wrong thing to say and the exact wrong time to say it. She deactivated her holodrive, got up, and quietly walked back to camp.

"What?" said Hollins to me. "Girls. Am I right?"

"No, you're not right," I said, and I followed Nicki.

We returned to find the others in the throes of an argument.

"No fire," said Eyf. "No, no, no."

"But the Eka aren't going to give us any more trouble," said Little Gus. "They said so. Don't you want to eat hot food? We can tell ghost stories! You're going to love the one about the haunted mini-fridge."

"No fire," said Eyf. "It's still dangerous. Very, very, very dangerous."

"We should eat more wryv," said Taius, ignoring her.

"But who knows what beastly things live in this new jungle forest!" cried Eyf.

"Oh," said Little Gus to Taius, also ignoring Eyf, "so you're the head chef now? You want to choose the menu?" It seemed an awfully churlish response to what amounted to praise for his cooking. "If you want more *Little Gus*

226

Soup"—Little Gus refused to use the Vorem word—"you can make it yourself, Taius!"

Taius glared at Little Gus. "Fine," he said, "maybe I will."

"Oh, no you won't!" squealed Little Gus. "Little Gus Soup is a registered trademark of LG Enterprises Incorporated, a limited liability corporation!"

"Can both of you shut it, please?" asked Becky, rubbing her temples. Then, in human: "Can't we all just leave the pointless arguing to me and Hollins, like the good old days?"

"Hey!" said Hollins. "I don't argue for no reason. Shut up!"

"Don't you talk to her like that!" snarled Taius, standing and facing Hollins.

"Whoa! Taius, you don't even know he's talking to me," said Becky in Xotonian. "You can't understand what he's saying!"

"I know but—but he . . . sounded . . . upset," said Taius, scratching his head. "I was just trying to . . ." He trailed off.

"You heard the lady," said Little Gus.

"I'm talking too. No one is listening to me," squeaked Eyf despondently. "It is just like Oru." She slumped to the ground.

And so our moment of triumph and unity seemed to have passed.

Becky tried to comfort Eyf. "We can sleep inside the *Phryxus II*," she said. "We can seal the hatches. The ship is mostly intact. We'll be safe from 'beastly things' or whatever."

Eyf nodded. She seemed a little mollified. "Can we vote on it?" she asked.

Becky nodded.

"Can we vote on what to have for dinner?"

Becky sighed and nodded.

"Can we vote on what is the best smell?"

Meanwhile, Taius and Little Gus continued to argue. "And when I cook it, maybe you'll be one of the ingredients," growled Taius. "After all, you can't make Little Gus Soup without the Little Gus."

"Are you guys hearing this?" whined Gus. "He's threatening me. I just want this to go on the record. He's threatening to cook me in a soup that would probably be *delicious*!"

Hollins and I ignored them and joined Nicki as she surveyed the crashed starfighter.

"Looks like it would take a week of work, at least, to bring her back online," said Hollins. "What do you think, Nick?"

"I guess I know everything because I'm the smart one, huh?" said Nicki.

"No." Hollins sighed. "Check that out," he said to me. He pointed to several blackened holes on the wing of the *Phryxus II*.

"Blaster marks," I said.

"Looks like some angry Aeaki got a lucky shot off and brought the ship down."

"I hope it was the Aeaki," I said.

Practically everyone was sulking now. To cheer up Eyf, Hollins actually did call for a vote on what we would have for dinner. Though Little Gus himself voted against it, everyone else wanted more borscht/wryv/Little Gus Soup. I volunteered to try to make it, but Little Gus had some choice remarks about the sophistication of the Xotonian palate. He declared he'd do it himself.

Eyf, Hollins, and Becky went out to find the required herbs. Taius set about building a fire. Nicki studied her holodrive map of Kyral. I stayed behind and helped Little Gus peel and chop a pile of the reddish roots.

"Man, I thought I didn't like that guy before," said Little Gus, glancing toward Taius. "But I really don't like him now."

"Why?" I asked. "I mean, I know he stowed away on our ship, but—"

"Just look at his dumb face," grumbled Little Gus.

I shrugged. Taius's face didn't look particularly dumb to me as he kindled a small flame with a bit of dried grass. Sad, perhaps. Dangerous, certainly. But not dumb.

As we watched, Little Gus pretended to narrate Taius's internal monologue. "Duuuuuh, I'm Taius, I'm a mysterious loner with a troubled past," he said, affecting an extremely stupid voice. "Duuuuuh. Look at my little gold badge. It gets me ten percent off movie tickets at select theaters. Duuuuuh."

"Dude, what?" I said, genuinely confused. "Are you . . . jealous of him or something? Is this about—"

"No! What? No!" snapped Little Gus, hacking a reddish root in half. "I just don't like him, that's all. And I'm just glad we don't need him anymore."

Until Little Gus said it, I hadn't realized. It was true, though. We didn't need Taius now. His zowul had led us to the distress beacon. But Kalac and the others had traveled onward toward Hykaro Roost. We would have to find them on our own.

I walked toward Taius. He now had a small fire blazing away in a little pit surrounded by stones. He stared into the flames, his face expressionless. I sat down beside him.

"I know," said Taius.

I sighed. "It's just that—"

"I understand," he said. "I remember the terms of our bargain: You help me get back to General Ridian if I guide you to your Xotonian leader. But I can't help you anymore. Taius Ridian fails again." He jabbed at the fire with a stick, causing a little flare and plume of sparks.

"I'll go my own way in the morning," he said. "Believe me, if I were in your position, I would do the same. Why keep an enemy close by if you have nothing to gain?"

"I don't consider you an enemy," I said. "Not anymore."

"You don't?" Taius stared at me for a moment. Then he looked away.

"My grand-originator once said, 'Nobody is all bad. Not Xotonians. Not humans.'" I said, "Well, I'm extending it to Vorem too. Even if we are on different sides of a war, you tried your best to help us. That means something."

"It was in my self-interest," he said.

"As far as I'm concerned, you held up your end of our deal. So I still intend to help you get back to your father. Except . . ." I trailed off.

"Except what?" he said.

"Except I don't know if the others feel the same way."

I caught up with Becky, who was busy tightening one of

231

the damaged hatches of the *Phryxus II*. After Little Gus, she seemed to have the biggest problem with Taius, so I wanted to ask her opinion.

When I did, she said, "Taius should go."

"His society is harsh, and his father is, as we know, basically a wad," I said. "I know he's rude and kind of rough around the edges, but deep down . . . I think he's not all bad."

"No, he's not bad," she said. "He's sad. But he should still go. It's dangerous to have him around."

"What do you mean?" I asked.

"I don't know," she said, and she stared at the ground.

• • • •

The pot of Little Gus Soup simmered over the fire. All seven of us stood around it. We prepared to vote on something more important than the dinner menu: Taius's future.

"We've found the *Phryxus II*. We no longer need Taius's tracker," I said. "But he still needs our help. He led us here. That's all we could have asked of him. I vote that he stays with us." I held out my thol'graz with a frib pointed upward. One vote in favor. I turned toward Taius. "You get a vote too."

He seemed a little embarrassed. "Then I vote to stay with you as well," he said. "You're still my best hope of getting off this world, so I pledge to help you however I can. You see, over time I've . . . that is . . . spending time with you all, I've come to regard you as . . . strategic . . . allies."

"Strategic allies?" said Nicki, wrinkling her forehead.

Taius glanced at Becky. "I mean . . ." He trailed off and simply held out his hand and pointed a clawed thumb skyward. That was two votes in favor.

"Aw, boohoo," sneered Little Gus. "Can we ditch this guy already?" He gave a thumbs-down accompanied by a raspberry sound. One vote against.

Becky gave a second thumbs-down. She declined to state her reasons. That put the count at two to two. Little Gus's jaw fell open when he saw her choice. I guess he'd expected her to vote a different way.

Eyf cocked her head. "I'm an Aeaki, and I'm supposed to hate him for what the Vorem ones did a very, very, very long time ago," she said. "But that's not his fault. He might be grumpy and scary, but he helped us. I vote for him to stay." Three in favor.

"Kyral is incredibly dangerous," said Nicki. "Hostile clans of Aeaki, terrifying beasts, raging dust storms. Any of these hazards could easily prove fatal. . . ." She noticed that we were all frowning at her. "Sorry. Thinking out loud. Point is: We stand a better chance of survival if Taius is with us."

That was four votes in favor, a majority of the seven. Taius would stay.

Though Hollins didn't have to, he voted yes as well. He said a deal was a deal.

At the last second, Little Gus even changed his vote, flipping his thumb upward with a chuckle.

"Maybe I was a little hasty before," said Little Gus. "Anybody who likes my soup that much can't be all bad. Glad you'll be staying with us, Tai. . . . Can I call you Tai?"

"No," said Taius.

The final count was six to one. Becky remained resolutely in the "nay" column. This made for a somewhat awkward dinner. However, the Little Gus Soup was more delicious than ever.

We slept inside the downed *Phryxus II*, with the hatches sealed against any wildlife. I was reasonably confident they'd be strong enough to stop an angry rahk.

After the others had gone to sleep, I laid awake and thought of Kalac. I missed my originator terribly, but I was glad to know that it was alive. The humans' parents were on the other side of the galaxy. The pain I felt—the young humans had had to live with it every day since their vessel took off without them. I listened to their sleep sounds and the muffled noises of the alien jungle. Outside, it started to rain.

"Hey," came a whisper. It was Taius. I could see his eyes gleaming in the darkness. "Thank you," he said.

At the first light of dawn, I deactivated the ship's distress beacon. And we set out for Hykaro Roost.

CHAPTER SIXTEEN

"Ugh, my foot!" cried Little Gus. I turned back to see him stuck up to his knee in the mud. The same thing had happened to all of us, many times, as we crossed the fetid marsh.

Hollins and Taius yanked Gus free with a squelching sound and a spray of slime, some of which got on my face. I didn't even try to clean it off. All of us were caked with centimeters of mud. It brought an odd kinship to the group. Vorem, human, or Xotonian, we were all equally filthy. Only Eyf stayed (relatively) clean as she circled overhead, landing only occasionally to point us in the right direction.

Eyf said that—like the Glass Desert—no Aeaki dared to live in the fetid marshes of Kyral. Not because they were cursed, but because they stank. Indeed, she was right. If I'd discharged my own stink gland, no one would have even noticed. If an usk-lizard had choked on some rotten stink-pods and dropped dead in front of us, it might have improved the air quality a little.

Other than a putrid stench and slimy weeds, the nameless marsh had little to offer. Once, we gazed into an oddly clear pool and saw that it was filled with tiny, scuttling arthropods. Eyf said they were edible. None of us was particularly tempted to do a taste test.

The good news was that, according to Eyf, we were most of the way across. I could even see the dark smudge of the tree line on the horizon.

Taius was checking his zowul when he made a false step and fell face-first into a puddle of murky water. It was a pretty undignified move for a patrician legate of the Vorem Dominion. Little Gus giggled. Gus had face-planted six times already, so perhaps he'd earned a laugh. Nicki and I went to help Taius up. When we did, we found that his arms and neck were covered in fine vines. They were a shockingly bright shade of pink.

"What is this stuff?" growled Taius as he ripped them off. They didn't come away easily. Nicki and I tried to help. The vines were sticky, and they seemed to be covered with tiny suction cups.

"No," said Eyf, when she saw what we were doing. "No, no, no, no, no! Don't touch it!"

"We already touched it," I said. I felt a subtle tickling around my fel'grazes. I looked down to see more of the strange vines snaking out of the murky water of the marsh. Slowly and subtly, they were coiling themselves around me! I tried to kick them away.

"Eyf, your planet is super gross," said Little Gus, hanging back with Becky and Hollins.

"That is the creeping sleem!" said Eyf as she hovered a few meters off the ground. "You must not touch it!"

"But I need to get a sample," said Nicki as she held up a mass of the stuff. It writhed gently in her bare hand. "A sample. Sample? Sample. Ssssssssaaaaaaaample. That's a funny word. Isn't it?" Nicki's speech sounded strange— slow and a little slurred.

"What's happening?" I asked Eyf.

"If the sleem touches your skin," cried Eyf, "it will spread a poison that makes your brain go weird! And then you won't even care when it pulls you under the mud!"

"What's under the mud?" I asked, flopping down. "Is it something cool? Maybe we should, uh . . . check it out."

"Everybody get up!" said Becky, yanking me back up off the ground. She was careful not to touch any of the vines.

"Why are you yelling?" Taius asked her. He had an idiot grin on his face. "Just be . . . cool."

"Yeah," I said, "be cool, Becky. Wait, are you Becky or Nicki? Or Bicki? I mean . . ."

Taius and Nicki laughed hysterically.

"Look, that's Nicki," said Nicki. She had put her glasses on a writhing wad of the creeping sleem.

Nicki and Taius and I laughed again. Becky sighed and used a stick to retrieve her sister's glasses. The creeping sleem had wound itself around my fel'grazes once more. It suddenly looked very beautiful to me. Such a nice shade of pink, just like my own sunburnt skin. For some reason, Hollins, Becky, and Little Gus were panicking.

"You guys are too stressed," I said to them.

"We must go!" cried Eyf from above. "Quickly "

"Okay," said Hollins. He yanked Taius up by the collar of his uniform, avoiding the sleem.

"Sorry I kicked you in the face . . . that one time," said Taius slowly enough for Hollins to understand. "We cool?"

Hollins nodded and pulled Taius behind him.

"Come on, sis," said Becky, lifting Nicki to her feet. "Time to go."

"But I'm happy here," said Nicki. "I was thinking: If we don't make it back to Earth . . . this can be our new home."

She waved at the marsh around us.

"I know. It's great," said Becky, leading her sister by the arm. "Maybe we can get a timeshare. Let's talk about it later."

"What, are you scared?" asked Nicki. "I'm not scared. . . . I'm saaaaample."

"Chorkle," said Little Gus. "On your fel'grazes, my second-best friend. You can't stay here."

"You're no fun," I said as he pulled me along behind the others. "I thought you were supposed to be the fun one."

We ran toward the forest now with big sloshing steps. All around us the pink vines were wriggling out of the mud. The creeping sleem was moving faster now, twitching and curling and whipping as we passed. It almost seemed frustrated. We avoided touching it, though now I couldn't quite remember why.

"Yikes! Not cool!" said Little Gus as a wet tangle of vines flopped across the path ahead of us. We stopped fast and gingerly stepped around it.

"Bye-bye," I said, turning backward as Gus pulled me. The creeping sleem looked so pathetic, so lonely, just squirming there on the ground.

At last we reached the dry embankment of the forest on the edge of the marsh. The others sat Taius, Nicki, and me together on the ground. They eyed us nervously. It made me feel very uncomfortable.

"What's wrong with them?" whispered Nicki. I shook my head. I couldn't figure out why they were acting so heartlessly toward the creeping sleem. "Bet *they're* scared. Scared of my power."

"Don't worry," said Eyf to the others. "The effects are not permanent. They should be back to normal in their brains in a few hours, I hope. In the meantime, though, they might feel more, uh, *emotional* than usual." Hollins, Becky, and Little Gus nodded knowingly.

"Can the three of you handle staying in one place?" asked Hollins, slowly and in human.

"Chorkle," Taius said to me in Xotonian, "am I freaking out, or is that guy speaking some weird, alien language?"

"Habla inglés," said Nicki.

"Whoa," said Taius, more freaked out than ever.

"Just stay put!" said Becky. She repeated it in both languages for good measure. And the others set about building a fire and foraging for dinner.

Taius looked around furtively. No one was watching. "Hey," he whispered to Nicki and me, "check this out." He reached into the breast pocket of his black uniform and pulled something out. There, wriggling in his palm, was the broken tip of a creeping sleem vine, just a few centimeters long. "I saved one."

"You got a sample!" cried Nicki, grabbing it from him. It curled and uncurled around her fingers, leaving tiny red marks where its suction cups had attached. She pulled out her notepad.

"Um, I'd like to hold it now," I said, taking it from her. It wriggled in my thol'graz. It was so cute! "I'm going to name it Hudka II."

"But I haven't catalogued its morphololo—morlopho—molorph—what it looks like yet," whined Nicki.

"It's mine," said Taius as he snatched it from me. He held it in his hands and cooed to it a little.

"Ooh, can I see?" asked Becky.

Taius looked at her. He looked at the little vine. Then he held it out.

Becky grabbed it—her hand covered by one of Nicki's inverted sample bags. "Come on, guys. Get it together," she said. Then she tossed the creeping sleem into the fire.

"What are you doing!" cried Nicki. "The loss to astrobiology is inestimable!"

Becky shook her head in disappointment. "'Astrobiology.' That's not even a real word, sis," she said. And she went back to collecting firewood.

The sleem had shriveled to ash. Tears welled in my eyes. I missed the pretty vines very much. By their miserable faces, Nicki and Taius felt exactly the same way.

"Why would she do that?" muttered Nicki. "Deeply incurious."

"She hates me," said Taius, pointing to Becky. "I thought we were friends—I mean . . . strategic allies."

"She can be mean sometimes," said Nicki, wiping her eyes. "But he's the worst!" She pointed to Hollins as he made camp. "He gave me a statue! That stands for wisdom! Can you believe the nerve?"

"It's okay. Becky *should* hate me," said Taius with a choked sob. "Everyone should. I'm a failure. I can't do anything right. My uniform is covered in mud. I suck."

"You think you're a failure?" I said. "Somehow I got all these humans trapped on the wrong side of the universe! And my originator's in danger, and I don't know where it is! It might even be . . ." I started to weep.

"It's okay, Chorkle," said Nicki. "It's not your fault. Me? I'm afraid of everything." She hugged me, and I realized that she was crying too.

"If I can get back to the Vorem Dominion," said Taius, suddenly filled with hope, "we have ships with hyperdrives. I could take you humans back to Earth! Then Becky wouldn't—I mean *the humans* wouldn't . . . but my father . . ." He trailed off.

"Don't worry about your father," I said.

Taius stared at the ground for a long time. "Chorkle, you have to know that I betrayed—"

"You didn't betray him!" I said. "Maybe—maybe he's just kind of a jerk. Maybe you're better than him."

"No, I'm not," said Taius, shaking his head. "I'm not." And he was silent after that.

It took hours for the effects of the creeping sleem's toxin to wear off. Afterward, Nicki and I felt vaguely embarrassed. Taius seemed positively humiliated. He refused to speak at all.

It didn't help that whenever our backs were turned, the others seemed to be doing impressions of us in our sleem-altered state. Once, I turned around to see Little Gus sitting on the ground, eyes crossed and petting his shoelace and drooling. Eyf and Hollins were giggling.

I slept fitfully, perhaps due to residual effects of the toxin. I dreamed I was chasing Kalac forever through an endless marsh. When I finally caught up with my originator, it withered to ash in my thol'grazes, just like the little sleem vine in the fire.

I was awakened in the night by the mournful wailing of some beast. Eyf had no idea what the creature might be. But I had the strange feeling I'd heard it somewhere before.

CHAPTER SEVENTEEN

The next day, the forest opened onto a wide and misty plain. Several kilometers ahead of us, a towering mass began to resolve itself through the murk.

"That is great Hykaro Roost," said Eyf with awe in her voice. "I always, always, always hoped I would see it."

As we approached, we saw signs of civilization. The shattered remnants of a road snaking through the grass. The burned-out shell of some vehicle covered in weeds. The warped, half-melted girders of long-destroyed buildings. The place reminded me of the Xotonian ruins of Flowing-Stone.

"You ever get the feeling you're being watched?" asked Little Gus as he stared back the way we had come. The fog was too thick for us to see more than ten meters in any direction.

Directly afterward, we nearly bumped into a group of purple-and-gold-feathered Aeaki. They were Uji— the ancient enemies (and occasional allies) of the Oru— on a pilgrimage to Hykaro to trade with the other clans. The Uji hopped and squawked and squinted at us—at Eyf most of all—and fingered their energy blasters.

"What clan are you?" they asked her.

"No clan," whispered Eyf.

The Uji gave each other sidelong glances. But they didn't attempt to hinder our passage. Even Taius the Vorem was met with nothing more than dirty looks.

"Good thing we are close to the city," said Eyf after we passed them. "By custom, the Aeaki are forbidden to fight with one another at Hykaro Roost. The clans from all over Kyral send traders here."

Soon we saw more Aeaki swooping through the mist, three or four at a time. Some had the telltale drab feathers of males. Most were female warriors with blazing plumage in every color combination. They represented dozens of clans for which Eyf didn't know the names.

The day wore on, and the fog parted. We saw Hykaro Roost clearly at last. It was a massive city, thousands of skyscrapers all jumbled together.

"It's like New York times Hong Kong," said Nicki, shaking her head in awe. "Or it was."

Big chunks of the buildings had crumbled, leaving them open to the elements. Some had fallen in on themselves. But their superstructure remained. Hundreds of meters off the ground, these ruins were connected by a web of rope bridges and makeshift wooden platforms. Above us, dark specks flitted among them: more Aeaki.

My is'pog was racing. Somewhere in this great ruined city, we would find Kalac, Ornim, and Chayl.

"My originator is here. I know it," I said, turning to face the others. "I want to thank all of you."

"You didn't have to come here and risk your lives yet again," I said to Nicki, Becky, Hollins, and Little Gus. "But I'm glad you did. Now I know the pain you must feel every day, how much you must miss your own parents."

"We'll get back to them," said Hollins with a catch in his throat. "But let's worry about finding Kalac and the others first."

I turned to Eyf. "We never would have made it here from Oru without your help. Thank you."

"You know, I think I wanted to help someone for a very, very, very long time," said Eyf. "You finally gave me the chance."

"Thank you too, Taius," I said, "You did more than your share. We couldn't have done it without you either."

He looked like he was about to say something, but instead he just nodded. His purple skin was slick with sweat. Perhaps he was still feeling some residual effects of the creeping sleem's poison.

I turned back toward the ruined metropolis. "Now where do we start looking?" I asked. Locating Kalac in this place would be like finding a tilvri in a yehl'nerm stack.

"First we must visit the Midden," said Eyf. "To make an offering to the gods for good luck."

"Let's go," I said. "We'll need all the luck we can get."

We had the streets of Hykaro to ourselves as we walked. There were wide boulevards of grass—sometimes grown taller than Hollins—between the crumbling skyscrapers. Above us, the fog burned off to reveal a clear violet sky. Eyf soared among the buildings. Every few blocks, Taius fiddled with his zowul. The rest of us hacked our way through the weeds.

Abruptly, the ground ahead ended. Stretching out into the distance was a vast pit, a dozen meters deep but bigger than all of Core-of-Rock. It was filled with garbage.

"The Midden," announced Eyf dramatically as she landed on the edge of it.

"It's, uh, beautiful?" said Nicki.

"If filling up landfills with trash is what pleases the gods," said Little Gus, "the human race is crushing it."

"Not trash," said Eyf. "It is all things from the time before the burning. Before the Vorem ones."

I looked again. She was right. Down in the Midden, I saw sleek metal vehicles and computer screens and furniture and even kitchen utensils. They were objects that had, against all odds, survived the Vorem attack. These things were the products of thousands of years of artistic and technological advancement—now useless on Kyral.

"Every Aeaki must bring something here," said Eyf as she carefully removed her little necklace of nuts and bolts. Then she threw it as hard as she could down into the pit. It landed without a sound. Eyf closed her eyes and bowed her head for a moment of silence.

"Are they paying their respects too?" asked Nicki. She pointed to a group of Aeaki—several different clans, by their feathers—standing out in the Midden. They seemed to be picking through the offerings.

"I do not know," said Eyf, noticing them for the first time. "The Midden is a very, very, very sacred place. Once something goes in, it is never taken out. All Aeaki know this. It is very odd that they would be there."

"We need to go," said Taius suddenly, startling us. He was clutching the zowul, and his eyes were darting wildly from empty window to empty window in the buildings around us. "This way," he said, pointing. It was the first he'd spoken all day.

"What?" asked Nicki. "Where are we going?"

"I'm picking up Xotonian life signs," said Taius, indicating the tracker. "But they're faint. . . . It might be your originator."

We followed him through the grassy streets of Hykaro Roost.

"In here," said Taius. "Hurry!"

He'd stopped at the doorway of a low, ruined building, only a few stories tall. Inside was a crumbling corridor, as dark as night. It took a moment for my eyes to adjust.

"Follow me. We're close now," he said, and he waved us inside.

The corridor led to a vast indoor space lit by glancing sunlight. It was a bowl-shaped room that sloped downward in the middle. Trees, probably hundreds of years old, grew skyward through the ragged holes in the roof. Three other corridors, just like the one we had used, also led to this room.

"It was a theater," said Nicki, shining her flashlight

around. She was right. I could imagine rows of seats where weeds now grew.

"Look!" cried Hollins.

At the bottom of the bowl—the area that must have once been the stage—I saw a shape slumped on the ground in a pool of sunlight. It was a Xotonian, facing away from us.

"Kalac?" I cried. The Xotonian squirmed a little, but there was no response.

"Something's not right," whispered Nicki.

I barely heard her. I was already racing toward the figure.

"Chorkle, wait!" Becky cried behind me. I didn't look back.

I reached the Xotonian and placed a thol'graz on its back. It turned toward me, and I could see that it was Chayl. But there was something across its gul'orp, a glossy black band. Chayl's five eyes frantically pointed back the way I had come.

"Chayl, are you hurt?" I said. "Where's Kalac?"

Chayl shifted a little and made a muffled murmur. It couldn't speak. I tried to remove the band around its gul'orp, and that's when I saw the manacles. All four thol'grazes and both its fel'grazes had been restrained with heavy chains.

"Now!" shrieked Taius. I turned. For some reason, he was holding the zowul up to his mouth.

From each of the four corridors burst two armored Vorem legionaries, pointing blaster rifles at us. We were completely surrounded.

"What's happening?" I asked.

"I'm sorry," said Taius. He closed his eyes and dropped the Vorem tracker.

I realized then that the zowul was not only a tracker; it was also a communicator. We'd been led into a trap.

CHAPTER EIGHTEEN

There was a burst of green light. Hollins fired on one of the legionaries who blocked the corridor from which we had come. The Vorem tumbled backward in a shower of sparks—hit in the shoulder. His partner growled something and returned fire. Bolts of red energy whizzed Hollins's way. He narrowly managed to duck behind one of the trees growing through the floor of the theater.

"Don't kill them," screamed Taius. "Take them alive! They—"

He never got to finish the sentence. Becky's fist smashed into Taius's mouth, and he crumpled backward. Two legionaries rushed forward and tried to pull her off him.

Eyf screeched in terror. The other legionary guarding the nearest corridor went down, the leg of his armor smoking where Hollins had shot him. "Go!" screamed Hollins, but he couldn't move without getting hit. He was pinned down by the hail of energy blasts from the others. The rest of the Vorem were all firing now. I saw Eyf flapping up toward the holes in the roof as red blasts cut through the air all around her.

Little Gus, Nicki, and I ran for it. We leaped over the two wounded legionaries and raced back down the darkened corridor. I heard heavy footsteps behind us.

We burst out into the grass and daylight. The languid, sunny day outside was completely indifferent to the fight in the theater. Perched in the windows of the nearby buildings were several Aeaki.

"Help!" cried Nicki. "Help us!" A few looked around uncomfortably, but they didn't move.

"Come on!" I cried. "Don't stop!"

The tall grass whipped at us as we ran. Nicki was in the lead, followed by Little Gus and me. I looked back to see two Vorem behind us. They were gaining on us.

Up ahead, Nicki skidded to a halt. Two more legionaries leaped out of the grass in front of her, blasters at the ready. She froze, then slowly she put her hands up and knelt on the ground. Somewhere nearby I heard a roar. It seemed familiar somehow.

"I knew we were being followed," said Little Gus. But he didn't mean the Vorem.

A massive blue shape launched out of the weeds. It smashed the two Vorem ahead of us right off their feet.

"Piiiiiiiiiizzzzzzzaaaaaaaaaa!" howled Little Gus in triumph.

Nicki looked up to see the thyss-cat wrestling with the legionaries on the ground. Pizza had the armored calf of one of them locked in his jaws. He clawed the other with all six of his legs. Both of the unlucky Vorem were screaming in fear and struggling to get away.

Nicki jumped to her feet and dove into the weeds. Gus ran after her. I followed, but I immediately lost them. I stumbled blindly through the tall grass now. I could hear someone behind me—running, breathing—but I couldn't see who it was. Was it Hollins or Becky or a Vorem legionary ready to blow a hole in my back?

I came to a clearing—an old patch of asphalt that hadn't crumbled to pieces. A red blast of energy knocked a smoking crater in the ground beside me. A legionary stepped out of the grass in front of me, and I stumbled backward. I nearly bumped into another behind me. Two more emerged from the brush. Now I was surrounded. Four Vorem legionaries—each with a rifle trained on me—

advanced with military precision. There was nowhere to go. I froze.

"What have we here?" said a familiar voice, cold and arrogant.

General Ridian strode into the clearing. He wore the same massive, insectoid black armor that I had seen before, but now he held his helmet under one arm. He looked like an older version of Taius, with harder, sharper features. He wore a close-cropped beard on his jaw, and his black hair was graying a bit.

Ridian squinted at me. Then he laughed. It was about as happy as the sound of bones breaking. "I know you," he said. "You're the little Xotonian who talked to me on the view-screen. As I recall, you weren't very *polite*."

He turned to the legionaries and gave a nod. They cocked their weapons.

"Father!" there came a cry. "Don't kill that one!" Taius stumbled into the clearing. Amber-colored blood trickled from his lip, and one of his eyes was ringed with a dark bruise. Good, I thought, Becky must have gotten at least one more good shot in.

Ridian turned toward his son. "Taius," he said. "I see you survived." It was a simple statement of fact. There was no emotion in his voice.

"Yes, Fa—General," said Taius. He gave an awkward salute.

Ridian snorted. "Where is your armor?" he asked.

"I—I had to leave it," said Taius. "On the asteroid."

"That suit was *priceless*," hissed Ridian. "It has been passed down in our family for generations. It was worth more than your life."

"Leaving it was the only way for me to survive, sir," said Taius, "to keep up the fight." His face remained expressionless, but I thought I heard something crack in his voice. He didn't make eye contact with me.

"Your survival was not my top priority. Victory was," said Ridian. "You lost the battle on Gelo. You humiliated your name. My name. You were defeated by a pack of"— he gestured toward me with contempt—"*these* things. The considerate move would have been to die."

"I lost," admitted Taius, "but I will redeem my reputation as a legate."

"That will be very difficult," said Ridian, "since you are not a legate anymore."

"But now you have the humans and this Xotonian as prisoners," said Taius, "thanks to me."

"You led a bunch of children into a trap," scoffed Ridian. "Capturing them is barely worth the effort."

"That one is the offspring of the Xotonian leader!" cried Taius.

Ridian glanced at me. Then back to Taius. "Hmm. Finally, you've provided me with a reason not to have you executed for gross incompetence," he said. "Still, you must give me your badge." Ridian held out a black-gloved hand.

Taius hesitated. Then he reached into his uniform and pulled out the gold legate's insignia and placed it in his father's palm. General Ridian regarded it for a moment. Then he crushed it.

"You have no rank," said Ridian. "You're nothing now. Get out of my sight."

Taius said nothing. He merely bowed his head and left.

"Now," said Ridian, turning to me, "back to you. Offspring of the Xotonian leader, eh?"

"Where is Kalac?" I asked.

"Kalac is staying on the top floor of my *palace*," said Ridian with a chuckle. He gestured toward a massive skyscraper of broken black glass—towering ominously above its neighbors—a few kilometers away. "We are becoming very close friends, Kalac and I."

"Huh. What do you two talk about?" I was quickly formulating a plan, and I needed to keep him preoccupied. "Sports? The weather? That time we kicked your butt and totally embarrassed your whole stupid space empire?"

"No," snapped Ridian. "We talk about the Q-sik!"

"Oh," I said, one thol'graz slowly creeping behind my back. "You mean that thing you totally failed to get? Sorry about that. Seems like you spent *your whole life* looking for it. And then to completely *blow it* at the last second? That's got to sting, right?"

"I will have the Q-sik yet," snarled Ridian.

"If you just let me speak to Kalac," I said, "maybe we can work something out."

"You know," said Ridian stroking his chin with an amused look on his face, "that's not a bad idea." He held up something toward me—another zowul, identical to Tai-us's—and punched something into it.

"Say hello to your 'originator,'" said Ridian, turning the screen to show me. On it, I saw Kalac. It was wrapped in black chains, bruises on its face. Its eyes were only open halfway. Despite my best efforts, I started to cry.

"Chorkle?" said Kalac, alarm and confusion growing on its face. "What are you doing here?" Its voice sounded small and weak.

"Kalac, are you all right?" I cried.

"Chorkle, I—"

The screen went black. "That's enough for now," said Ridian, pocketing the device.

"No, please!" I cried.

"You have served your purpose," said Ridian. "Now that Kalac knows you are my prisoner, it will give up the Q-sik."

It took everything I had to control the emotion in my voice. "Sounds like a foolproof plan," I said. "Tell me, how did your last plan work out?"

"That was not my fault!" roared Ridian, suddenly enraged. "My son is a weakling and an idiot! He squandered our every advantage! We should have won! Taius was defeated, not me!"

Ridian continued to bellow excuses, flecks of foam spraying from his mouth. It was now or never. Inside my pack, I reached for the Q-sik. Though Great Jalasu Jhuk itself had warned that the device always brought destruction to its user, I had no choice. I couldn't allow myself to be captured and the weapon to fall into Ridian's hands. I would fire it once. A blast on its minimum power setting would disintegrate Ridian and the legionaries. . . .

My thol'graz fumbled around inside the pack. My is'pog sank.

The Q-sik wasn't there.

Ridian cocked his head midtantrum, suddenly aware of me once more. "Reaching for something? A weapon, perhaps?" he asked.

I was utterly speechless. My mind was numb.

"Brave," said Ridian, stroking his chin, "but not smart."

A Vorem rifle butt smashed into my face. All was black.

CHAPTER NINETEEN

"Remember," said the Vorem centurion, "this is what you are looking for." He held up a sheet of parchment. It was a schematic diagram of a cylindrical object: a complex technological jumble of wires and coils and turbines with four curved tubes radiating from its sides. It was the same image we'd been shown every day for two weeks.

And so we set about our work. On General Ridian's orders, we were searching the Midden for a salvageable hyperdrive.

"I do not like this," I heard an Aeaki hiss under her breath. She was heavyset, with cyan-and-pink plumage. An Eka, I remembered. I wasn't sure what she didn't like: being conscripted by the Vorem, being forced to work with enemy Aeaki clans, or desecrating the sacred Midden of Hykaro Roost. Perhaps it was all three.

From listening to the Aeaki chatter among themselves, we'd learned that as soon as the Vorem landed on Kyral, they'd started searching the Midden. Presumably, this was Ridian's whole purpose in traveling to the planet. He needed a hyperdrive to get back to Voryx Prime.

At first, emissaries from various Aeaki clans complained to Ridian about this violation of their ancient customs. As Eyf had said, once something was offered into the Midden, tradition dictated that it should never be removed. These Aeaki asked why the great and powerful Vorem Dominion needed to sift through the relics of their past anyway. Ridian gave no answers.

The next day his thirty legionaries rounded up two hundred Aeaki—both from clans that were loyal to the Dominion and clans that had never surrendered—and took them prisoner. From now on, said Ridian, the natives would do his digging for him. Whichever of them found a hyperdrive would earn an unspecified reward. Those who complained would be made permanent slaves. Or worse, disintegrated.

The Aeaki feared the Vorem, and so they accepted the indignity. Some were glad to see their rivals imprisoned. Others whispered darkly among their own clans.

Meanwhile, the conscripts dug through Kyral's past, looking for a hyperdrive that matched the diagram. Lately, they had been joined by four new prisoners: Little Gus, Hollins, Becky, and me. Nicki and Eyf hadn't been captured with us in the theater. Other than that, we krew nothing of their whereabouts.

Each morning we were led up from our coops and out into the Midden. Armed legionaries watched us, as we spent the day poking through the last remnants of a bygone civilization. The Midden was huge, a rolling landscape of offerings from countless generations of Aeaki, heaped dozens of meters high in some places.

Ornim and Chayl searched beside us. Despite the circumstances, I was glad to see a couple of familiar faces. In bits and pieces, I'd been able to glean the story of what happened to them on Kyral.

As the *Phryxus II* approached the planet's surface, it was attacked by Ridian's trireme and shot down over the jungle. Luckily, they all survived the crash landing. Unluckily, their communications systems were critically damaged—which was the reason they never contacted Gelo. They decided that Hykaro Roost was their best hope for repairing the ship and possibly still finding a nyrine quantum inducer, which is what they'd been sent for. But as they approached the city, they were ambushed by a group of legionaries. After fierce fighting, the three of them were taken prisoner. This was the last they'd seen of Kalac.

As I dug through a pile of ancient furniture, I could see the black skyscraper—the place Ridian had called his "palace"—towering above the other buildings of Hykaro Roost. Kalac was in there, somewhere. Still alive, I hoped. Lately, though, I was finding hope in short supply.

"Look, a toaster," said Little Gus, startling me. He was prodding a shiny metallic object with his foot. "Wait . . . " he said. "Guys, there's still toast inside."

"Please don't eat eight-hundred-year-old toast," sighed Hollins.

"Too late," said Little Gus as he chomped into what looked like a black doorstop. His smile faded. "You know . . . I don't think it was toast after all," he said quietly.

"Get back to work," yelled the nearest guard.

The humans and I could talk among ourselves in their native language, as the Vorem had no idea what we were saying. Still, the legionaries wouldn't tolerate too much idle chatter. We had a job to do.

Nearby, Becky called out in Xotonian: "Oh my gosh! Is that a hyperdrive? Oh wow!" She waved at something under a mound of debris. Dutifully, the legionary took a look. Becky was pointing at an old bathtub.

"No," said the guard. "That's a bathtub."

"Are you sure?" asked Becky. "Isn't that the antimatter intake valve?"

"That's the faucet!" growled the guard. "Stop wasting our time!"

"Sorry," said Becky, feigning innocence. "I was confused. Can I see that picture again?"

"No," said the legionary.

Becky pulled some variation of the same trick at least five times a day. It had no purpose, really, other than to annoy our captors. She considered that an end unto itself.

"One of these days," she said quietly in human as the legionary returned to his post, "I'm going to find an energy blaster in this pile of junk. Then I'm going to vaporize these creeps."

"I doubt it," I said. "No Aeaki would toss a weapon into the Midden. Not while there were other Aeaki left to shoot."

"Come on," said Becky, "you haven't given up that easily, have you, Chorkle?"

Another day passed without a hyperdrive. As the sun dipped low, the legionaries rounded all of us up to return us to our cells. After a thorough pat-down—they wanted to make sure we weren't hiding anything dangerous—we marched through Hykaro Roost in a long single-file line. Every twenty prisoners or so, a pair of armed Vorem marched beside us.

"I don't get it," said Little Gus as we walked. "Why isn't Ridian looking for some sort of communication equipment? He could contact another Vorem ship to come and rescue him."

"I don't think he wants to call home," said Becky. "After all, he screwed up pretty big back on Gelo. The only thing he wants is to return with the Q-sik."

"Where do you think it is, anyway?" Hollins whispered to me, as if the legionaries could suddenly understand his language.

He'd asked me before, and I had no answer. All I could do was shrug. I had no idea where the Q-sik was. I guessed it had fallen out of my pack somewhere on Kyral. This was, without a doubt, the single stupidest thing I'd ever done. When you misplace something—an umbrella, your keys, maybe even a Feeney's Original Astronaut Ice Cream bar—it might seem important. But the fate of the universe doesn't usually hang in the balance. I wondered if this was the worst mistake ever made in the history of Gelo.

The guards led us through the darkening streets toward our new home. Hykaro's skyscrapers loomed above us. But instead of going up, we descended broken stairs into the ground.

We followed a dark, moldy passage past several rusty doors. At last this passage opened into a vast underground chamber lit by a few dim Vorem lanterns. The remnants of gilded tile clung to the ceiling in scattered patches, offering no clue as to what the entire design might have been. Around the walls were six arched shapes, about five meters high and built of slightly different masonry. To one who has spent most of its life underground, they looked very much like walled-up tunnels.

This was our prison. Our captors had filled the space with rows of temporary cells. Each one was a box of fine metal mesh with a heavy door on it. Apparently, mobile internment camps were a specialty of the Vorem Dominion. As a dark joke, the humans referred to these cells as "the coops"—mainly because of the two hundred birdlike Aeaki who were caged around us. The sound of their squawking and flapping and occasional fights filled the air with noise. Our fellow prisoners were only scared into silence when a loud roar echoed through the chamber.

That was Pizza, locked away in his own cage. After the fight we'd had in the theater, the thyss-cat had been captured too. As Little Gus recounted, proudly and often, it took six Vorem to drag him down here, and he fought them every centimeter of the way.

A legionary opened the door to our own coop and waved us in.

"Home, sweet home," said Hollins, stepping inside.

"Did you want us to fill out a timesheet, or are you guys keeping track of our hours?" Little Gus asked the legionary.

"Shut up," he said. Then he locked the coop behind us with a little octagonal key that he kept on his belt.

After all the prisoners had been secured, most of the guards marched back up to the surface. They always left two legionaries to stand watch throughout the night. Whether these were the same two night guards each time was a matter of some debate. It was impossible to tell, as all the Vorem legionaries wore identical black armor.

We sat down and tried to make ourselves comfortable—as much as that was possible in a six-meter-by-six-meter wire cell—while we waited for our dinner. The contents of our coop were modest: a couple of woven Aeaki blankets and a plastic jug of water. If "nature called"—as Becky had said—you had to persuade one of the legionaries to take you out of your cell and lead you a little ways off to take care of it. Usually, you just had to hold it. It was a miserable place, and so it matched my mood.

Soon came the familiar sound of a squeaky wheel. Our food was delivered by an old male Aeaki rolling a rusty cart between the rows of coops. His eyes were cloudy, and his feathers were brown with faded highlights of red and orange on his wings and throat. He never spoke, and none seemed to know his name. The old Aeaki didn't occupy one of the cells, and he returned to the surface once his duties were done. The other prisoners despised him for being a "Vorem collaborator."

The old-timer distributed the typical Aeaki fare—seeds, nuts, and berries wrapped in leaves. Twice a day, he pushed four of these packets through the slot in the door of our cell. We ate them eagerly. Picking through mounds of refuse was hard work, and we had nothing else.

Since our capture, we hadn't seen any sign of General Ridian himself. Neither had we seen Taius. I hated General Ridian, but somehow my feelings toward Taius were even worse. I tried my best not to think about him. When I did, such anger swelled in my z'iuk that I thought I might be sick. The others felt the same way. Yet somehow they couldn't stop talking about him.

"I totally called it with Taius," said Little Gus, not for

the first time. "Remember? Red eyes: evil. When I say stuff, you all should be writing it down."

"You also said anyone who liked your soup couldn't be all bad," said Hollins as he cracked hard seeds between his teeth.

"But did he like the soup? Did he *really*?" asked Little Gus. "Or was it all part of his cover?"

"I can't believe I had a crush on that guy," said Becky with a sigh.

"Wait . . . you *did* have a crush on him after all?" said Little Gus, deflating like a punctured oog-ball. "Come on! He's not even human, and you voted against him, and he's— he's got pointed teeth!"

"Mysterious loner," said Hollins with his mouth full.

"Shut up," said Becky. "Doesn't matter anyway. When we break out of here, he *won't* have pointed teeth anymore. I'm going to knock all of them right down his throat."

This brought them to their second most frequent topic of conversation: escape.

"If only we could sneak something down here from the Midden," said Hollins. "A piece of metal or something. Maybe we could pry the door off its hinges."

"How?" I asked. "The guards search us every day before we return to the coops. Even if they didn't, the two night guards would hardly stand by and allow us to remove the door of our cell. Not to mention the fact that the door looks like it could withstand an awful lot of prying."

"All right, fine," said Hollins.

"Maybe, when they're leading us back for the night, we could make a break for it," said Becky.

"And what's to stop the Vorem from shooting us in the backs?" I asked. None of the humans had an answer. I will admit, I was hardly a font of optimism these days. And it was easier to shoot down their ideas than to come up with any of my own.

"Well, I guess it's up to Nicki and Eyf," said Little Gus, shrugging.

Perhaps they were still out there somewhere, hiding among the ruined buildings of Hykaro Roost. Once, a few days earlier, I thought I'd seen a little white speck soaring high in the sky above the Midden. It might have been my imagination or a fluttering piece of plastic refuse, but maybe . . .

I refused to let myself think of it. After all, we'd had such incredibly bad luck—ever since the Core-of-Rock reactor had failed, now that I thought of it—why should I expect it to stop anytime soon? Nicki and Eyf were probably dead. Kalac too. The rest of us would be next. Then, after that, Ridian would locate the Q-Sik—wherever I had managed to drop it—and destroy the universe.

Good, I secretly thought, because I was angry at the universe, but mostly I was angry at myself. I scowled and ate my dinner in silence.

• • • •

Days passed. Up in the morning. A leafy packet of food. Search the Midden. Back to the coops. Another packet of food. Sleep. Repeat.

The Aeaki around us grew more and more restless with their imprisonment. Those who were deemed to be a flight risk (literally) were forced to work with heavy manacles chained to their legs. More fights broke out among them. Once, one of the prisoners even attacked a Vorem guard. She tried to peck right through his black helmet—and actually succeeded in putting a big spiderweb crack in the visor—before three other legionaries dragged her away. No one ever saw her again.

Those Aeaki who hadn't been imprisoned watched us— from perches in nearby buildings—toil in the Midden. The hostility in the air was palpable. The Aeaki prisoners hated their free brethren and probably vice versa. The prisoners hated one another owing to a mix of old clan rivalries and a general mistrust for anyone who didn't have the same color feathers. Together, they all hated the Vorem.

"Maybe the free Aeaki will rise up," said Hollins one morning as we walked to the Midden. Hundreds of Aeaki in little clan groups watched us from above as we marched through the city.

"Ha. That would mean different clans working together," I scoffed. "It will never happen."

You see, my anger had faded to resentment, then to self-pity, and finally to hopelessness. I found myself barely talking all day long. My mind was constantly wandering yet somehow always empty. Slight changes in my daily routine—such as the Vorem leading us by a different route to the Midden—vexed me greatly. The details of our journey across Kyral had become fuzzy in my mind. I could only remember the Midden and the coops. And reaching for the Q-sik, only to find it gone.

Sometimes I'd suddenly realize that one of the humans had been speaking to me for minutes at a time and I hadn't been listening at all.

"So what do you think?" said Becky, glancing at a nearby legionary. He had his back to us.

"About what?" I asked. It was midday on Kyral, and the

sun was beating down on us as we sifted through more of-ferings. Needless to say, my sunburn was worse than ever, which hardly helped my mood.

"About that," said Becky, wiping more dirt off it.

I took a closer look. It was a poster that showed an im-possibly complicated snarl of brightly colored lines. The lines were speckled with hundreds of little white dots. All were labeled.

"I don't know," I said. "I wouldn't hang it in my dwell-ing. But what is art, really?"

"It's not supposed to be *art*, Chorkle," said Becky. "It's a map. I think—I think it's, like, an old subway map. Of Hykaro Roost."

"Ah," I said. I hadn't been much of a conversationalist of late. And truth be told, I wasn't particularly interested in the history of Aeaki public transportation.

"Don't you get it?" she whispered, looking around once again.

I shrugged.

"That's where the coops are," she said, "down in one of these old train stations. That's how we could escape. Through the tunnels."

"Those tunnels are all walled up now," I said, trying to burst her bubble.

"So we break through. I've broken tons of stuff in my day: lamps, teeth, promises to get better grades. Breaking a wall should be easy enough," she said. "And then we use this map to figure out where to go."

"How?" I said. "We can't take it with us."

"I can't," said Becky. "But you can." She tapped her head.

I sighed. She apparently expected me to somehow memorize what looked to me like a plate of rainbow svur-noodles.

"Impossible," I said. "It's just a mess of squirmy colored lines."

"No, Chorkle," said Becky. "They're not lines. They're tunnels. They're *turns*."

I blinked. She was right. Once I imagined the colored lines as different passages intersecting one another underground, some fundamental part of my brain kicked in. It wasn't hard for a Xotonian to memorize a bunch of turns.

Becky studied the map. "There are six walled-up tunnels leading out from the coops—"

"Here," I said, pointing to a white dot where three lines intersected: purple, yellow, and green. I checked the label beneath. "It's called Central Crossing."

"Yeah, that's it," said Becky, nodding.

Mentally, I tried to place myself inside the tunnels and

orient myself to the geography I knew of Hykaro Roost. With my frib, I traced the lines of the tunnels.

"And that's where Ridian is keeping Kalac," I said, pointing to another station thirteen turns from Central Crossing. Its name on the map was "League Tower."

Becky smiled. "Good eye, Chorkle," she said. "I was afraid we might have lost you, pal."

"Sorry," I said, shaking my head and feeling the fog clear a little. "I don't know what's been wrong with me. It's just, I trusted Taius. And I can't believe I lost the . . ."

"It's okay, Chorkle," said Becky, placing a hand on my i'arda. "If things always worked out, just imagine how boring life would be."

Just then, we heard a nearby Aeaki squawk. It sounded like there might be another fight about to break out. Becky and I followed the noise. Hollins and Little Gus joined us.

Several Vorem legionaries had surrounded the shrieking Aeaki, but there was no fight. I gasped. There, beneath a mound of sports equipment and broken crockery and industrial cables was a complex cylindrical object with four curved tubes radiating out from it. All of us recognized it immediately.

"The one hyperdrive on this whole planet," said Hollins. "And now Ridian has it."

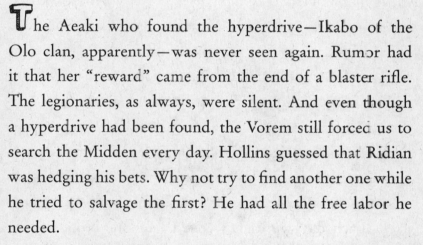

CHAPTER TWENTY

The Aeaki who found the hyperdrive—Ikabo of the Olo clan, apparently—was never seen again. Rumor had it that her "reward" came from the end of a blaster rifle. The legionaries, as always, were silent. And even though a hyperdrive had been found, the Vorem still forced us to search the Midden every day. Hollins guessed that Ridian was hedging his bets. Why not try to find another one while he tried to salvage the first? He had all the free labor he needed.

All of this drove prisoner morale to a new low. Fights among Aeaki were an hourly occurrence now. There were two more incidents of Aeaki attacking the guards. One male tried to fly away from the Midden and was shot down by the legionaries, in front of everyone. After this incident, all of them wore chains.

The situation in Hykaro Roost was deteriorating fast. But then something happened that pushed it from unpleasant to urgent.

One afternoon, while we were returning from the Midden, we passed several Vorem in the passageway that led to the coops. They were installing something around one of the support pillars: a black box with a single blinking red light. The Aeaki had no sense of what they were doing, but the humans understood immediately: The Vorem had wired the tunnel with explosives. With the push of a button, they could destroy our only way out and leave all of us prisoners sealed underground. I didn't doubt that the instant Ridian knew his hyperdrive was functional, he would do just that.

With still no sign of Nicki or Eyf, the humans and I prepared for our escape. We didn't have an exact plan, but we wanted to be ready when the opportunity presented itself. Each day we each secreted half our food away. I figured that to find the Q-sik, we might need to retrace our steps all the way back to Oru. Hollins did push-ups in our cell, for "strength conditioning." Becky said he was just doing them to prove he could. I drew and redrew the subway map each night in the dirt of our coop so the humans could study it.

One evening, the old Oru was pushing his squeaky cart through Central Crossing and enduring the usual verbal abuse of the other prisoners.

"Oh boy, oh boy! I sure hope it's seeds!" said Becky, her voice thick with sarcasm.

"If you like seeds," said Little Gus, "you should really try the nuts."

As usual, the old Oru said nothing as he pushed four packets through the slot. I thought I caught him giving me a strange look. I was about to say something, but he was already gone, wheeling his old cart to the next coop. He probably wouldn't have answered anyway.

I noticed that my leafy food packet was larger and heavier than normal. Perhaps I'd accidentally gotten a double or even triple helping. I wasn't sure I wanted extra seeds, but even so, I unwrapped the folded leaves.

There—instead of my usual dinner—was a small home-made technological device. It took me a moment to recognize Taius's static electricity gun.

On the inside of the leafy wrapping, one word was scratched in faint human letters: "Tomorrow."

• • • •

"Help!" pleaded Little Gus to the guard. "Please, I think it's choking!"

The legionary waved him off. Compassion was not the Vorem legion's guiding principle.

"Choking! It does having choking!" repeated Hollins. The guard was still unmoved.

"Look, you have to help," said Becky, pressed against the mesh of our coop. "This is the offspring of the Xotonian leader. If it dies, don't you think Ridian is going to be mad at you?"

The guard cocked his head. This approach seemed to strike a chord with him. He looked around, but his overnight comrade was off somewhere, patrolling the far side of the chamber. He cautiously approached our cell, blaster rifle out.

"Everyone get back!" ordered the guard. The humans did. The legionary unlocked the door of our cell and peeked inside.

He found me lying on the ground, not breathing, my skin an oxygen-deprived shade of blue. The Vorem prodded me with the tip of his heavy boot. I didn't move. He looked to the humans for support. They stared back at him, terrified.

"Is it . . . dead?" asked Little Gus, his voice quavering.

"Shut up," said the guard.

"Please, that's my second-best friend there!"

The Vorem knelt beside me to feel for a pulse. But then he realized that his hand was covered with a heavy armor gauntlet. He removed the gauntlet and—

An arc of electricity jumped from Becky's hand to the Vorem guard's bare skin. He convulsed for a few seconds and then flopped on the ground.

"No fun, is it?" said Becky to the unconscious guard.

I sat up and changed my skin back to its normal color. Hollins had already grabbed the legionary's blaster rifle. He tossed the octagonal coop key to Little Gus.

"Go get Ornim and Chayl," said Hollins. Gus turned to run, but then froze. The other guard was jogging toward us, blaster out. He must have heard something.

Hollins fired at him but missed. The guard stopped and then ducked behind a row of coops. He returned fire, knocking a chunk out of the concrete wall behind us.

"Damn," said Hollins, trying to get a sight. "I can't shoot him without hitting the other prisoners."

Hollins leaped to his feet and ran after the legionary. I followed him. Little Gus and Becky closed the door to our coop, locking the unconscious guard inside.

Hollins fired and missed again. The legionary now

crouched behind a big pile of rubble. All around us, the Aeaki prisoners were squawking wildly. More red laser blasts flew our way.

Hollins fired back, but the legionary was already gone. He'd made a break for the long passage to the surface—the only way out.

"He's going to leave and come back with reinforcements!" I cried.

Hollins gave a nod, and we ran after the fleeing guard, up the tunnel, and toward the city above. Hollins sent laser blasts whizzing past him as we went.

We lost sight of him. But around the next bend, he popped out from behind a concrete pylon and returned fire. Hollins screamed and tumbled to the ground.

"I'm fine. I'm fine," said Hollins, scrambling for cover behind a broken chunk of asphalt as I caught up to him. "Except . . ." He held up the blaster rifle—or what was left of it. It had been blown to pieces.

The legionary knew we were unarmed, and he wasn't running anymore. He walked back toward us now, leading with a hail of red laser blasts. We were pinned down, totally defenseless. All we could do was wait for him to arrive and disintegrate us.

"Well, we gave it a shot," whispered Hollins. "'It is hard

to fail, but it is worse never to have tried to succeed.' Teddy Roo—"

Just then, I heard something: a familiar voice echoing down the passage behind the legionary.

"But if igneous is formed below the surface, it is called *intrusive*. There are more than seven hundred types of igneous rocks. Most of them are formed beneath the planet's crust."

The Vorem whipped around to see someone standing in the hallway between him and the surface—a lone, frizzy-haired figure clad in a sensible sweater.

"Can it be?" I whispered.

It was none other than my fifth-grade geology teacher, Ms. Neubauer.

The Vorem grunted with surprise and started wildly shooting at her.

"Now if you'll please sync your workdrives to location seventy-six, you'll find a quiz covering today's material," continued Ms. Neubauer impassively while dozens of laser blasts whizzed harmlessly through her. "Please complete it by the beginning of class tomorrow."

The Vorem realized too late what was happening. A rusty door burst open beside him, and Becky flew out. With a wordless battle cry, she charged the guard. Fully armored, he must have weighed at least three times as much as she did. But she hit him just below the knees and took his legs right out from under him.

He tumbled to the ground, and his blaster rifle bounced away down the corridor. Two seconds later, Hollins was pointing it right at his face. The confused legionary slowly put his hands up.

"Nice work, Becky!" I cried.

"Not Becky," she said, brushing her hair back from her face.

"What?" cried Hollins, doing a double take.

"Eyf, can you hand me my glasses, please?" she said. Eyf stepped out of the darkened doorway, trembling.

"Hi," said the little Aeaki as she handed Nicki her glasses.

"Nicki?" cried Hollins in disbelief. "But—but you tackled that guy like some kind of maniac. That's not really . . ." He trailed off.

"Not really something 'the smart one' would do?" She finished his sentence as she deactivated Ms. Neubauer and collected her holodrive from the floor of the tunnel.

"Well . . . yeah," said Hollins.

"Well, maybe I'm not so *smart* after all," she said, smiling. Then she frowned. "Wait. No, that's not what I meant."

"No, I know what you meant," said Hollins. "You're capable of more than I gave you credit for."

Nicki nodded.

"But how did you manage to get the static gun into our food?" I asked.

"That was all Eyf," said Nicki, smiling. "She managed to persuade Rezuro—that's the name of the old-timer who pushes the food cart—to help. He's an Oru, you know."

"Finally, an Oru who isn't a jerk or a mold-brain!" I said. "Thanks, Eyf!"

Eyf shrugged modestly. "I just kept talking and talking until he finally agreed to help. . . . I can talk a long time." If she hadn't been covered in feathers, we might have seen her blush. "I think there are many Aeaki in Hykaro who do not like what is happening," she said. "I've tried to tell them what you said. That they don't have to fight each other."

"Um . . . can I go?" asked the Vorem legionary, startling us all.

"No!" we cried in unison. We'd all temporarily forgotten he was still there.

"But . . . they've detonated the tunnel," said the legionary. His hands were shaking now.

"What?" I asked.

He nervously pointed. There, on the wall, was the black explosive device. The red light on it was no longer blinking.

Eyf, Nicki, Hollins, and I looked at one another for a split second.

"The rest of the prisoners are still down there!" I cried.

And we ran as fast as we could, back down toward the coops. The legionary leaped to his feet and made for the surface.

I don't know whether he got out or not. Ten seconds later, we heard an ear-splitting boom echoing down the corridor behind us. The walls of the passage started to shake and splinter. There was a great rumbling noise, and I felt a wave of heat.

We reached the end of the tunnel just as it collapsed with a deafening crash. Shards of metal and chunks of concrete as big as me whistled past us. The air was filled with choking dust, even thicker than the storm in the Glass Desert.

Hollins, Nicki, and Eyf were beside me, coughing. Hollins's mouth was moving, but no words came out. All I heard was ringing.

As the dust settled, I realized we were sealed inside the old train station. But worse than that, the walls of the chamber now wobbled uncertainly. Huge cracks were spreading through the structure. The collapse of the tunnel had severely damaged the chamber. The whole place might fall in on itself at any moment.

As the ringing in my ears faded, it was replaced by the sounds of Aeaki shrieking in terror. I looked around. About half were now out of their coops, but the other half remained caged. Some were flapping around blindly through the dusty air of the chamber, colliding with the walls and each other in their panic.

We found Becky, with Ornim and Chayl, surrounded by an angry mob.

"Stand back!" cried Chayl. It had a length of old pipe clutched in its thol'grazes. Though much smaller than an Aeaki, Ornim and Chayl were no pushovers in a fight.

"Come on! We freed you!" cried Becky. "This is super ungrateful!" She was ready to fight too, but there were far too many of them.

"You outlanders don't belong here!" screeched an Aeaki.

"We're going to die in this hole!" screeched another.

"Do not!" cried Hollins, waving the energy blaster over his head. "Staying calm!"

A big Aeaki went for Ornim, who ducked out of the way and grappled at her feet. Chayl swung the pipe, and it thudded off her wing. She squawked in pain and stumbled back.

"Everyone, please!" cried Nicki. "Just quit fighting for a second! We have to . . ." No one was listening to her. Another crack spread up the wall.

Hollins fired an energy blast at the roof, temporarily bathing the dark chamber in red light. And for a moment the Aeaki did stop fighting. As one, they all turned and stared at the weapon. Then they rushed Hollins.

"I don't . . . want . . . to shoot them!" Hollins screamed desperately. All around him, Aeaki were pummeling and jostling him from every angle, each one of them trying to pull the weapon from his hands. A wing battered his face, leaving his nose bloody. A clawed foot kicked me in the back, and I fell. Aeaki wrestled and pecked one another in the dirt around me.

One of them emerged from the scrum, holding the blaster. She flapped up on top of an empty coop, screeched once, and began firing wildly around the chamber. Someone hit her with a rock, and she went down.

I heard another deep rumble and saw the roof shift. "Please," I cried, "the whole place is about to fall. . . ." No one could hear me.

A wild-eyed Aeaki was looming over me now. She'd picked up a heavy chunk of masonry, and she was ready to bash my brains in with it. Then, for some reason, she cocked her head at me and blinked.

I realized my skin had automatically camouflaged itself to the mottled gray of the concrete upon which I lay. The Aeaki looked up, surprised, just as a heavy blue paw swatted her out of the way.

Little Gus pulled me to my fel'grazes. Pizza stood beside him, hackles raised, snarling at the other prisoners.

The scene around us was pure chaos. Aeaki were fighting Aeaki. Dozens of them were piled on the floor, scrabbling after the blaster rifle. They would still be fighting each other when the station caved in, I realized.

"Stop it!" a voice cried. It was an Aeaki voice, loud and commanding. The other Aeaki turned to see the speaker, perhaps to challenge her authority. Those still locked in their coops quieted their wild screeching.

"Just stop!" the clear voice cried again. "Stop fighting among yourselves!" The chamber fell quiet. She had their attention now. I could finally see who was speaking. It was little Eyf. She was using a voice far bigger than herself.

"Why should we listen to you?" cried a tall Aeaki warrior with green and burgundy feathers. A cut above her eye was oozing blood. Apparently, she had won the blaster rifle, which she pointed at Eyf. "You're just a hatchling of the—the . . ."

"What clan is she?" cried someone else, ready to meet whatever answer with derision.

"What clan?" called others.

Eyf held out her wings for all to see. Plain white. "No clan," she said.

A whisper ran through the crowd.

"I've answered a question. Now I'll ask one," said Eyf. "Where are we?"

"In a Vorem prison," someone cried.

"In a tomb!" shrieked another.

"In *your* tomb, you Yko traitor!" snapped a third.

"No," said Eyf. "We are in Hykaro Roost. . . . So why are you fighting?"

The crowd grew uncomfortable now. None of the Aeaki wanted to answer her.

"The rule," said Eyf, "practically the *only* rule we have left on Kyral, is that when we are here, we don't fight one another."

"Now that the Vorem are back, all bets are off," said someone. "It's the end of the world!"

More of the Aeaki cried out in rage and fear.

Eyf held out her wings for quiet. "Enough," she said. "History is very, very, very long. Everybody attacked somebody. But at some point, instead of looking back all the time, we have to look forward. It's our only hope."

"Hope?" shrieked the Aeaki warrior holding the blaster rifle. "The Vorem have burned all the hope. They left us with the ashes. There is no hope on Kyral."

Eyf thought about this for a moment. "If we don't like what the Vorem ones are doing, there is only one thing we can do to try to stop them."

"Oh?" demanded the one with the blaster rifle. "You know what we need to do? A child. You have it all figured out, do you? You can tell a warrior how to defeat the mighty Vorem?" A few others around the chamber laughed with derision.

"Yes," said Eyf. "We have to work together."

They were all quiet now.

"The Yko will never work with the Esu!" someone cried. But their voice sounded weak and unsure.

"How?" cried someone else.

"I'm not sure, exactly," admitted Eyf. "But the Xotonians have figured out a way to work together. So have the humans. I think we can too. All I know is the first step."

"What is it?" someone cried.

"Tell us!"

"Look around you," said Eyf. "You see other Aeaki. Strangers—enemies, maybe. But you must imagine whomever you are looking at has the same color feathers as you do. Or that you have the same feathers as them. Or, if it makes it easier, imagine that both of your feathers are like mine, with no color at all."

Some of them shook their heads in disbelief or anger. Others listened though. They glanced or stared right at one another. They cocked their heads, and their shiny little eyes glinted in the darkness.

"Imagine that we are all one clan," said Eyf. "Aeaki."

A few of them were nodding now. I couldn't believe it. They were heeding Eyf's words. After all the centuries of bloodshed, were they finally tired of killing each other?

"The legends say that Kyral was a very, very, very great place long ago," said Eyf. "If we can forget the old grudges, forget who attacked whom and who robbed whose hunting traps, then maybe it could be great again."

Just then, there was another rumble. A massive chunk dropped from the ceiling and crushed four coops flat. Thank Jalasu Jhuk all were empty. This set the prisoners panicking anew. Central Crossing swayed and wobbled.

"Now, does anyone know of a way out?" asked Eyf, her voice calm.

"That way!" I cried. I pointed to one of the walled-up arches. "It's a tunnel."

Eyf looked at the arch, then she turned toward the Aea-ki who held the Vorem blaster rifle. "You, with the energy blaster," she said. "What is your name?"

"I am Tanihi of the Ati," said the warrior proudly. Here was at least one Aeaki who wasn't ready to give up her clan yet.

Eyf looked back to the arch. "Well, Tanihi, my friend says we need to break through that wall to escape. Otherwise, all of us will die."

Tanihi looked at the blaster she held. Then she looked at the two hundred Aeaki around her, their dusty feathers every color of the rainbow—some of them sworn enemies, no doubt.

She lowered the blaster rifle, and she fired. A blast knocked a chunk out of the center of the walled-up arch. I saw pure darkness behind it—a way out.

Carefully—stone by stone, so as not to destabilize the arch—we widened the hole until it was large enough for an Aeaki to fit through. Meanwhile, Little Gus and Becky worked to free the rest of the prisoners. With Pizza present, though, many of the Aeaki had to be coaxed out of their coops.

Recalling the subway map, I described the escape route to Ornim and Chayl. True Xotonians, they only needed to be told once. They took the lead, and one by one the Aeaki followed them through the hole and into darkness. Meanwhile, Central Crossing was falling to pieces around us. Eyf, the humans, and I waited until the last of the Aeaki were through. We were about to follow when I suddenly remembered.

"Wait," I said, cursing myself. "There's still a Vorem guard locked in our cell. We can't just leave him there."

"Really?" said Becky quietly. "He didn't seem like a great guy."

"Yeah, dude," said Little Gus. "Remember what happened *last time* you rescued a Vorem?"

"I know. I know," I said with a sigh. "But I've thought about it a lot, and I can't really explain it, but . . . I *still* believe that saving Taius was the right thing to do. Even if he did turn out to be a lying—"

"Fine," said Hollins, cutting me off. "But we better hurry." A nearby wall shifted ominously.

Eyf and the humans followed me as we ran back to our coop. The Vorem was still inside, awake and pressed against the wire mesh. Hollins opened the gate, and the guard made a mad dash for the tunnel.

"Ugh. Didn't even say thank you!" said Becky.

"Vorem," said Little Gus. "More like Vo-rude."

"Just stop," said Becky.

The Vorem disappeared through the hole in the archway just as an avalanche of rubble crashed down behind him, nearly crushing us. We were alive, but our way was completely blocked. Huge sections of the ceiling were landing all around us, spraying dirt and gravel into the air.

"There!" cried Hollins. A falling girder had punched a ragged hole in another one of the walled-up arches.

We ran for it and just managed to scramble through the opening as Central Crossing shuddered its last and collapsed.

CHAPTER TWENTY-ONE

The six of us walked through an ancient tunnel by the light of Nicki's flashlight. According to the map in my head, we were now on the purple line instead of the green line. This would mean an extra two turns before we could rejoin the original route with the others.

"Chorkle leading the rest of us around in the dark," said Little Gus. "It sure brings back some memories, doesn't it, guys?"

The humans said that by the looks of the old machinery, these tunnels had formerly held some sort of train system. The air smelled of decay, and all around us, we heard the quiet scuttling sounds of vermin. Once, Pizza dashed off to chase whatever was scurrying in the darkness.

"Are you sure that beast is friendly?" asked Eyf once the thyss-cat was gone. "It has very, very, very pointy teeth."

"Nah, Pizza's cool," said Little Gus. "He's never eaten a friend. Just a couple of acquaintances."

"Eleven is more than a couple," said Becky with a grin.

Eyf chirped in fear until Nicki made them admit that it wasn't true. Eyf was almost calm when Pizza trotted back, licking his chops. He had apparently caught whatever he was chasing.

It was odd. After Eyf's speech, she had reverted to her same old bubbly, talkative self. I realized that she too was capable of so much more than we had imagined.

We followed the tunnel to another underground station, far smaller than Central Crossing.

"This way," I said, leading us down an intersecting track.

"Hey, what's that?" asked Nicki. She was looking at a metal door, now mostly covered with rust.

"On my planet, we call it a door," said Becky.

We'd passed dozens of others like it down here. The humans assumed they were for maintenance, back when the transit system was operational.

"No. Look," said Nicki. And she cut off her flashlight, leaving us all in darkness.

You didn't need five Xotonian eyes to see what Nicki was talking about. There was a faint slice of light shining from beneath the door.

On the wall beside it, I noticed some graffiti scratched in chalk. It was so faded, it was almost impossible to see. But it looked like a crudely drawn eight-pointed star.

Hollins kicked at the door—which made a frightfully loud clang. He kicked again, and it swung open with a dry creak.

Inside was a short corridor leading to a second door. This one was made of steel and had no trace of rust on it. It looked thick, perhaps even sturdy enough to withstand a nuclear blast. On its surface was a subtle inlaid design—abstract but somehow similar to the Aeaki murals we had seen in Oru. Beside the door was a touchpad with each of the Xotonian letters on it. It bathed the small room in a soft blue glow.

"It looks like the Vorem ones never found this place when they plundered Kyral," said Eyf with wonder.

"Azusu mentioned some sort of Aeaki resistance in Hykaro Roost when the Vorem invaded," said Nicki. "Maybe this was one of their hideouts."

I pulled on the door's big handle. Of course, it didn't open.

"Look," said Hollins. On the floor in front of the door were four lines scrawled in the same chalk graffiti—all in Xotonian. "Of course, I can read it," said Hollins, "but maybe, uh, you should translate it into human . . . you know, for Becky's sake."

Becky snorted, but I did so anyway. In human-ese, it roughly translated to:

> *Found by the restless*
> *Kept by the state*
> *Made by its breakers*
> *And valued too late.*

"Huh," said Hollins.

"They're song lyrics," said Little Gus. "If we sing the song right, then the door will open. It's the ultimate karaoke challenge!"

The humans all stared at him. He shrugged.

"I think it's a riddle," said Nicki. "And the solution is the password."

"Then it's probably 'Love,'" said Becky. "Fact: The answer to ninety-eight percent of all riddles is 'Love.'"

"Love isn't kept by the state," said Nicki quietly.

Still, it was worth a try. I punched the characters for the Xotonian word into the touchpad. The door didn't open.

"Well, the answer to the remaining two percent of riddles is 'Time,'" offered Becky. "Give that a shot."

I did. No luck. I also punched in "Sleep," "Prisoners," "Waves," "Life," "Pizza," "Little Gus Is the Original King," and about a dozen more suggestions from the humans. None of them unlocked the massive door.

"I hate to say it," said Becky, "but we're kind of in a hurry here. . . ."

"No, please," pleaded Eyf. "This is one small corner of the whole planet that was never broken. . . . I need to see what is behind that door. I need to know what we once were."

The humans and I nodded to one another. If I was in her place, I would feel the same way.

"Okay, then, let's think about this out loud," said Nicki, stroking her chin. "Whatever is locked away—if it's still there—is valuable. That's why this place is hidden down here. That's why the door is so thick. But assuming that the riddle is the answer to the pass code, they wanted someone to be able to open it."

"Seems like a bad idea," said Hollins. "What's to stop some Vorem from figuring the riddle out?"

"I guess the answer would need to be something no Vorem would think of," I said.

We all stood in silence, bathed in the light of the touchpad, trying to think of an answer.

"I know what it is," said Eyf. We all turned to look at her. Her eyes twinkled in the darkness.

"'Peace,'" she said.

With the grinding of heavy tumblers, the door unlocked. It took both Hollins and Becky to pull it open.

Behind it was a bunker with reinforced metal walls. It was carpeted with several centimeters of dust.

"It was a command center," said Nicki, shining her light around inside.

Indeed, it looked like whoever had occupied it last— hundreds of years ago, at least—was fighting a secret war. The walls were covered with maps of all scales: street maps of Hykaro Roost, topographical maps of Kyral, star maps of the cluster the planet occupied. Huge stacks of files— brittle and curling at the edges—filled the place. They had labels like "Tactical Vulnerability of Dominion on Kyral" and "Theory of Vorem Leadership Structure" and "League Assets on Danis IV."

"I can't believe we made all this," said Eyf. She was marveling at a simple piece of paper, something that the Aeaki of today were incapable of creating. "We were as advanced as the Vorem ones. Maybe even more!"

"What are these?" asked Little Gus. He was holding up a shiny purple metal bar. There were several stacks of them.

"Phanium to power starships," said Eyf. "It's why the Vorem ones attacked."

Scattered around the bunker were several computers and pieces of high-tech equipment, the purpose of which I could only guess. One such device was a screen with an articulated, spiraling cone projecting out of it.

Nicki gasped. "I can't believe it," she said. She picked up a heavy book that was sitting beside the device and blew the dust off its cover. Then she showed it to us. In Xotonian, it read: *Operating Instructions for Tachyonic Ansible*.

"Huh. I prefer mystery novels, but okay," said Becky.

"Guys, it's a tachyonic ansible," said Nicki. We all stared back at her blankly.

"The Observers told me about them. I told you," she said, a touch of exasperation in her voice. "They exploit the synchronicity of tachyons for instantaneous conveyance across astronomical distances. . . . Anybody?"

"Nerd," said Little Gus.

"Fine, maybe. But bottom line," said Nicki, "is that I think we can use this thing to call home."

The other humans let out a simultaneous cry of joy, and much celebration ensued. Eyf learned what an Earth standard high five was. Finally, it seemed, we'd had a little bit of good luck. And it didn't stop there. In the back of the bun-

FOR THE LOVE OF GELO!

ker, Hollins found a metal locker containing several energy blasters.

"They still work," he said as he flicked the power switch on one and heard the high whine of electricity. He shoved a pistol in his belt. He offered a weapon to the rest of us as well.

Eyf refused. "I don't want to shoot anybody," she said, shaking her little head. "Not even a Vorem one."

I didn't either, really. But I took an energy blaster anyway. As Hollins distributed weapons to the other humans, I noticed that one of the maps on the wall was curling up at the edge. Instead of solid metal, I saw empty space behind it.

I peeled back the map to reveal a hole cut crudely into the wall of the bunker. Inside, there was a small lead box. Its lid bore a familiar inset: an eight-pointed star, just like the doors of the Vault and the hangar back on Gelo.

I slid the box—incredibly heavy—out of the wall and onto the floor with a dull clank. With great effort, Nicki and I managed to pull the lid off.

The object inside it was alien, yet instantly familiar. It was a technological device made of odd, iridescent metal. Instantly I knew: Whoever created the Q-sik had made this object too. Somehow, though, it looked like the opposite of the ancient superweapon to me. Or maybe the companion piece. I reached for it and—

Suddenly, Becky called out. "Hey, sis. I think I can beat your, uh, pachydermic runcible." She was looking underneath a tarp that covered a big irregular shape in the corner.

"Tachyonic ansible," corrected Nicki.

"Sure, whatever you say," said Becky. "This is better." She had all of our attention now. She waited, a huge grin on her face.

Finally, Hollins couldn't stand it any longer. "All right, enough showmanship, Becky. What's under there?"

"Instead of calling home," said Becky, throwing the tarp aside with a flourish, "how about we just fly there?"

She revealed a second hyperdrive. This one showed none of the wear and tear of the one Ridian had extracted from the Midden. It looked to be in perfect working order, exactly to the specifications of the schematic we had studied every day for weeks.

"Wow," said Nicki, going for it like I might a Feeney's Original. "We might be able to install it into one of the starfighters! Faster-than-light travel! It's been the dream of humanity for so long. And we have it. Right in front of us."

She stroked the hyperdrive lovingly. I could almost see Pizza getting jealous.

"I mean, it could take years to figure out how to understand it. Maybe even decades. It's possible that we humans lack the ability to truly conceive of more than three or four dimensions, which might be necessary to utilize something like this. . . ." She trailed off when she noticed that we were all staring at her.

"Whatever," she said. "This is awesome!"

The humans cheered and danced. Armed with her new-found knowledge, Eyf high-fived them all. Little Gus tried to kiss Becky on the cheek, but she ducked out of the way. Pizza rolled over on his back for a belly rub. I felt tears welling in my eyes.

I couldn't believe it. The humans finally had a chance, a real chance, at making it back to Earth. They would no longer be separated from their parents. I could finally put right my mistake and repay them for everything they had done for my fellow Xotonians and me.

"Why are you crying?" asked Nicki, noticing me.

"You're going home," I said.

"Not yet," said Hollins. "First we've got to save Kalac."

CHAPTER TWENTY-TWO

As we neared the surface, we heard blaster fire. We exited the tunnel into daylight and found ourselves at the base of League Tower—in the middle of a battle!

Five Vorem legionaries were trading fire with Aeaki of all colors—some on the ground and some circling in the sky above. While the Vorem had superior training and equipment, the Aeaki had numbers on their side. I recognized some of the attackers from the coops. Beside them, though, were just as many Aeaki who had never been captured. And they had armed their newly free brethren with energy blasters. The Aeaki of Hykaro Roost had risen up. They were finally working together.

"Prisoners, return to your cells immediately. . . . Prisoners, return to your cells immediately . . ." an automated voice repeated from a speaker somewhere—a difficult command to obey, considering the cells were now under a hundred tons of rock and dirt.

"Vorem, return to your own world!" cried an Aeaki in response. "Immediately!"

The fighters cheered when they saw Eyf step out of the tunnel. Their morale boosted, they pressed the attack.

"I'll see you at the top of the tower," cried Eyf and she took wing, soaring high above the fight.

The humans and I ran for the entrance of the black skyscraper as energy blasts sliced through the air around us. The two Vorem guarding the doorway literally threw down their weapons and ran when they saw Pizza bounding toward them. Even Dominion military discipline had its limits.

We entered a crumbling lobby of black marble, strewn with rubble. A large metal sigil had fallen from the wall and lay half-embedded in the floor: another eight-pointed star.

From an alcove, a concealed Vorem shot his blaster, sending a burst of energy whizzing past my head. Becky returned fire, and he ducked back into his hiding place.

We made for the stairs and ran upward. One flight. Two flights. Ten flights. The sounds of fighting continued as the Aeaki attacked the tower from the sky. Soon all of us were huffing and puffing. Even Pizza's coat glistened with sweat.

"Hisuda . . . was . . . right. . . . We . . . really should . . . be able to fly," said Becky.

"This is . . . worse than . . . Dynusk's Column," wheezed Little Gus, leaning heavily on the thyss-cat. Pizza shook him off.

The climb was not only exhausting but treacherous too. Many steps were missing. Others would crack and fall away at the slightest pressure. The whole flight between the eighteenth and nineteenth floors was gone. Pizza and I made the jump, but the humans were forced to use their nylon rope and haul themselves up one at a time.

On the thirty-fourth floor, we heard the sound of blasters close by. In a hallway off the stairs, we saw three legionaries exchanging fire with five Aeaki hunched down behind a pile of broken furniture. Big Tanihi was among them, still gripping her hard-won Vorem blaster rifle. Hollins and Little Gus sent two energy blasts flying the way of the Vorem. Flanked, they retreated farther down the hallway. The Aeaki saluted and followed their enemies.

We continued upward. On the sixty-third floor, we met two Vorem legionaries running down. They were surprised to see us and started to shoot. Laser fire pounded the stairs all around us, and we huddled backward. Our path was blocked.

From further up, I heard a battle cry: "For Jalasu Jhuk!"

There was a flash of sparks. One of the legionaries toppled over the railing and fell down the shaft at the center of the stairwell with a muffled scream. Someone was shooting at them from above.

I peeked upward. On the landing of the floor above the Vorem were two Xotonians with energy blasters. It was Ornim and Chayl! The remaining legionary was pinned between them and us.

Pizza saw his chance. He dashed up the stairs, headed for the other Vorem. By the time we got there, the poor soldier was flailing on the ground and pleading for his life, his armor studded with bite-shaped dents. Pizza held his foot immobile in his jaws. Becky picked up the legionary's blaster rifle, and Little Gus called the thysscat off.

"Kalac is on the top floor," cried Chayl. "We must hurry. Ridian has his hyperdrive up and running now."

On the eightieth floor, the stairs finally ended. We had reached the top of League Tower. This high up, I could feel the building itself swaying in the wind.

We burst out into a hallway guarded by four Vorem legionaries. This hallway led thirty yards toward two massive black doors with polished steel handles, some-how still bright after centuries. Behind those doors, I knew we would find General Ridian. We would find Kalac too.

All the guards fired at once, forcing us back into the stairwell. I took a deep breath.

"We'll cover you," said Hollins.

I nodded. Then I ran for it. A hail of red energy blasts shredded the hallway as I zigged, zagged, flipped, and ducked—across the floor, the walls, and even the ceiling—toward the doors.

Ornim, Chayl, and the humans charged out of the stair-well behind me, weapons blazing. A legionary just ahead of me fell, his armored knee joint smoking. With a roar, Pizza tackled another unlucky Vorem right through the wall and into an adjacent room.

I heard Becky scream. An energy blast had grazed her arm. Ornim went down, a smoking wound in its z'iuk.

I smashed through the black doors and past the two befuddled guards, who nearly shot each other trying to hit me. The battle continued in the hall as the guards held my companions back. The sounds of the fight were muffled now as the heavy doors swung closed behind me.

I found myself in a huge penthouse chamber at the top of the tower. I could tell it had been beautiful once, but now it was a ruin. Sleek statues lay toppled. The floor was strewn with paintings, now black with rot. One wall and a large portion of the ceiling had broken away, leaving the room open to the sky. Outside, I saw Aeaki wheeling and swooping. Two legionaries faced the gap, firing blaster rifles at them.

Ahead of me stood General Ridian, armored but still without his helmet. He faced a small slumped figure bound in chains. In his hand he held a scrap of parchment.

"9-1-5-6-7-2-3-4," yelled Ridian. "What does it mean?"

"Nothing," rasped Kalac.

"Yes it does. It *does* mean something!" Ridian bellowed at his prisoner. There was a note of panic in his voice. The Aeaki uprising must have caught him off guard. "Don't you understand? This is your last chance! Command the Xotonians to give it to me!"

The small figure turned to him. "I told you. Even if I wanted to . . . the Xotonians would never turn it over," said Kalac, its voice barely a whisper. "You won't get the Q-sik, Ridian."

"If they don't give it to me, then you die!"

"So be it," said Kalac.

Ridian punched my originator hard in the face. Kalac grunted.

"And it won't just be you!" cried Ridian. "I have your offspring—"

"Not anymore, you don't!" I cried, firing my blaster pistol at Ridian. I cursed as the shot flew wide of its mark.

"Chorkle?" said Kalac, blood dripping from its gul'orp.

Ridian turned, his red eyes wide. "Capture it!" he shrieked to his guards, ducking and fumbling to get his own blaster pistol from its holster.

Both the legionaries turned and fired at me. I scrambled behind a mound of debris while laser fire pummeled the floor nearby.

"Don't *kill* it! I said *capture* it! It's no use to me dead, you idiots!" screamed Ridian from across the room. "You! Worm! Redeem yourself!"

It took me an instant to realize that his last command wasn't for either of the legionaries. I whipped around as a swift kick knocked the blaster pistol from my thol'graz. My weapon skidded across the broken floor.

Before me stood Taius Ridian in a battle stance. He was unarmored, still wearing the same filthy, tattered uniform as when I'd seen him last. His cheeks were sunken, his hair greasy. He looked even worse than when he'd first emerged from the cargo hold of our starfighter.

"Taius," I said.

"Chorkle," he said in a cold monotone.

Then he kicked me hard in the z'iuk, and I slid backward across the floor. I leaped to my fel'grazes and discharged my stink gland. Lithe as ever, Taius ducked out of the way as the spray flew harmlessly past.

"What are you doing, you weakling?" bellowed Ridian to his son. "Why are you not engaging the Xotonian! It's half your size, you coward. Is this how you acted when you lost on Gelo?"

Taius swiped at me with his claws, and I sprang backward. He was bigger, stronger, and a fully trained warrior. He wasn't holding a weapon though. If I could get to my blaster pistol, I might have a chance.

"You shouldn't have saved my life," said Taius. With a snarl, he lunged at me again, and I somehow managed to somersault over him.

"You owe that *thing* your life?" hissed General Ridian with disbelief. "How is that possible? You're a *disgrace*."

Taius spun around and hit me with a roundhouse kick that sent me sprawling in the opposite direction.

I lay on the floor for a moment, dazed. I blinked and saw Taius at the apex of a high jump. I just managed to roll out of the way as he stomped the ground where my head had been. I heard him growl with rage.

"That little Xotonian is making a fool out of you," said Ridian. Odd, considering I felt like I was barely staying alive.

Taius swung his fist and cracked me hard across the gul'orp. He swung again, and I ducked. Overbalanced, he stumbled forward.

"You're not a warrior," said Ridian.

Somehow I managed to scramble through Taius's legs and get behind him.

"You're not my son," said Ridian.

My blaster pistol was close now—just a few meters away on the floor. I dove for it and felt my fribs brush its handle when a hard armored hand clamped onto my thol'graz and yanked me back. One of the legionaries held me firm in his grasp. I wriggled, but it was no use. His grip was like iron.

"Got the Xotonian!" the legionary cried, hoisting me up. And an energy blast to the shoulder promptly knocked him off his feet.

"'Sup, dudes," said Little Gus.

I turned to see him standing in the doorway with Chayl,

Hollins, Becky, and Nicki. They all pointed their weapons right at General Ridian. They had defeated all the guards in the hallway.

"No!" shrieked Ridian.

The other legionary crouched to fire, but before he could raise his blaster rifle, Pizza came hurtling over the heads of the humans and landed hard on his chest.

I caught movement from the corner of my third and fourth eyes. Taius charged at me. I sprang into the air and somehow caught a dangling light fixture. He growled as I hung just out of his reach.

"No, no, no, no, no," said Ridian, looking around the room frantically. With both legionaries neutralized, he was outnumbered and outgunned. Outside, the Aeaki were routing his troops. His plans on Kyral were falling to pieces.

"Everyone back!" cried Ridian, and he yanked Kalac to its fel'grazes and pointed his blaster pistol right at my originator's head. "Stay back, or I will end Kalac's life!" He inched toward the open ledge.

The humans looked at one another uncertainly. At last, they lowered their weapons.

Taius stood below me, panting hard. He reached into his pack and pulled something out. It was a small device: a glowing tetrahedron that spun slowly inside several concentric rings of tarnished, iridescent metal, mounted on a complex base.

"No," I heard Nicki gasp.

With a choked noise of wordless hatred, Taius aimed the Q-sik at me.

CHAPTER TWENTY-THREE

I could feel the Q-sik drawing energy to itself. It was powering up to fire. When it did, a white light would burn through me. A beam powerful enough to punch a hole through a planet would blast my body into its constituent particles.

"You—you have the Q-sik?" said Ridian in disbelief.

"Yes," said Taius. "I've had it since I came here. I took it from this one while it slept. Not so stupid, am I?"

He must have stolen it the night after we crossed the marsh. He must have known I had it all along. I realized that the dream I had in the village of Oru was real.

"Shoot him!" croaked Kalac. My originator's face held a look of despair.

Neither Chayl nor the humans moved though.

"You had it, but . . . why didn't you give it over to me,

my son?" asked Ridian. His voice was kind now, paternal.

"Quiet," said Taius. General Ridian blinked.

Taius's face had contorted into a grotesque mask of pure rage. He stared at me, past the Q-sik, as tears streamed down his cheeks.

"No matter," said Ridian. "If you want to be the first to fire it, go ahead. After all, you've earned it. You're a clever boy. A good boy. Blast that Xotonian out of existence. Be careful, though. I've studied the Q-sik, and the lowest power setting will suffice. Otherwise you might kill us all." Ridian chuckled. "That thing can shatter suns, you know."

"Shoot him," whispered Kalac. The others remained frozen where they stood.

"Do it, Taius," said Ridian, ignoring my originator. "You've more than redeemed your failures on Gelo. Now you can erase your debt to that creature too. You'll be a general. More than a general. You'll command your own fleets. Together we'll return to Voryx Prime and take what is rightfully ours. Fire the Q-sik and then hand it over to me. With it, I will be imperator: Stentorus Sovyrius Ridian I. And you will take the throne after me."

Taius nodded slowly. I could tell he was picturing the future his father laid out for him: wealth, honor, glory. The

Q-sik continued to power up. I realized that he'd set it to its maximum setting.

"Why?" he asked.

"Why . . . what?" I asked.

"Why did you pull me out of that burning ship?"

"I thought it was the right thing to do," I said.

"Are you a fool?" he cried. "Why did you help me? It doesn't make any sense. We're at war! I'm your enemy! I'm your enemy. . . ." His pointed teeth were clenched.

"You didn't have to be," I said. "You still don't."

Taius and I stared at each other. The Q-sik hummed and crackled. Slowly, he closed his eyes.

"What are you waiting for?" asked General Ridian. "Stop jabbering and shoot. Or give the Q-sik to me. Enough dawdling, boy. You need to—"

"Shut up!" screamed Taius.

General Ridian's eyes grew wide. Taius now pointed the Q-sik at his father.

"What?" laughed Ridian, backing closer to the ledge. "What do you think you're doing, Taius? Is this a joke? Give that thing to me right now."

"Stop telling me what to do," said Taius in a dangerous voice. The Q-sik continued to power up.

"You are an officer of the Vorem legion, subordinate to

me," said Ridian. "I have every right under Dominion law to tell you what to do."

"No," said Taius. "I'm not a military officer. I have no rank. You took that from me."

"As punishment for your failure," said Ridian.

"My failure? My failure!" he cried. "What about your failure?"

"I don't know what you're talking about," said Ridian.

"Look around. The Aeaki are routing your troops."

"I'm not—my objective is not to defeat the Aeaki. It is to obtain the Q-sik."

"That was your objective on Gelo too," cried Taius. "Ten triremes and a battle cruiser, beaten by three antique Xotonian starfighters! Pathetic! Anyone who couldn't win that battle would flunk out their first year at war college."

"They fired the device!" snapped Ridian.

"You knew they had it! How could your strategy not account for that possibility?" cried Taius.

"I thought—our simulations determined that there was a ninety-seven percent chance that they lacked the will to use it," stammered Ridian.

"But you were wrong! They *did* use it!"

"Yes," said Ridian, his voice now thick with contempt. "And that's what makes them braver than you."

"What?" cried Taius, his eyes suddenly crazed. The Q-sik was drawing power still—it radiated dizzying waves of energy. If Taius fired it at this setting, the blast would surely destroy us all.

"You heard me, boy," sneered General Ridian, moving toward the ledge, his blaster pistol still pointed at Kalac's head. "You won't shoot that thing at me."

"What makes you so sure?" asked Taius.

"Because what I said was true: You aren't a true warrior. You lack the courage," said Ridian.

"Do I?" he snarled.

"Yes," he said. "If you stood in *my* way, I would destroy you without a second thought."

"Don't do it," I said quietly to Taius.

"Shut up!" he yelled at me.

"You're weak," said Ridian. "You can't."

"When does it end?" asked Taius.

"What?" asked Ridian.

"When does it end?" repeated Taius.

"When does *what* end?" asked Ridian.

"The Vorem Domion has conquered thousands of worlds. But we always want more. . . . More killing. More fighting. More taking. When does it end?"

Ridian laughed. "It never ends," he said. "Now I'm telling you, boy, this is your last chance. Give me the Q-sik and I won't put you to death for this sad treason."

"No," cried Taius. "I hate you!"

"You may hate me," said Ridian, "but I'm everything to you. Without me, there is nothing."

Taius and his father stared at each other for a long moment. Taius bellowed with anguish and gripped the Q-sik with both hands. I closed my eyes.

"Yes. There. Is," said Taius. And he lowered the weapon.

"Just as I thought," said Ridian. "Pathetic." And he stepped off the ledge, taking Kalac with him.

"No!" I cried, dropping to the floor and running toward the edge.

Slowly, a black shape rose. It was the Vorem trireme, hovering about five meters from the building. Ridian stood on the wing, clinging to its open hatchway, the wind whipping his black hair. He still clutched Kalac by its chains.

"When you wish to make an exchange," said Ridian, "my *son* knows how to reach me."

I raced toward them. Kalac turned, and our eyes met. I could somehow hear my originator over the roar of the ship's thrusters. "Don't give up the Q-sik," it said. "Whatever happens, Chorkle, know that I love you."

The trireme nosed skyward.

"Kalac!" I screamed. And with all my strength, I leaped.

"Chorkle, don't!" yelled someone from behind me. Was it Taius?

My thol'grazes flailed as I sailed through the void. I desperately reached for the trireme.

But I missed.

The Vorem ship fell away toward the sky. It took me an instant to realize that it was I who was falling. I'd jumped from the top of League Tower, and now I had two hundred fifty meters to drop before I smashed to bits on the ground below.

Time seemed to slow as I plummeted toward my death. It was oddly quiet. I found myself blinking back tears, half from racing air and half from being so close to Kalac and yet losing my originator again. I don't think I felt scared, particularly. Perhaps the fear of dying hadn't registered yet. Some oddly logical corner of my brain hoped that I would land before it did.

The ground was rushing up at me very quickly. I could even see the shapes of tiny armored Vorem legionaries fleeing before the Aeaki. Above me, the trireme had dwindled to a black speck. And beside it, I saw a little white speck about the same size.

I blinked again. The white speck grew. Something was hurtling through the sky of Kyral toward me, approaching faster than I was falling.

It was Eyf.

"Chorkle!" she shrieked. She swooped and caught my thol'graz with her feet. She flapped her wings hard, but she wasn't strong enough to lift me. Now the two of us were both falling together. But instead of falling straight down, her momentum was carrying us forward too.

Another ruined skyscraper—maybe a third the height of League Tower—grew ahead of us. We were approaching it fast. Too fast. I heard Eyf shriek.

The last thing I remembered was smashing through a wall.

CHAPTER TWENTY-FOUR

Darkness.

Silence.

So this is what it feels like to be dead, I thought, to cross over to the Nebula Beyond.

I heard a faint noise ringing in the void. A growl. It was my own z'iuk. I felt . . . hungry.

But that wasn't right. How could I be hungry after I'd died? Perhaps . . . perhaps I wasn't dead.

To test the hypothesis, I opened a single eye. The world was painfully bright. After a moment, this formless light began to resolve itself into a room. It was made of old broken concrete. I was lying on a woven grass pallet with a short wooden table beside me. On the table was a small crystal statue: a woman with a shield and spear. A few vines crept in through the open window. Outside, the sun was shining.

A big blue shape in the corner shifted, and I felt a surge of panic. I was sharing the room with a thyss-cat, the most fearsome predator on all of Gelo. The beast tilted its head, and its yellow eyes locked with mine.

"Hamburger," it said.

"Aaaaaaaaaaagh!" I screamed, startling the thyss-cat.

Just then, an old brown-feathered Aeaki came bustling in. Somehow I knew his name was Rezuro, and he was a member of the Oru clan. He didn't seem to be afraid of the beast.

"Shoo! Go on! Get out of here," he said to Pizza. Chastened, the thyss-cat whined and slunk off.

"I heard it . . . It was . . . It said . . . " I mumbled. My head felt foggy, and I suddenly realized that everything hurt.

"It's all right," said Rezuro, easing me back onto the pallet. "Relax. You need to rest."

"But . . . I . . ." It was hard to argue with him. I felt as though I'd been sat on by an usk-lizard.

"Is Chorkle awake?" cried Nicki, bursting into the room. She was followed by Hollins, Little Gus, and Becky, who had one of her arms in a sling.

"Yes, but please try not to agitate it," said Rezuro as it left.

"Chorkle!" cried Nicki, hugging me tightly. There were

several spots on my body that I hadn't realized were in pain.

"How are you doing?" asked Hollins.

"Pretty banged up," I said.

"You should see the wall you hit," said Becky.

"What happened to Eyf?" I asked, remembering my fall.

The humans looked at one another. Hollins held up his hand to quiet the others. He stared at me. At last, he spoke slowly in Xotonian. "Eyf is . . ." He trailed off, shaking his head.

I felt my is'pog sink. I opened my gul'orp to say something, but no words would come out.

Becky punched Hollins in the arm. "Dude, say 'fine'!" she yelled.

"Ow. Sorry," said Hollins. "I always blank on that word. 'Phaeti' means 'fine,' right?"

"Seriously, just do the homework," sighed Nicki.

"Anyway, Eyf is fine," said Hollins. "A few bruises and scrapes, but she's fine."

"And Taius?" I asked.

"He gave us back the . . . " said Hollins, catching himself and then lowering his voice. "He gave us back the *you-know-what*, and he surrendered. Just offered himself up as a prisoner."

"Becky zapped him with his little electricity gun anyway, though," chuckled Little Gus. "You should've seen it." Little Gus pantomimed putting his hands up, then snapping his body totally rigid and flopping onto the ground.

Becky shrugged. "Well, I owed him one," she said.

"He also gave us this," said Nicki, removing something from her pocket and handing it to me. It was a small metal device with multiple wire and tubular outputs. "I guess he had it in a hidden pocket the whole time."

"What is it?" I asked.

"The nyrine quantum inducer," she said. "He stole it to sabotage Core-of-Rock's reactor. He thought the Vorem prisoners could escape if he disabled the city's power supply. I guess it didn't work."

"Another brilliant plan by Taius Ridian," scoffed Little Gus. "I'm being sarcastic," he clarified. "That guy is dumb, and I hate him."

"Eh . . . he's okay," I said. I could tell by the looks on their faces that the humans didn't agree, but they weren't going to argue with a sick patient.

"Well, you might need to convince him of that," said Nicki. "I think he's lost the will to live."

"Good," said Becky.

"Anyway," said Hollins, "with the nyrine quantum inducer, Ydar should be able to fix the reactor and get the Stealth Shield up and running again."

"And you'll be able to contact Earth," I said, "with that, uh, thing we found. . . ."

"Tachyonic ansible," said Nicki, grinning.

"Right," said Hollins. "And maybe we can even figure out how to install that hyperdrive into one of the Xotonian starfighters!"

"'We'?" said Becky. "Just say 'Nicki.'"

"I can't believe it," I said. "You'll be able to go home. Finally, you're going to see your parents." I choked up as I said it. The humans looked at one another with concern.

"Don't worry," said Becky, placing a hand on my thol'graz. "We'll get Kalac back."

I nodded and wiped my eyes. I hoped that what she said was true.

Rezuro poked his head back in. "All right, I'm afraid Chorkle has had enough excitement for now," he said. "It just woke up, you know."

The humans nodded, and one by one, they filed out of the room. Little Gus was the last to go.

"Gus, wait," I said.

He turned.

"I heard it," I said.

"Heard what?"

"I heard Pizza say 'hamburger.'"

He smiled. "Sure you did, little buddy," said Little Gus, patting me on the i'arda. "Sure you did." And he was gone.

· · · ·

We spent two more weeks on Kyral. The day after I awoke, Nicki and Hollins left Hykaro Roost accompanied by an armed escort of Aeaki from several clans. They hoped to return after they repaired the *Phryxus II*.

Rezuro continued to treat me using traditional Aeaki remedies—herbs and foul-smelling poultices. He even told me something of his past. It turned out that Azusu the Raefec was his cousin. He told a few embarrassing stories about her younger days that I'm sure she would have tossed me from the top of Oru for even knowing.

Eyf came to visit me often and told me long stories, most of which had no ending. In fact, they often didn't seem to have a beginning either. The stories were mostly middle. I didn't mind, though. I found her happy presence a great comfort, and I didn't feel like talking much anyway. Little Gus brought me warm bowls of his eponymous soup—

far superior to the seeds and berries that Rezuro fed me—and taught me to sing some of Pizza's "favorite" jazz standards. Becky came too, and we spun out elaborate predictions for what we thought might happen next on *Vampire Band Camp*. We were both pretty sure that Clyve wasn't *actually* dead.

At last Rezuro allowed me to leave the chamber. Becky, Little Gus, Eyf, and I walked between the old skyscrapers of the city on swinging rope bridges. Hykaro really was a different city from above.

Everywhere we went, the Aeaki cheered Eyf when they saw her. As she got closer to each one, they bowed low as if she were their leader, and they fumbled their words. It was strange to see her treated with such deference.

"In the past, nobody ever, ever talked to me because they didn't like me," she laughed to the humans and me. "Now they don't talk to me because they do!"

Eyf had become the symbol of a new movement in Hykaro Roost. Formerly, it had been a place to trade goods, where peace was just a means to an end. Now, I saw members of different clans socializing. Mixed groups of them traveled the city together. Sometimes I heard them laughing among themselves and singing strange old songs. They even deigned to interact with the odd flightless outlanders from

Kyral's new moon. Ornim and Chayl tried to teach them oog-ball, but the sport didn't take.

In short, the city seemed less like the remnant of a lost world and more like the seed of a new one.

I visited Taius once by myself (none of the humans cared to accompany me). He occupied a drafty room on the tenth story of an empty building. Though there was nothing keeping him there, he never left. Taius was a prisoner in his own mind.

I brought him a portion of Little Gus Soup or "wryv," as the Vorem called it. He barely ate. He spoke even less.

"You know, by keeping the Q-sik from your—from General Ridian, you might have saved the universe," I said. "The universe is pretty important."

He nodded, but nothing would cheer him up. I sighed. At last, I rose to leave.

"You know," he said, "I think . . . I miss him. How stupid is that? He said he'd destroy me, but I still miss him."

"Not stupid," I said, shrugging. "I know how you feel."

"Because what if he is right?" said Taius. "Without him, what am I? I don't know."

"I do," I said. And I left.

A few days later, the *Phryxus II*—patched and repaired—landed in Hykaro Roost. Nicki and Hollins exited the craft,

followed by a boisterous pack of Aeaki. They were thrilled
to have flown in an actual starship.

"What's the big deal?" asked Becky, shaking her
head. "They fly every day. They don't even need a ship to
do it."

Ornim, Chayl, the humans, and I loaded the starfighter for departure. We packed the tachyonic ansible and the
hyperdrive, as well as several boxes of files from the underground bunker. I wanted to learn more about the history
of the war against the Vorem. Inside one of these file boxes,
discreetly wrapped in a sheet of parchment, I smuggled the
strange device that I'd found inside the lead box marked
with the eight-pointed star. I'd come to think of it as the
Q-sik's companion piece, though its purpose was anyone's
guess.

A crowd of Aeaki gathered to see us off. Eyf stood at
the front with old Rezuro and the warrior Tanihi at her side.
It seemed as if the Aeaki wanted her to say something. She
looked around sheepishly and cleared her throat.

"The Aeaki and the Xotonians were good friends a very
long time ago—members of a League of Free Civilizations,"
she declared in her loud, sonorous voice. "Today our two
peoples are friends again. Today a new league is born!"

I gave Eyf a big hug, and the Aeaki cheered.

Beside us, Hollins stepped forward as though he meant to address the crowd. The other humans glanced at one another nervously. If he was going to speak to them, it would have to be in Xotonian. Hollins cleared his throat, and I winced. A hush fell over the crowd. The Aeaki might have put aside their differences, but what would happen if some strange outlander accidentally called them all "pudding" for no good reason? Nicki placed a gentle hand on Hollins's shoulder to stop him.

"Look, Hollins," said Nicki, "maybe you shouldn't—"

He smiled and waved her off. Then he turned and spoke to the crowd in Xotonian. "Hello," he said. "A human leader from long ago once said: 'There is no good reason why we should fear the future, but there is every reason why we should face it seriously, neither hiding from ourselves the gravity of the problems before us nor fearing to approach these problems with the unbending, unflinching purpose to solve them aright.' The Aeaki are now on a long and difficult road to rebuilding your world. But you've already done the hardest part. You've taken the first step."

At this, the crowd exploded. I couldn't believe it. His Xotonian—even the translation—was flawless, poetic even!

"What? How did you . . . I mean you're not . . . " whispered Nicki, dumbstruck.

"Maybe I'm capable of more than *you* know too," said Hollins with a grin.

"I take it back," said Eyf, impressed. "This big one is not simple at all!"

"Are you sure you don't want to come with us back to Gelo?" I asked her. "We have fried cave slugs!"

Eyf made a face, which hardly seemed fair since I'd seen her gorge on squealing yellow grubs.

"No, Hollins is right. There is very, very, very much to do here," she said. "The Aeaki here have learned to work together, but there are many, many more out there." She waved toward the horizon, the rest of Kyral. "I think it is my duty to help them figure out that they do not have to fight one another."

"We must be united," said Rezuro.

"For when the Vorem return," said Tanihi, finishing his thought.

"When they do," I said, "the Xotonians will stand beside you. If you need us, we'll be right up there." I pointed toward Gelo's pale outline in the afternoon sky.

"Ugh. Speaking of Vorem," said Becky, turning away and heading toward the cockpit.

The crowd parted as Taius silently walked toward the ship. I'd asked him to come back to Gelo with us, and he said it made no difference where he went. Hollins privately described this attitude as "super emo."

Now he boarded the ship as the humans stared at him. Pizza gave a low growl.

"Would you be more comfortable hiding in the cargo hold?" asked Little Gus.

Taius said nothing as he took his seat.

The *Phryxus II*'s thrusters rumbled as we climbed into the sky. Below us, the green world of Kyral shrank away as we flew back toward Gelo.

CHAPTER TWENTY-FIVE

"Exit the starship with your thol'grazes up!"

The hatch of the *Phryxus II* slid open with a hiss. I stepped out into the hangar, reaching toward the ceiling. Ornim and Chayl followed behind me, looking defiant.

"Um, we don't have thol'grazes," said Becky, shrugging as she stepped out, followed by Nicki, Hollins, and Little Gus.

"Quiet, hoo-min!" yelled Sheln. The Chief of Council stood before us. Beside it was Zenyk, in full "Commissioner of the Guards" getup. The other three members of the Xotonian Council were there too, looking distraught. So were Eromu and a dozen other city guards who seemed embarrassed by our cold welcome. I sensed that things had somehow gotten even worse in Core-of-Rock since we left. Sheln pointed an energy blaster right at my head.

"Nice to see you too, Sheln," I said.

"I'll thank you to refer to me by my proper title," cried Sheln, "you insolent little—yaaaaargh!" Sheln shrieked and jumped backward—now involuntarily camouflaged—as Pizza disembarked from the ship. A few of the guards snickered.

"Apologies," I said, scratching the thyss-cat behind the ears. "Nice to see you, *imperator*." And I bowed, which prompted another chuckle from the guards.

"Everybody shut your gul'orps," snapped Sheln. "I'm not imperator, I'm Chief of Council! And you, Chorkle, you don't even know how much trouble you're in. You stole a starfighter for some personal lark down on Kyral."

"It was a rescue mission," I said.

"No, it was treason! You disobeyed my orders in a time of war—during a *state of emergency*! I'll have you locked away for the rest of your life for it."

"Oh, right. About that war," I said. "Taius?"

The assembled Xotonians gasped as Taius stepped out of the ship, hands on his head. Several of the guards raised their weapons. He was indifferent though. He stared at the ground and repeated the lines I'd asked him to.

"Greetings," he said in a flat monotone. "I am Taius Sovyrius Ridian, the legate who led the invasion of Gelo.

As a representative of the Vorem Dominion, I'm here to declare that our war against you is officially over. We surrender."

A hush fell over the assembled Xotonians, and they looked at one another, confused.

"Now does somebody want to arrest me or something?" said Taius. He sounded like he didn't particularly care either way. At last Eromu stepped forward and took him by the arm.

"You heard him," I said to Sheln. "The war is over."

"Wait just a minute!" cried Sheln, slowly grasping the implications. "He can't just—"

"And since it's no longer a time of war," I continued, "I believe your state of emergency has ended too."

"Guano!" sputtered Sheln. "Just because you trot out some Vorem to say there's no more war doesn't make it true!" It looked to the guards for support. They offered nothing.

"This legate has surrendered," said Loghoz, shrugging. "Unless there is another Dominion representative who outranks him, we must accept his word."

"No!" bellowed Sheln. "No, no, no, no! This is ridiculous. That's just one Vorem. The war's not over. Ask anyone. They'll tell you! The whole Dominion is still out there, waiting to attack us for the Q-sik. And speaking of which, Chorkle, I *command* you to give me the code to the Vault! I know you know it you—"

The rest of the Xotonians stared at Sheln.

"But, uh, let's not get sidetracked," it said, perhaps conscious of how it was coming across. Sheln calmed its voice and continued. "Point is: Nobody needs to worry, the war is still going strong, folks."

"Nope. We surrender," repeated Taius.

"Who asked you?" snapped Sheln.

"Sorry, Sheln," I said. "You too, Zenyk. I think your state-of-emergency appointment to Commissioner of the Guards just expired."

"What?" said Zenyk, crestfallen. It wistfully regarded its medals and badges.

"Time to put away the Christmas decorations for another year," said Little Gus.

"Nobody listen to Chorkle or the Vorem!" cried Sheln. "This is madness! The people will have something to say about this! They know the truth!" It waved back in the general direction of Core-of-Rock.

"How do you mean?" I said, feigning confusion.

"The rest of the Xotonians on Gelo! I'll gather them all together, and—and I'll call a Grand Conclave, and we'll see if *they* think the war's over!"

I smiled. Sheln realized too late that it had taken my bait.

"You're calling a Grand Conclave?" I said. "Fantastic."

"No, I mean, uh," Sheln stammered, "I didn't actually intend to say that, because I was actually—"

"Let the record show that the Chief of Council called a Grand Conclave!" said Glyac.

"Wait, hold on. You're putting words in my gul'orp. I said I *will* call one, not that I *am* calling one. And it was a figure of speech anyway. I'm sorry if it caused any confusion," said Sheln.

"Loghoz," said Dyves, interrupting it. "Tell us: Under the law, may the Chief of Council *un-call* a Grand Conclave once it has been called?"

"Most certainly not," said Loghoz primly.

"Guano," sighed Sheln.

· · · ·

Three hours later, the Xotonian populace stood gathered in Ryzz Plaza at the center of the dark city of Core-of-Rock. Sheln cowered behind the other three members of the Council for safety. The crowd was angry. They called out complaints and curses and outright threats against the

Chief of the Council. None of the guards even pretended to protect Sheln this time. Loghoz was having a difficult time quieting everyone down.

"Hey, Chork-a-zoid!" cried Linod, shoving its way through the crowd toward the humans and me.

"Linod-tron!" I said. "Any important news while we were away?"

"Absolutely!" cried Linod. "I found two new yeasts and this truffle that kind of looks like Gatas. My new fascinating fungi collection is really coming—whoa, check it out!"

Linod was pointing to Zenyk, who was standing nearby in the crowd. It was already dressed as a civilian again, as though it had never been elevated to a fictional rank within the city guard. Even Zenyk had abandoned Sheln. When it noticed we were staring, it muttered something and slunk off.

At last Loghoz quieted the crowd enough to begin. "By Great Jalasu Jhuk of the Stars," it cried in a piercing voice, "let this, the eight hundred twentieth Grand Conclave of the Xotonian people, commence! The first to speak shall be Chorkle. . . ."

I greeted the crowd and recounted the events on Kyral—with a few key omissions, of course. The humans stepped in at points to help tell the tale. Little Gus was particularly excited to describe the contribution of Pizza, who had apparently defeated a hundred Vorem legionaries all by himself. The crowd gasped and many wept as they heard what happened to Kalac. I found it hard not to cry myself. But when they learned that we had recovered the nyrine quantum inducer, a huge cheer went up over the plaza.

Four resolutions were proposed that day. The first was to hold a new election for the position of Chief of Council in three weeks' time. In the interim, Loghoz, the Custodian of the Council, would assume the duties of the Chief. This passed almost unanimously. Loghoz cried a little and tried to give a speech but somehow got sidetracked and descended into an extended rant about the importance of proper hygiene. At some point, Glyac nodded off.

The second resolution was for the immediate release of Hudka and the dismissal of the charge of sedition that had been leveled against it. This too passed easily, though not with as many votes as the first one. Hudka had irritated enough Xotonians in its day that more than a few were happy to see it rot in jail for a while longer.

The third resolution proposed was for the immediate and permanent imprisonment of Sheln. Loghoz would not allow it to come to a vote, though, since Sheln had technically violated no law. I have no doubt it would have passed. I can't say for sure how I would have voted.

The fourth and final resolution was to hold a complete performance of the Jalasad the following day. At this, the crowd gave another wild cheer.

After the Conclave broke up, we proceeded to the Hall of Wonok for Hudka's release.

"I missed you," I said.

"Eh, it's not the first time I've been arrested, and it won't be the last," said Hudka as it gave me a big hug.

"Yo, Hudka!" said Little Gus. "You get any cool tattoos while you were on the inside?"

"Yup, I got one of me kicking your butt at Xenostryfe III."

"That sounds like a very complicated tattoo," said Nicki.

When we were alone, the humans and I told Hudka everything that had happened. This time we held nothing back. And this time I did cry when I spoke of Kalac's capture. Hudka cried too. It was the only time I'd ever seen it do so.

"Don't worry," said my grand-originator, drying its eyes. "Kalac will be all right."

"How can you be sure?" I asked.

Hudka stared at me. "Because it's got an offspring like you looking out for it."

Just then, Eromu walked past us toward the hall. The guard captain was leading Taius Ridian by the arm. Taius turned, and for a second his red eyes met mine. I wanted to say something to him, but I didn't know what. He turned away, though, and the heavy doors closed behind him.

CHAPTER TWENTY-SIX

We looked out from the Observatory on a sea of lights twinkling in the darkness. We weren't looking through some telescope at the stars though. We were staring out a window, down upon Core-of-Rock. The nyrine quantum inducer had been successfully reinstalled, and the ancient reactor had hummed back to life. Again, the Stealth Shield concealed us from outsiders. The city glowed once more.

"It's kind of beautiful, isn't it?" said Becky.

"Yep," I said.

"Are you guys talking about my hair again?" said Little Gus, sidling up to us.

"Nope," said Becky, "I've never actually looked directly at your hair. I'm worried about retina damage."

"Witty repartee!" said Little Gus. "We're having fun! I love it!"

Becky cocked her head and squinted at him. "Dude, you're a special case, you know that?" And she left to join the others.

Little Gus beamed. "You hear that, Chorkle?" he whispered, nudging me with his elbow. "She said I'm special to her."

"Well, that's not exactly what she—"

"She. Said. I'm. Special. To. Her," he repeated.

"She sure did," I said, clapping him on the back. Gus smiled and nodded.

"Are you two ready?" asked Hollins.

We joined him and the twins in the center of the Observatory. Nicki was fiddling with the tachyonic ansible we'd recovered from Kyral, adjusting various nobs and sliders. Hudka stood beside her, "supervising" (acting as if it knew what was going on). So did Ydar, the High Observer, who was a nervous wreck.

The Observers had spent weeks studying the device's manual and connecting it to various power sources, intakes, and outputs within the Observatory. In fact, there was every indication that the chamber had held its own ansible once, but it had been deliberately removed. Still, the High Observer feared that activating the device would cause some irreparable damage to the other systems.

"I just need to make sure that the synchronistic convergence is set to zero," Nicki muttered to herself.

"If possible, please set it *below* zero," offered Ydar.

"Aw, lighten up, Ydar. It's all just stuff," said Hudka, waving at the priceless technology that filled Observatory. "You can't take it with you to the Nebula Beyond." Ydar was not comforted.

Nicki and the Observers had calculated Gelo's approximate distance and direction from Earth and calibrated the device accordingly. If the ansible functioned properly, it would transmit a message instantaneously, where it could be received as radio waves. Likewise, it could detect a reply along the same radio frequency. The humans' anticipation was palpable.

Becky took a deep breath. "So . . . shall we phone home?"

"Absolutely," said Nicki. "I just hope this thing doesn't blow up."

"Wait, what?" said Ydar. But she'd already activated the ansible. It made an oscillating whine as the screen lit up with red static.

"My dad is never going to believe it," said Little Gus quietly. "I made soup on another planet."

Nicki made one small adjustment to a particular dial, then nodded to Hollins. He began his familiar message:

"Hello. This is Daniel Hollins, Nicole García, Rebecca García, and Augustus Zaleski of the Nolan-Amaral mining vessel *Phryxus*. We are safe on the asteroid Gelo, orbiting a habitable planet called Kyral, approximately forty-two light-years from earth. Is anyone out there? Over."

There was silence.

Hollins began again. "Hello, this is Daniel Hollins, Nicole—"

"Did you say . . . forty-two light-years?" crackled the ansible.

The static on the screen resolved itself into a face. It was a human face, kind and female and somewhat more lined than the faces of the children. Tears shone in the woman's eyes.

"Hi, Mom," said Hollins.

"Danny, you're alive," she said. "I can't believe it. You're all alive."

"Yes. And we're coming home."

"No. No, Danny. Listen to me. You can't come home," said Commander Hollins. "Not yet."

The human children looked at one another.

"Why?" asked Hollins.

"Because," she said, "Earth has been conquered."

LOOKING FOR ANOTHER OUT OF THIS WORLD ADVENTURE?

More secrets await behind the second-to-last door at the end of the hall in Robert Paul Weston's fantastic series:

THE CREATURE DEPARTMENT

By Robert Paul Weston

"Stunning. . . a bit like if you took *Charlie and the Chocolate Factory* and *Monsters Inc.* and shoved them in a TARDIS."
—*BUZZFEED*

CHAPTER 1

In which Elliot doesn't want to go to Food e School, and Leslie would rather be in Paris

Elliot von Doppler, you come down here right now or I swear, I'll boil you in soup and serve you to your father!"

Elliot pulled the covers over his head. This soup ultimatum was the third such threat in the last five minutes (his mother had also promised to flash-fry one of his kidneys and pickle his fingers in vinegar).

Of course, it is important to stress that Elliot von Doppler's parents had never eaten anyone, nor did they intend to. They weren't cannibals. They were food critics.

Peter and Marjorie von Doppler edited the Food section of the *Bickleburgh Bugle*. Together, they wrote a daily column called "Chew on This," offering reviews of local restaurants. Occasionally, they even went on tasting trips across the country and around the world. In short, they had haute cuisine on the brain (even when they were trying to get their son out of bed in the morning).

"I'm not kidding, Elliot. You know how much your father likes a good borscht!"

Elliot groaned.

"I'm going to count to three, young man. After that, I'm coming up there to drown you in hollandaise sauce."

(Don't worry, Elliot's mother would never do this. In fact, she doesn't know how to make hollandaise sauce. In spite of their jobs, both Elliot's parents are terrible chefs.)

"*One!*"

Elliot rolled out of bed and dressed himself. He put on shorts and a T-shirt, topping them off (as always) with a bright green fishing vest.

"*Two!*"

Elliot reached for his most prized possession: an original DENKi-3000 Electric Pencil with Retractable Telescopic Lens. It had been a gift from his uncle Archie, and it was an antique. The electric pencil was the first product DENKi-3000 ever produced.

"*THREE!* That's it, young man. I'm sending your father up there with a garlic press."

"I'm coming!" Elliot called back. He slunk down the stairs to the kitchen and saw breakfast was on the table. Soggy boiled tomatoes and burnt toast.

"We spent a lot of time on this breakfast," his father informed him. He sat at the head of the table, the morning's *Bickleburgh Bugle* in his hands. "So I don't want to hear any complaints."

"Have a seat," said Elliot's mother, eyeing him carefully. "Tell us what you think."

Elliot did his best to moisten the blackened, rock-hard toast with the juice of the tomatoes. It didn't help.

He was halfway through eating (more like forcing down) his breakfast when he noticed an envelope sitting in the middle of the table.

It had his name on it.

"What's that?"

"Your uncle stopped by on the way to work this morning," his mother told him.

"*What?* He was here?" Elliot was astonished.

His mother nodded ruefully. "He vanishes for weeks on end, *as usual*, and then—POOF!—he shows up looking for you."

"*Me?*" Now Elliot was *even more* astonished. Uncle Archie practically lived at DENKi-3000 headquarters. The company's unusual buildings were just on the other side of Bickleburgh Park, but Uncle Archie never "stopped by," not for anything. He was famous for missing birthdays, Christmases, soccer games . . . all the usual stuff. "Why didn't you wake me up?"

"I have enough trouble getting you up at the *regular* time. Anyway, he left you that note."

Elliot (happily) gave up on his breakfast and tore open the envelope. Inside was a brief, hastily jotted letter.

Dear Elliot,

For years, you've been asking me for a tour of the company, but I've always been too busy.   With the way things are going, though, I've decided that now is the time. Why don't you stop by today and I'll show you around.

Yours truly,

Uncle Archie

PS: You'd better bring your friend, Leslie, too.

Elliot squinted at the letter, his mouth hanging open.

"What does it say?" asked his father.

"Uncle Archie wants to give me a tour—*today*."

Perhaps noting his bewildered expression, his mother asked, "Shouldn't you be happy about that?"

"I am, but . . ."

"But what?"

"But *who's* Leslie?"

"I'm not sure I follow," said his mother.

"Look," said Elliot, pointing to the bottom of the letter. "It says, '*PS: You'd better bring your friend, Leslie, too.*'"

"Nice of him to invite her as well," said his father from

behind his newspaper.

"But *I don't have* a friend named Leslie." Elliot didn't want to admit it, but he didn't have many friends at all (or any).

"Wait," said his mother. "Isn't that the name of the girl from the science fair?"

"*Leslie Fang?*"

"Of course," said his mother. "That must be who he means."

"It can't be," said Elliot. He hardly knew Leslie Fang. She had arrived only a couple months before school let out for the summer, so there wasn't time for *anyone* to make friends with her. "Why would he want me to bring her along? We're not even in the same class."

It was true. The only reason Elliot knew Leslie was because they had tied for third place in the Bickleburgh City Science Fair. (They had both designed nearly identical model rocket ships, which was kind of embarrassing, even if you ended up tying for third place.)

His mother thought about the question for a moment. "I often see that girl on my way to work, just sitting all by herself in the park. She's been there nearly every day since school let out for summer, and to be honest, she looks quite lonely. Maybe Uncle Archie noticed the same thing."

Elliot slumped in his chair. He didn't much like the idea of sharing his uncle with someone else, but what could he do? Leslie Fang was the only Leslie he knew, and there was *no way* he was going to pass up a once-in-a-lifetime tour of DENKi-3000.

"Fine," he mumbled. "I'll ask her. *If* I see her. Can I go now?"

"Not until you finish your breakfast," said his father.

"*And* give us your review," added his mother.

Elliot looked glumly down at his plate. He pushed some black crumbs across a puddle of tomato juice. Struggling to gulp down the rest of the meal, his eyes wandered to the front page of the newspaper in his father's hands.

There was a large photograph of the DENKi-3000 headquarters. Spanning across it was a headline:

Technology Giant to Close Its Doors?

Elliot choked on a mouthful of breakfast (which wasn't hard to do at all). "*Close its doors?*" he spluttered. "As in shut down?"

His father nodded. "That's probably why Uncle Archie is finally giving you a tour. It's now or never."

"What does that mean?"

"There's another company," his father explained. "Some big investment firm. They're gonna buy the whole thing. People expect them to move the headquarters overseas."

"But. . ." Elliot couldn't believe what he was hearing. "What will happen to Uncle Archie?"

"Hard to say," said Elliot's mother. "Nobody really knows."

Elliot stared at the newspaper. In the bottom corner of the majestic image of DENKi-3000 was an inset photo of a very old man. He had shaggy gray hair and a thick gray beard and he was dressed in a brown cardigan and circular, gold-rimmed spectacles. The caption below the old man said: *Sir William Sniffledon, DENKi-3000's longtime*

CEO, *admits serious financial difficulty.*

It was odd to think this old man, who looked more like a doddering librarian, was the high-powered CEO of a company as big as DENKi-3000. Elliot's eyes moved to the first few lines of the article:

The head office of DENKi-3000, the fifth-largest technology producer in the world and one of Bickleburgh's largest employers, could be set to close its doors in a matter of months.

Following a year of less-than-stellar profits, the company seems ripe for acquisition by Quazicom Holdings, a private capital investment firm. DENKi-3000 CEO Sir William Sniffledon said, "It would be a sad day for Bickleburgh if . . .

Elliot returned his eyes to the photograph. The DENKi-3000 buildings were the most interesting things in the city: four glass towers climbing up from a vast oval of land. In spite of having an uncle who was head of the company's Research and Development Department, Elliot had never set foot inside the heavily secured gates.

He pushed his plate away, finally finished. "If Uncle Archie invited me, I'd better not keep him waiting."

"Not so fast, mister." His father pointed to the red-and-black mash drizzling across his plate. "Not until we get our review."

"Do I have to?"

All his parents cared about was *describing* food. Was it really so crazy to just want to eat it?

"How are you going to get into Foodie School if you don't start practicing?" asked his father.

"What if I don't want to go to Foodie School?"

"Don't you want to grow up to be a famous food critic, like your parents?"

"Maybe I'd rather be more like Uncle Archie."

"I'm not sure he's someone you want to emulate." His mother glanced at the newspaper.

Elliot, of course, had no intention of becoming a famous food critic. However, he knew if he wanted to see his uncle, he would first have to appease his parents.

"So?" asked his mother.

"Be as descriptive as possible," said his father.

Both of them leaned anxiously across the table.

"Well . . . it was . . ." Elliot struggled to find the words. "Crunchy. And wet."

His father frowned. "That'll *never* get you into Foodie School."

"Can I go now?"

"I suppose," said his mother, a little reluctantly. "Say hi to your uncle for us."